THE SPECTRE OF SUICIDE SWAMP

By
E. K. JARVIS

I0541530

ARMCHAIR FICTION
PO Box 4369, Medford, Oregon   97501-0168

A FREAK ACCIDENT IN TIME AND SPACE

Duke Harley was a Hollywood has-been and Kathie Dawn wasn't too far behind. Their time as Hollywood stars was definitely on the wane. And now they were both set to star in every former big star's greatest nightmare…a cheap Hollywood horror movie. It was a schlocky movie about bank robbers and a mad robot prowling through a snake-infested swamp. The script would surely be filled with inane dialogue that would make any seasoned thespian cringe. But when you're on the skids and someone offers you seven hundred and fifty a week, it's hard to say no.

But on the set something happened. The two fading stars saw reality fade and found themselves face-to-face with "the Spectre of Suicide Swamp."

FOR A COMPLETE SECOND NOVEL, TURN TO PAGE 75

CAST OF CHARACTERS

DUKE HARLEY
He was essentially a washed-up movie actor, now forced to take parts in cheap grade B horror movies.

KATHIE DAWN
She never let up her façade of stardom in Hollywood's inner circles—even if her career was on the skids.

TOM LEWIT
What happens when a country-bumpkin is suddenly given the lead part in a Hollywood movie? This kid found out the hard way.

GINNY HAYS
She may not have had money and position, but she was quick on her feet and ready to leap at every opportunity

THE PROPHET
A self-styled Rasputin of the swamp country. His maniacal grip was a death sentence—and could break a man in half!

FRANKY LEWIT
As Tom's kid brother, he was often an exasperating nuisance, but there was courage in this kid, a courage born in the swamp.

THE BEAST
This steely creature had crimson eyes, was fifteen feet tall, and could rip buildings apart with ease!

CHAPTER ONE

HARLEY HAD about given up hope for the day when the phone rang. He picked it up. "Duke Harley speaking." He was careful to keep a superior, *prosperous* tone in his voice.

"Hello, Duke. This is Marty French."

"Oh...Marty." The tone became cordial as hope welled up. Marty French was casting director at Epic. Casting directors were God's chosen people. They gave you a job sometimes, and when you had a job you could eat.

"You working?"

Duke glanced at the frayed cuff of his dressing gown. He laughed with just the right note of amusement. "I'm getting a little rest, thank heaven. Turned down some eastern video appearances. Too tired. I'm starting a western at Tri-Art next month."

The sound over the phone might have been a sigh. "Oh...Well. I figured you wouldn't be interested, but I thought I'd call."

"Interested in what?"

"We're doing a quickie to cash in on this science-fiction boom. The script's all ready. Five weeks at seven-fifty per. Didn't think you'd be interested."

Duke continued to study his frayed cuff. Now he switched his attention to the other cuff. It was frayed too. He said, "Let's cut out the crap now, huh? That western at Tri-Art is the same one every out-of-work actor has been starting for the past ten years. It never gets made. I want that job and you damn well know I do. When do I start?"

"We begin shooting Thursday."

"How about a hundred bucks advance? I'm bust."

"Okay. I'll send it over."

"Who's the sex interest?"

"Kathie Dawn."

"Okay. I need the job so bad I can even put up with her."

"Come down tomorrow and sign the contract."

"Will do. So long."

Duke hung up, realizing he'd committed the cardinal sin of filmdom: he'd dropped his front. No matter how bad off you were in Hollywood, you were always working or resting between pictures. You were never out of a job and you always took a job as a favor to the producer. You were never hungry and you were always hard to get.

Duke had broken the rule—dropped his front—and he didn't care. What the hell! You couldn't be a phony all your life. You had to tell the truth at least once a year, or you got so you didn't know the difference between the truth and the lie.

Duke banged a cigarette viciously against his thumbnail and thought of Kathie Dawn. She'd evidently come down a long way—just as had he himself—to take five weeks in a quickie. He blew out a cloud of smoke and grinned at it. A hard dame, Kathie, but you had to give her credit. She'd never bought a part the easy way.

ACTING ON sudden impulse Duke picked up the phone, dialed a number, thinking as he did so that it might be the wrong one. It probably was the wrong one with Kathie taking a grade-B assignment. Kathie wouldn't live there any more.

"Park Royal."

"Is Miss Kathie Dawn in?"

"Just a moment. I will connect you."

Kathie was still keeping up the front. Duke waited.

"Hello—Miss Dawn's suite."

"Hello Kathie. Duke Harley."

"Oh, Duke." The voice sounded more natural. "You were lucky to catch me. I was just—"

"I know—headed for Ciro's. Look, I understand you signed with Epic for a—"

She wouldn't let him say it. Her laugh was silvery. "For some reason, I've never been able to turn Marty down. He's such a dear."

"Oh—doing him a favor, huh?"

"Yes—a favor." Something in her tone dared Duke to imply it was anything else. Duke said, "I'm doing the lead in the same stinker, hon, but they're doing me the favor—"

"Why—Duke!" Kathie's surprise was sincere. "Do you mean—?"

"I mean I decided to be honest about it. First time in years, and it's such a novel feeling I had to have more. Look—I've got ten bucks to my name and I'll shoot in on dinner. Not at Ciro's, though."

"Well—I have a date, but—"

"Like hell you have. Listen—do you want a five-buck steak or don't you?"

A pause—then another change in tone. "I'm drooling."

Duke laughed. "Twenty minutes."

KATHIE DAWN sopped up the last of her gravy with a piece of bread. "They're calling it *The Spectre of Suicide Swamp.*"

Duke shuddered. "Oh, good lord, no! If Marty had told me that—"

"It's all about a robot out in a swamp."

"Location?"

"No. They've got a set from an old horror picture they never tore down."

Duke held out a pack of cigarettes. "Kathie, there's a reason I don't care if anybody knows I'm broke or not."

Kathie took a cigarette and questioned with her beautiful eyes.

"I'm quitting pictures."

"Duke!"

"I'm fed up. I'm sick of all the shallow, phony pretense. Besides, I'm starving to death."

"But what are you going to do?"

"I think maybe I'll open a gas station."

"You're kidding?"

"Why do you say that? There's a living in a good gas station…some money every day."

"You're insane."

"Uh-huh. Five years ago I made ten thousand a week. I was a kid then, I didn't know what to do with it. Now I'm washed up and still this side of thirty. I'm still looking forward to five weeks of seven-fifty. That's a lot of money. It'll buy me a nice gas station."

"You're just feeling low, Duke. You'll get over it."

"Kathie—after this picture, why don't we get married? We can have a lunchroom with the gas station. We'd do all right."

She whitened under her rouge. Duke thought she was going to slap him. She got up from the table. "Thanks for the dinner. I'll see you on the set."

Kathie left. Duke stared into his coffee Clip. "Oh, well," he muttered. "It was a silly idea anyway."

THE SET was an old one Epic had used for scenes from *Swamp Angel*. It had lain idle too long to suit Joe Parker, Epic's president. It covered about ten acres and was, Duke thought, as full of phony atmosphere and horror as any other section of this phony movie lot in the phony town called Hollywood.

Duke got down early Thursday morning and found an assistant director, Pete Cooper, waiting for the cast. Pete Cooper did most of Sam Corwin's worrying for him. Sam was a big director. He was so big he could afford to do a stinker like *The Spectre of Suicide Swamp* once in a while. And he was big enough to rate a first-class worrier like Pete.

Pete said, "Good morning, Mr. Harley. Are you familiar with the story we're going to shoot?"

"The hell with the story, I know my part."

Pete was hurt. "That's not the right attitude, Mr. Harley. How do you expect to do your best if you haven't got the story line?"

"I'm getting seven-fifty a week. That's how good I'm going to be. Right to the penny. Then I'm going to open a gas station."

Pete smiled, "You're a great kidder, Mr. Harley. Let me brief you on the story. It's about a robot built by a scientist in a big city. Four hoodlums steal the robot. They use it to smash in the brick wall of a loan company and carry away the safe."

"They put the robot and the safe in a six-wheel trailer truck and head south," Duke said. "They kill off a few of each other and sink the truck in four hundred and eighty feet of quicksand. Then the robot wanders off into the swamp. The gentle swamp folk take one look and go nuts."

Pete was a little hurt. "Oh, you do know the story."

"Uh-huh. A minor classic. They should call it *Gone with the Slight Breeze*. Good morning, Kathie."

Kathie came over and sat down in Sam Corwin's chair. She'd already been to makeup. She wore a pair of ballet slippers over bare feet and a plain ragged dress. It just happened to reveal every luscious line of her body.

Pete Cooper wore a worried look. He was hoping Kathie would get out of Corwin's chair before the director showed up. Kathie shivered and rubbed the goose flesh on her arms. "Talk about realism! I haven't got a blessed stitch on under this thing. No room."

Duke took off his coat and handed it to her. It was ragged too, but it helped. Duke said, "You'd look nice in a dress like that—in our lunchroom next to the gas station."

"I thought maybe you'd recaptured your sanity. I guess not." She glanced out over the dismal prop-swamp. I hope that water's warm in there—and no snakes."

"We have four cottonmouths," Pete said. "They're caged up when we aren't using them."

Kathie shuddered again, but for a different reason. "I wish they'd cut that scene where I get bit."

"Oh, we couldn't do that. It's one of the high points of drama," Pete assured her.

Duke eyed Kathie critically. "Let's get a cup of coffee—unless you're afraid it'll show under that dress."

CHAPTER TWO

DUKE'S first scene with Kathie came at ten o'clock. It was the scene where Duke, passing by sheerest happenstance through the thickest and most impenetrable part of Suicide Swamp, came upon Kathie taking a swim. An alligator also happened by at that moment and craved Kathie for dinner. It was Duke's job to prevent this, and thus strike up an acquaintance with the swamp girl. A good scene.

All would have gone well, but the alligator they'd rented was well into its late hundreds and not interested in dinner. It had been too well fed. Its owner used a goad on its soft underbelly, but by the time he had the reptile functioning, Sam Corwin had become interested in dinner himself.

"An hour for lunch!" Pete Cooper screamed, and everybody went tearing out of the jungle toward the cafeteria, leaving Kathie waist-deep in water.

"Hey—help me out of this—somebody!"

The arms that reached for her belonged to Duke Harley. Duke said, "Baby, can't you see the writing on the wall? When they all run out and leave you standing in the swamp, you're about washed up. Now, that gas station I have in mind…"

Kathie's eyes blazed fire. "Damn you, Duke." She raked a set of nails at his face—missed—fell back in the water. Again Duke reached down and fished her out. He was laughing. He lifted her, his hands against the curves of her back.

Kathie, anchored there—her feet against the bank, her body arched out over the water, resting against his hands.

And, to Duke, it was very strange—indescribable—except to call it a moment between heaven and earth. Only a moment, surely, but yet a lifetime. The passing of lazy clouds over a blue sky. Slowly. Long years in a moment? Or a moment in long years?

Duke couldn't be sure, but he remembered pondering upon the subject—on that and many other things, with the warm flesh under his hands, the ripple of muscles under his fingers.

And it was within him to know that Kathie was also bemused; that Kathie, too, pondered many deep problems. Like—does a queen bee dress for dinner? And, where do the warm breezes go in wintertime?

"PUT ME down." Duke lowered his eyes to gaze dully into Kathie's face. Slowly, very slowly, it dawned on him that he had lifted her up from the water and was holding her in his arms like a child.

"Put me down." Not peremptorily, but with a sense of wonder.

"Oh, sure—sure."

He set her down carefully on her bare feet. Her eyes held his, afraid to turn elsewhere. She asked, "What were you looking at?"

"The sound boom."

"Where?"

"Overhead—where it always is."

"Is it there?"

"No. It's gone. That's why I was looking. It seems so damn silly that they'd take the sound-boom to lunch with them."

"Duke—they wouldn't do that."

"No. Nor the cameras. You don't go to lunch with cameras. But they're gone too."

Kathie came close and leaned against him. She put her face on his chest and closed her eyes. "Duke—it's different. It's all—different.

"How can you tell? You aren't looking."

"I can tell. It's a feeling—it's how I felt and what I was thinking about when you pulled me out of the water. It took so long. I had a wild, crazy thought."

"What thought did you have, Kathie?"

"It was so silly, I'm ashamed to say."

"What thought?"

"An old man bent and twisted. He came hobbling over with a needle and thread in his hand. He sewed up a hole in the sky." Kathie pushed hard on his chest. *"Duke. I'm going mad…"*

"No, angel. I saw him too. It was the old lamplighter doing some extra work to earn a few pennies."

"Duke! Duke! For God's sake!"

"Take it easy, angel."

"It's all changed, Duke—all changed." Kathie's nails were biting into the flesh of his arms. Her teeth were set and he knew her lower lip was between them. He knew if he didn't do something about it, pretty soon there'd be blood.

He pushed her back and slapped her face.

Her eyes spat fire. She said, "Damn you!" But she wasn't tense any more.

Duke said, "Sit down—there—on that log."

Kathie sat down and Duke dropped beside her. There was the passing of time. Silence. Kathie said, "Why are we sitting here?"

"I don't know. It just seems the thing to do. We've got to say things. There are things waiting to be said. Let's get them over with."

"What things?"

"Things like this isn't a movie set. This is a swamp. That alligator over there wasn't leased for the day. And we aren't actors. Somebody pulled the plug. We went down the drain."

"Duke—who are we? Where are we?"

"That's what doesn't seem right. If we were somebody else we should know it."

"I'm not anybody else—I'm *me*. Me! Do you understand?"

DUKE WAS staring pensively at the dark water below the bank on which they sat.

"Duke—where *are* we?"

"In a swamp, baby."

"That's no answer."

"It's the best one I've got at the moment. Listen—I've got another hunch. I think we belong here—at least, the people we've become belong here. Is that too tough to follow?"

"No—no I guess not. But what makes you so sure we're two other people? If this had to happen, couldn't it just happen to us?"

"I don't think so. I don't think people are dropped through holes in the sky for no reason at all."

"That old man—"

"Skip it—forget him. He was nothing but a rationalization."

"What's that?"

"Something entirely different from what it appears to be. You see it the way you do because it has to be put into some form you're familiar with or your mind can't grasp it."

"I'm not grasping anything."

"Your subconscious is, but quit arguing with me. I was saying that we couldn't just be dropped here willy-nilly.

There had to be two places for us to fill. Otherwise there wouldn't have been room."

"What happened to the people who occupied this space before we came along?"

Duke got abruptly to his feet. "How the hell do I know? Come on. Let's start walking. I think when we come to the place we're supposed to go we'll recognize it."

Duke took a step—stopped. Kathie was looking down. Duke asked, "What's wrong?"

"My dress—it's wet. And there's still nothing under it."

"Interesting," Duke said. "I'll file the information away. Come on."

THE PATH was narrow and thickly overgrown with grass. It wound through trees thick trunked, and heavy with dank moss.

They walked and walked and it seemed there was no way out. Nothing but a path that turned and twisted through a swamp; a swamp not sad and melancholy by Hollywood design, but because it had grown that way.

"Be careful," Duke said. "The snakes in this place don't come in boxes. And they haven't had their teeth pulled."

Kathie stopped, stood rigid, staring up at Duke.

"What's the matter, baby?" He knew even as he asked. He could sense the hysteria bubbling up.

"Duke—it's not real. It doesn't matter what we do. You're not here. This isn't here. It's not real. I'm all alone in a dream!"

He took her by the shoulders and shook her roughly. "Baby! Get that foolishness out of your mind. This is real! You're flesh and blood and you can get hurt. Remember that. You can bloat all up if a snake bites you. You can die, baby! Snap out of it!"

Duke had help in snapping her out of it. This help came from the biggest man he had ever seen. A huge man with a flowing white beard and piercing eyes who could move through the swampland like a shadow. He appeared, as from nowhere, to skewer them with piercing eyes. "You two been out in the swamp alone?"

He thundered the last word, and the impact of his voice stunned them. Duke said, "We've been—"

"Silence!" The giant raised an arm like an angry Moses. "I—the new redeemer—have given the law! Thou shalt not commit adultery! You have disobeyed."

"Who—who said anything about adultery?" Two facts stood out starkly in Duke's mind. First, his reaction to this reeking character actor should have been strictly from a belly laugh. He'd never seen anything so rank as this in all his Hollywood days. But he didn't laugh and he was scared stiff. This giant was dangerous—a madman—and life and death could hang in the balance.

The second fact, dormant in his mind, was that there were two others here before them. Maybe they were like them, but not exact duplications. Yet, they were accepted as the other two. Is that how it would be—all eyes blinded to their differences?

"The tasting of the fleshpots is an abomination of the Lord! Down on your knees before I smite both of you to earth!"

He's just the guy who can do it too, Duke thought, and pulled Kathie down until the giant towered over them. Kathie was trembling. Duke could feel the terror within her. He whispered, "Take it easy, baby—easy."

"Pray now. Pray that you escape the boiling fires of hell!"

"We repent our sins," Duke croaked.

"But we didn't sin—"

The duke squeezed Kathie's hand to cut off the words. His head was lowered. He whispered, "Sure we did—don't disappoint this guy. He'll crack our skulls like eggs. Say it!"

"We repent our—sins."

Duke took a chance and raised his eyes. The giant stood staring up at the sky with arms flung wide. He bellowed, "Are the lives of these sinners forfeit, oh Lord? Give thy servant a sign. I would do thy will!"

"Duke," Kathie whispered. "He's—he's crazy!"

"Sure he's crazy. Why do you think we're kneeling here in the mud? This guy's a killer..."

The giant was saying, "Oh Lord—give me a sign. Are the lives of Ginny Hays and Tom Lewit forfeit in thy sight? Give thy servant a sign—a sign! I am thy vengeance, oh—"

CHAPTER THREE

GINNY HAYS giggled. "Tom—stop it. You stop it now!"

Tom Lewit took his hand away. He was somewhat confused. "But Ginny...you came out here with me. What for'd you come here if—?"

The girl sobered. "We shouldn't have, Tom. What if the Prophet found out? What if he followed us?"

"Don't worry about him, honey. He's—"

Ginny sat waiting for Tom's hands to come back. Having sent them away, she could hardly invite them. She could only wait. "Tom, there's some that say he's crazy. What do you think? Is he really a prophet like he says?"

"I don't know. He's sure a glory-be-to-God fire-eater. The way he whips them up at the prayer meetings—"

"I'm—I'm afraid of him."

"Who isn't?"

"When Laura Pritchard and Toe Davis disappeared—do you believe what the Prophet said about it?"

"What does it matter? Their folks must have. Nobody made any complaints. He's put the fear of the Lord into everybody—that's for sure..."

Ginny smiled most dreamily. "Tom—we ain't got much time—"

That should have helped, but it didn't. Tom said, "Ginny—"

"What?"

"That thing—that thing up there. Where'd it come from?"

"I don't know. I never saw it before. It wasn't here when we—"

"Ginny...something's wrong. Look at those other things—those boxes with—with eyes like. They weren't there before either."

Ginny had suddenly changed. She was no longer the languorous female preoccupied with the biological urge. Her eyes were bright, sharp, intense. She gripped Tom Lewit's wrist. "Tom—I know what those things are! Movie cameras! Remember when they had the picture show at Bate's Landing? The pictures they had of famous people getting off that ship and men with cameras were there? These are almost the same."

"But where'd they come from? Ginny—we'd better get out of here!"

"Sit still. Let me think! Something's happened."

"You sure ain't fooling about that. I got a feeling—"

"Be quiet! Tom—you know what this is? Where we are?"

"Why, sure—we're in Suicide Swamp on the bank of the—"

'We're not. We're on a movie set. It told all about movie sets in those magazines at the landing store!"

"But that don't make sense. How'd they get here without us hearing them?"

"They didn't come to us. We went to them." Ginny's eyes were sparkling. "Listen, Tom. I don't understand any of this, but I've got a feeling about it. You know how I always wanted to get out of the swamps—wanted to get where I could *be* somebody? Well, maybe wishes are prayers. And even the Prophet says prayers are answered. You just keep your mouth shut and let me do the talking."

"BUT GINNY—that's silly. If we're some place else, the people will know it no matter how we got here. We just won't belong. We're swamp folks…"

"I think maybe we will belong. I—I've got some instincts about all this. I think we took somebody else's place. Otherwise there wouldn't be room for us—"

"You mean the people that were here got out of our way—or died or something?"

"I don't know. It doesn't matter. Just keep—*somebody's coming.*"

A dozen technicians showed up, all wearing toothpicks in their mouths. Pete Cooper came down the walk. "What's the matter? Didn't you two eat?"

Tom gaped. Ginny smiled. "No, we were—were—"

But Pete interrupted, staring at Tom. "Gosh—you're sure going all out on this part, aren't you?"

"Huh?"

"I said you're sure absorbing your role. Man, you really got hold of the mood."

Tom turned his head to gaze at Ginny. She smiled and chucked him under the chin. It appeared to be a gesture of endearment. It served another purpose, however, when she pushed his lower jaw up and closed his mouth.

"That's what we've been doing," Ginny said. "Getting the mood."

Pete threw away his toothpick and yelled, "Everybody on set! Everybody on set!"

Things moved in kaleidoscopic fashion for Tom and Ginny after that. Sam Corwin strode up and took his chair. He consulted with his subordinates. Then everybody sat back while the alligator was brought back.

TOM STARED at the reptile with unbelieving eyes. He whispered, "Glory be... That old 'gator's ready for the soft mud. He couldn't bite his way out of a thick fog!"

"Quiet..." Ginny hissed. "Follow my lead."

"Where we going?"

"Shut *up...*"

"Scene Seven—Take four." Pete Cooper yelled, and faded back into the swamp while Corwin took over.

"This will be a take," Corwin bellowed. "Places please. Mr. Harley—Miss Dawn."

Tom looked around. "They must be waiting for somebody."

"That's us, stupid," Ginny hissed.

"Then what are we supposed to do?"

Pete Cooper materialized. "Duke—Kathie. Look alive. That's Mr. Corwin talking."

Ginny got slowly to her feet. "Your name is Duke Harley. Remember it," she whispered.

"Sure, but..." Tom stopped speaking to watch open-mouthed as Ginny passed a hand over her forehead and collapsed gently to the ground.

Pete Cooper rushed over, pushed the staring Tom out of the way. "What's wrong with you, Duke? She faints and you let her lie."

"Faint? That's silly. She's strong as a horse."

Pete, half bent over, did a double take. "Duke, you're letting your role go to your head."

Pete picked Ginny up and started off the set. Tom trotted along behind. "Where you taking her?"

"To First-aid. Where else?"

"Okay—I'll just come along."

Ginny came to just outside the first-aid room and handled the situation beautifully. "I'm sorry—awfully sorry. I can't work anymore today."

Pete Cooper put her down gently, regretfully. "Sure, Kathie. You feeling a little better, though?"

"Yes. Please take me to my dressing room."

With alacrity, Pete picked her up again and started across the lot. Tom again took up the rear. Pete turned. "I can handle it, Duke."

Tom stopped and watched the two of them disappear around a corner. He looked about dolefully. He was definitely not happy.

GINNY reappeared from around the corner half an hour later. Tom gasped anew, and with good reason. Ginny was dressed in apparel the like of which he'd seen only in pictures. Maybe Ginny had been backward, but she'd sure learned fast. There were stars in her eyes as she asked, "Like it?"

"I—I guess so."

"There's things under this," she said demurely, then frowned at Tom. "Why aren't you dressed?"

"Me? I'm dressed. I ain't got any clothes but these, Ginny—and a Sunday shirt back home."

Ginny pointed. "Over there, stupid. That little house on skids, with your name on the door. It's your dressing room."

Tom peered. "That ain't my name."

"It is too. And stop saying *ain't*. Your name is Duke Harley."

"Oh sure, I remember. You think it's all right to go in there?"

"Of course. You'll find clothes in there." She turned to eye him critically. "You *can* dress yourself, can't you?"

"Oh sure—sure. But—"

"Go on! Stop arguing."

Tom went into Duke Harley's dressing room and, fortunately, was not bewildered by any great array of clothing. There was just enough to clothe one man and no more. Tom put everything on, and in so doing he encountered another piece of luck. Duke had worn a sport shirt that morning, so there was no necktie to bewilder the swamp boy.

When he came out he found Ginny waiting for him. "I found out where you live!" she said triumphantly.

"You did? I was wondering about that. How'd you find out?"

"From that funny little man with the big hands that carried me over here. You live in the Sudbury apartments."

"Where's that?"

"On Wilshire Boulevard."

"Where's Wilshire Boulevard?"

"We'll take a taxi. The man will know."

"They charge for that, don't they?"

"Of course. Haven't you got any money?"

"I don't know."

Tom dug into his pockets and came up with a sparse handful of green bills. "Some, I guess."

"And there's some in my handbag."

"Your handbag?"

"Kathie Dawn's handbag—but it's mine now. Can't you get that through your head? What was theirs is now ours. Try to remember that."

"Sure—sure. I'll remember."

"Come on, let's hurry."

Tom came along, a step behind. "Why are you in such a sweat to get to Duke's—to my place?"

"There's a reason—an important one. Stop lagging behind."

TOM TOOK the dime the cab driver handed back. Tom said, "Thank you kindly," and put the dime into his pocket. The cab pulled away with a snort of tires. Tom and Ginny went into the Sudbury apartments.

Tom found a key to open the door of the shabby one-room walkup. He followed Ginny inside, stood looking about. "Sure a pretty place," he conceded.

Ginny was paying no attention. Her sharp eyes caught what she was looking for on the bed table. She went over and picked it up triumphantly. "This is it! Glory be! We found it."

"Found what?"

"The story! The parts we have to play in the movie they're making." She frowned at him. "Say—why do you think I fainted when I did?"

"I don't know. It seemed kind of funny. Didn't figure you was the kind that's plagued with the vapors."

"It was because we didn't know what we were supposed to do. It was the only way out. Now we've got the parts it'll be different. We'll study them—memorize them—"

Tom stared at the thick sheaf in her hand. "You mean we read that stuff and then remember it. Ginny! It'd take a lifetime."

"It's got to be done by morning."

"*Morning.* Good Lord. When night comes we got to sleep. You know that!"

"No sleep tonight. We're going to work."

Tom had all the appearances of a reprimanded dog. "Ginny—I don't like this. Let's go home."

Ginny slipped an arm around his neck and smiled up at him. "Darling, you are home. Duke, dear. This is your home."

Tom felt her fingers exploring the back of his neck. "The Prophet wouldn't like this," he muttered.

"But the Prophet isn't here, darling."

"How do we know?" Tom replied gloomily. "Maybe he can come the same way we did."

"Tom, forget the Prophet. You're going to be a great movie star. All you have to do is learn the part."

Misery shone from his eyes as he looked down at her. "You want me to do it, Ginny?"

"Yes. You know I do. This is our big opportunity. Our chance!"

"But—but what if the guy that owns these pants comes back? And the woman who belongs in that dress."

"I belong in this dress. Will you try to learn the part?"

Tom sighed. "I'll try. But some way I see trouble ahead. I ain't no actor, Ginny."

"You don't have to be. Just learn the part, darling. Then all you have to do is be yourself."

CHAPTER FOUR

THE GIANT with the white beard lowered his head. "God in his mercy has spared your lives," he rumbled.

Duke lifted his head. "Can we get up now?"

"Go to your homes. Never let me find you alone out here again." He lowered his great arms and stepped aside. Duke helped Kathie up and urged her along the path. When they were out of earshot, he said, "Who do you suppose that character was?"

Kathie clung tightly to his hand. "Duke—I'm scared. Let's get out of this place. Let's find a road and a bus and then a train. I don't like this country."

"He said to go to our homes. I wonder where they are?"

"Duke! Did you hear me?"

"I heard you. You want to leave this country. But it isn't as simple as that."

"Why not?"

"Because we don't know where we are. Where *is* this country? How do we get out of it? Besides, we aren't ourselves any more. We're two other people. You heard what he called us. Ginny Hays and Tom Lewit. We've got to find out where we live."

The path widened now and they came into what was evidently a settlement. There were a dozen or so weary, decrepit shacks and cabins. A teetering wharf beyond them nosing out into the black, still waters of a river.

"Maybe this is it," Duke said.

Evidently it was. A shapeless slattern appeared in one of the doorways to shrill, "Ginny! Ginny Hays—you get into this house this minute. I got something to say to you."

"That must be your mother," Duke whispered.

"Oh—God forbid! Duke, she's…"

"You'd better do as she says. Go ahead. I'll see you later."

"No! If I go, you come with me."

"I'll walk part way. Buck up! Don't look so scared."

Duke went most of the way. Far enough to meet the slattern who lumbered out into what passed as a street and took Kathie by the ear, but addressed her remarks to Duke. "You ought to be ashamed of yourself, Tom Lewit! Leading my little girl out into the swamp! Your pa ought to tan your hide."

A HALF DOZEN urchins had materialized to form a visible audience. Duke felt the eyes of a larger, invisible audience from the windows and doorways of the hovels.

One of the urchins bleated, "I saw 'em, Mizz Hays. I was a watchin'. They met the Prophet!"

Mrs. Hays paled and almost lost her grip on Ginny's ear. "Met the Prophet?"

"Yes," Kathie moaned. "He said it was all right."

Duke thought he saw relief in the renewed energy with which Mrs. Hays swung Ginny around and pointed her at the house. "Then you can be thankful for his mercy," the shapeless woman screamed. "Now, into that house with you."

The urchins were grinning. The half-pint spy chuckled with glee. "Ginny's going to get tanned good."

Duke looked down at the dirty face, viewed it with marked distaste. This was the kind of a child one would enjoy whaling regularly. The child grinned at Duke. "And you better come home. Pa's waitin' for you."

Oh, no! Duke moaned inwardly. Not the kid brother! "All right," he said aloud. "You lead the way."

Junior complied with obvious relish—a relish borne, no doubt, of anticipation. He moved up the street with Duke in his wake, and turned left around the end of the settlement. As they entered a thick grove, Duke heard a wail of anguish from the direction of the houses behind him. The voice belonged to Kathie.

Duke felt a little sorry for her, but not much. Maybe a spanking would do Kathie good. Duke almost smiled. If she'd had more of them earlier in life...

Another clearing opened before him. In its center was a house, somewhat larger than those in the settlement proper, but just as beaten and tumbledown.

And now Duke stopped short as the house erupted humanity. Out they came, large and small; from toddlers of two and three up to young men and women of both sexes in at least their early twenties. Duke began counting swiftly. He got to fourteen and gave up. "In heaven's name—what will pa and ma look like?" he muttered.

He was soon enlightened on this point. A heavy-faced, beetle-brewed man strode out scowling. He was followed by a thin wisp of a woman with a baby in her arms. "Now, Pa," the woman said, "don't lose your temper."

The scowling man strode out to meet Duke; stopped and stood spread-legged, his scowl deepening. "Where you been?"

The whole family waited in dead silence to hear.

"Why—why, out in the swamp."

"With that sheep-eyed Hays gal?"

"We were—"

The man's fist came up and around, to catch Duke flush on the mouth.

The woman cried, "Pa! Your temper! Don't lose your temper now!"

THE ADVICE came a little late, Duke thought as he lay on the ground looking up into the moss-laden trees.

"Get to your feet!"

"Why? So you can knock me down again?"

"None of your lip! What's this I hear about you meeting the Prophet?"

"We met him. He got us a fast trial and an acquittal."

The man frowned. Duke had been trying to judge his age. His hair was streaked with gray. There were deep lines in his face, but no softness in his muscle. "What are you talking about?"

"I'm not sure myself."

The man stood undecided. His words held further threat. "If you got us in bad with the Prophet—" He turned away suddenly. "Go in and eat your supper."

The man strode around the house and out of sight. Duke stood rubbing his jaw, looking over his new relatives. All brothers and sisters, he supposed, even though it seemed incredible. He wondered if children ever struck out for themselves in this weird country.

"Come in and eat your supper, son," the woman said. "It's getting cold." Duke grinned. That, at least, sounded sane and wholesome. It was what mothers said the world over.

He found a dim, crude room inside with a dirt floor and a long table down the middle. There was a fireplace at one end. Bunks ran along two walls. A ladder led to a loft above.

The fun having terminated, the family went about its business and left Duke pretty much alone. The food tasted good. He was hungry enough to overlook the greasiness of the meat and the sogginess of the bread. Covertly, Duke studied the members of the family. He wondered what their names were, where confidences should be attempted. He wondered also how Kathie was faring. Had she been sent to bed without her supper? This amused him at first. Then the absurdity of the whole thing struck him. Kathie had been right. They should get out of this horrible country. What were they doing here in the first place, anyhow?

CONTEMPLATION on this point sobered him. What *were* they doing there? By what freak accident in time or space had they been transplanted so suddenly from one environment to another? And whose places had they taken?

Duke chewed on a piece of salt pork and put this single item under the mental microscope. Why did his mind keep repeating that idea? How did he know they had replaced anyone? Maybe they hadn't.

But obviously they had. They'd walked into this strange world, had been taken by the ear, spanked, and knocked down with an unmistakable show of familiarity.

"You shouldn't anger your father, Tom. You know his temper."

Duke started, turned, and found the woman seated beside him, the baby lying, contented, over her shoulder. His heart suddenly warmed. She handled the baby as naturally as she breathed. She would always be handling one. She would probably leave a baby crying when she died.

"No—I guess I shouldn't."

"He isn't as hard as he seems. It's just that everybody's afraid since Laura Pritchard and Joe Davis disappeared."

Duke could remain silent no longer. He had to pry for an opening somewhere. This seemed as safe a place as any. "Ma—what happened to them? That is—what do you think happened?"

A strange, blank look came into her tired blue eyes. "It must be like the Prophet said. The Lord smote them down because they sinned."

"Ma—do you really believe that guff?"

Her eyes cleared, then widened. "Why Tom! I don't understand...what are you saying?"

"After all, why do you—we, take the Prophet's word for everything? He's only another man."

The woman glanced quickly around as though she feared her other children had overheard this heresy. "Tom! You don't mean that—any of it! The Prophet has brought us close to God. He's made us realize the horror of sin." Again she glanced around while the infant on her shoulder cooed happily. She lowered her voice. "And he controls The Beast. Don't forget that. He controls the instrument of God's vengeance."

Duke beat down the next logical question. But it wouldn't stay down. He sought the most innocent method of framing it. "Ma—do you think anybody ever really saw The Beast?"

"You know they did, Tom. When the beast went to Carter's place that night and tore it down, as a warning. The Carters saw The Beast when God's mercy let them escape with their lives. You heard them tell it in church. And a half dozen other people saw it walking through the swamp with its red eyes blazing!"

"But how do we know The Prophet controlled it?"

The woman turned worried eyes on him. "Tom—what's got into you? Do you want to bring God's vengeance down on all of us?"

"No, Ma. I guess I'm just upset. Think I'll take a walk and then go to bed."

DUKE FOUND relief in the darkness of the night outside. Night, it seemed, came quickly in this swamp country. He made his way toward the light of the settlement, was startled by the soft footsteps that came close.

"It's me...Franky."

Duke knew the voice. It was that of the urchin he'd have liked most to wallop. One of his many brothers.

"What do you want?"

"Looking for to see Ginny?"

"Maybe."

Franky giggled. "It still costs a penny."

Evidently there was a working arrangement here. Duke wondered if he had a penny. He dug into his pocket and found what felt to be several. He wondered how his predecessor had managed to acquire such wealth in this God-forsaken mire. "All right. There's the money."

"Wait here."

The light footsteps faded. Duke leaned against the dim bole of a tree; slapped a couple of mosquitoes; wished he were back in Hollywood. Then he again went over his conversation with Mrs. Lewit. Now he settled into deep thought. He was oblivious of time and place when Franky's voice brought him back. "I brung her this time," the youngster said. "Before I always told her where you was, but this time she wanted me to bring her."

Duke reached out and look Kathie's hand. "Thanks, Franky, but before you go, there's something I want to ask you."

"Got another penny?"

Again Duke doled out. "You get around plenty. Tell me—did you ever see The Beast?"

Franky did not reply for a moment. Then he said, "Gee, you talk funny."

"What do you mean?"

"The words you say. I dunno—they're different some way. Bigger."

"Never mind that. Answer my question."

"Sure I seen it."

"What did it look like?"

"Just like they said in church. It was fifteen feet high with red eyes and arms like tree trunks. It looked kind of like a man, only bigger'n any man I ever saw. I ran like anything."

"Did you see it in the daytime, or at night?"

"At night, when Willy Nickels and me was over in the slough after bull frogs. There was a moon."

"Okay, Franky. You earned your penny. Take a sneak, now."

"Huh?"

"Go on home."

"Gee, you talk funny lately."

DUKE WAITED until the brushing footsteps faded in the direction of the house and the pale form disappeared. He reached out and Kathie came into his arms. "How was it, baby?"

"Duke! I was never so glad to see anybody in my life!" She clung to him.

"Pretty bad, huh?"

"That old battle-axe spanked me! *Spanked* me, right over her knee in front of a dozen brats!"

Duke hoped the darkness hid his grin. "Your family?"

"On my bare skin, with nothing underneath this—this filthy rag I'm wearing. Duke, I want to go home."

"Sure, baby, sure. But listen. You know the plot of *The Spectre of Suicide Swamp?*"

"Of course I do."

"Was it an original? Any idea where it came from?"

"Epic bought it from some freelance, or so I heard. The way I got it, the story was inspired by a news story that broke in the east not long ago."

"Tell me what you know about it."

Kathie clung closer, as though for warmth. "Duke, does it matter? That was a thousand years ago in another world. A world I want to go back to."

"I know, but—"

"Here I am climbing all over you and nothing happens. You don't even kiss me. Duke—I'm cold and scared and weak. This is your big opportunity."

He kissed her lightly. "Tell me about the story."

She sighed. "One of us is slipping. Oh well…" She cuddled closer. "There was a bank robbery in some eastern town where some crackpot scientist was building a robot. By an odd coincidence, the scientist was killed and the robot disappeared the same night the bank was robbed. This writer took the two incidents and tied them together. He—he extra—extra—"

"Extrapolated. Took certain facts and built onto them to arrive at other pseudofacts."

"Or something. Anyhow, that's where the plot came from. This writer had a gang kill the scientist and steal the robot and break open the bank with it. Then they loaded a safe and the robot into a big trailer truck and headed south. They—"

"I know the rest. They dumped the truck into quicksand, after some of them were killed and the robot got loose. I wish I'd known about it before."

"About what?"

"The news-story angle. Kathie, I think I know why we're here. If there's any rhyme or reason to anything, there must be a reason for our being dropped into this swamp, and I've got a hunch I know what it is. There wasn't any Prophet in the *Spectre* script, was there?"

Kathie nuzzled Duke's cheek with her nose. "Uh-uh. What's happened to you? Are you a lot older than you look? Maybe you've turned senile."

Duke quit thinking about his problems and started to show Kathie he wasn't senile. The kiss didn't last long, however. It was interrupted by a crashing in the trees nearby. Then two red spotlights lit the area to a bloody glow.

Kathie screamed. Duke's blood froze as he goggled up at a huge monstrosity fresh from a Frankenstein set. He flung Kathie to the ground and fell on top of her.

CHAPTER FIVE

TOM SAT with elbows on knees, holding his head in his hands.

"Ginny—for Lord's sake! I'm tired. I want to go to bed."

"We can't go to bed, Tom. Not 'til we know these parts. Now say the words again. Say them."

"Oh, all right. Ah…let's see now…darling, I've got to tell you the truth. Our chances of getting out alive are…are…well, they ain't good."

"Tom! Say it right."

"—are very small."

"Oh, Harold. I'm afraid. I'm afraid!"

"We can't go through the slough. The 'gators are waiting there. The high grass is alive with cottonmouth snakes. And in the forest—the Spectre!"

"Oh Harold—Harold!"

Tom lapsed again into perplexed reality. "I just don't understand it. How in tarnation did they get theirselves into such a fuddle? Glory be! Scared of a few snakes and a toothless old bull 'gator."

"Tom! The writer knows better than you do."

"He knows better than me how people live in the swamp?"

"He gets paid for knowing—and writing about it."

"Well. I'll vow he couldn't sell much of his writing down Ogmulee way. They'd laugh him right out of the county." Tom leaned forward, frowning in puzzlement. "Ginny, you see anything funny about this story?"

"Funny? Of course not. It's serious drama."

"I don't mean funny that way. I mean the things it's got in it. The men coming south in the big truck with the—the robot and killing each other. That big truck could be the same one Joe Davis saw going into the quicksand. It goes into the quicksand in this story too."

"That doesn't matter. We've *got* to learn these parts."

"You know—I think that's what really happened to Joe and Laury. I think Joe went down there and dived, trying to find the truck. Then maybe Laury got scared and went in after him."

Ginny laid down the script. "The Prophet said it was the vengeance of the Lord."

"Somehow—now that I'm away from him—I don't take much stock in that Prophet. I always had the feeling there was something about his eyes that got a person. They bored into you peculiar-like."

"He said the Lord had him by the hand."

"Maybe—say, Ginny, this robot-thing in the story. Doesn't say what it looks like. Wonder if it could be anything like The Beast that tromped all over the Carter's house?"

"It might."

Tom's eyes saddened. "Kind of wish I was back there—Prophet or no Prophet. I'd sure like to find me a hill alive with cottonmouth like it says in this story. Never saw anything like that in my life."

"Tom, let's try it once more. Do it right this time and I'll let you go to sleep."

"All right, Ginny. I'll do my best. That looks like a mighty wonderful bed. I've been itching to get into it. Hope that other fellow don't come back and want it just when I get comfortable."

BUT, AFTER five minutes, Tom again became entangled in reality. He said, "You know, Ginny—since we got clean away from that Prophet, he kind of begins to interest me. Funny how he changed, isn't it?"

Ginny sighed and put the script on the table. "How do you mean *changed,* Tom?"

"Well, he wasn't always like he was then—is now—oh, tarnation! This here and there business gets me all mixed up. I wish I knew who I was—am."

Ginny was pondering also…It was a little strange, thinking back, how the Prophet changed. The people at Ogmulee never seemed to give that much mind."

"Too scared, probably."

"I can remember how he was before his wife died and his boy ran away. That must have been pretty hard on him, Tom."

"'The trouble was he always stayed above other folks. Never let them help him. Guess that's the way with people that depend on the Lord. When they need something and the Lord's taking a day off—out fishing or something—ordinary folks' help seems pretty stingy."

"His boy Louie was an odd one."

"Uh-huh. None of the kids liked him very much, maybe 'cause he was a preacher's son." Tom rubbed his chin reflectively. "Ginny…I wouldn't much like being a preacher's son. Must have been pretty lonely. Never going with the kids to swipe a chicken, or on Halloween. Never getting in a fight."

"No wonder he ran away. He was probably pretty lonesome."

"Uh-huh. And it ain't—"

"*—isn't—*"

"—isn't very hard to see why the Preacher went off kind of, getting two kicks in the face like that so close together."

Ginny picked up the script, but Tom reached out tensely and stayed her hand. "Ginny—I think I got it figured out!"

"What?"

"The real answer! What really happened! When you go crazy, you go one way or another—crazy over *something,* that is. Like old Moss Keeley went moon-crazy. Remember how he used to look at the moon all the time—and when it wasn't in the sky how he used to cry for it to come out?"

"What's that got to do with it?"

"Well—the Prophet went money-crazy!"

"But he never had more than fifteen cents at one time in his life. He lived off the land."

"That's it. After reading this story I can figure it out. There was money in the big truck Joe and Laury saw. It was the Prophet, I'll bet, that shoved it into the quicksand. But he'd snagged the money first. And I'll bet he killed Joe and Laury 'cause they saw him do it!"

"Tom! You're crazy!"

"Maybe I am—maybe I'm not. But I'll bet I know where the money is. You know that little shack by the slough, where old Ken Cooley lived? You know—Ken Cooley, who died when he drank too much and saw more snakes than they've even got in this story. Well—the Prophet chased the kids away from that shack three times. My little brother Franky told me about it. That's where the Prophet's got all that money hid, Ginny. You can take my word for it."

"But that doesn't make any difference to us, Tom. We don't care any more. We got more important things on our mind. We've got to learn these parts!"

Tom sighed. "All right, Ginny. Let's have another go at it. Glory be! I never see such a one-track woman in all my born days—"

CHAPTER SIX

"DUKE, WHEN are we going to leave this awful place? You keep saying tomorrow, and tomorrow, but it never comes. When, Duke?"

Duke smiled down at Kathie. The lipstick and the rouge were, of course, long gone. The mascara was about worn away. He was just finding out what Kathie really looked like. "One of these days, baby. Take it easy."

"But Duke—"

"I wonder if you realize how you've changed, Kathie?"

"Changed? How?"

"In the old days you'd have asked me once: 'You want to go? Then get the lead out.' You'd have given me ten minutes—maybe five. Then you'd have hit the road alone with never a backward glance."

Kathie seemed bewildered. "But this horrid swamp! I can't go alone. The snakes—"

"I've yet to meet the snake that could have scared the old Kathie."

She lowered her head; put her face in her hands.

Duke said, "We'll go, angel, but there are some things around here that interest me. I've got to have some answers first."

Kathie shuddered. "You must have gotten one the other night! That horrible—thing! With its terrible green eyes!"

Duke froze; then thawed slowly; reached down and raised Kathie's face. "What did you say?"

"That *thing!*"

"You said something else. With the terrible what?"

"Green eyes."

Duke pondered on this before he said, "That's funny. I saw terrible *red* eyes."

"What does it matter? Red, green, purple! It was still horrible."

"It may matter a lot. You stay here a while, I'll be back, I want to do some investigating."

They had a secluded nook between two huge trees where they met—a place the Prophet hadn't come upon. Duke hurried away from it, without a backward glance, toward the village. Breaking into the open he saw the swamp folk going about their various businesses, and it suddenly came to him that his status among them had gradually changed.

Changed so slowly, he'd scarcely realized it himself until this moment. Now they seemed to silently look to him for leadership. It was not a request for leadership exactly, more a matter of asking for it silently, by look and by manner.

For one thing, there were no more pennies needed to get favors from Franky. The penny thing had been dropped by common consent and without comment. Duke called, "Hey, Franky!"

The youngster looked up from his play and came running. "What you want. Tom?"

"The other night, when the Beast visited us. You remember?"

"Sure I remember."

"Tell me—what did it look like to you?"

"It looked like what it was, big and snorting, with a great big red eye in the middle of its forehead."

"One eye?"

"Sure—one big eye. You saw it, didn't you?"

"Uh-huh. It almost ran me down."

AMOS CARTER was patiently rebuilding his home. He straightened and said, "Afternoon, Tom. Ain't seen much of you lately."

"No. I've been up in the swamp a lot."

"Dangerous place to go, son."

"Uh-huh. Listen, Amos—the night that the Beast wrecked your place. Did you see it pretty clear?"

"Clear as a man can see anything ten feet away from him."

"Exactly what did it look like?"

"I told that at the church, it was about fifteen feet high. It had two red light bulbs for eyes and looked a lot like a man only a lot bigger. It was made of steel and it walked on two legs."

Duke rubbed his chin and stared at the house. "Well, anyhow, there's no doubt it busted up your house, Amos."

"And like to of killed my family and me. We was sure lucky. Sure didn't know we was so sinful, but we'll be more careful after this. Prayers every night and morning and at dinner, too. The Prophet says that's the ticket."

"I'D ALMOST given you up," Kathie said.

"It took me longer than I thought, but I think I'm getting somewhere. I talked to seven different people, Kathie, and it was amazing. Every one of them has a different idea as to what The Beast looks like."

"What's unusual about that? Did you ever read what seven different eyewitnesses to an accident have to say? You'd think they saw seven different accidents."

"Not quite that bad, but here's the interesting point. Only one man—Amos Carter—has the same description as you and I."

"But ours weren't the same."

"They were basically. We differed only on the color of the eyes. And Kathie—we're probably the only two people around here who actually know what a robot should look like. It's kind of complicated, Ginny—"

"Ginny? Now wait a minute!"

"Kathie. I'm sorry."

"That's better. Now I *know* we've got to get away from here."

"I think I'm getting this thing unraveled, but as I say, it's kind of complicated. We know the writer who did *The Spectre* script took certain facts, combined them, and projected a story. It could have been one of those rare cases where the projection followed actual facts to an astonishing degree. Look at the way it fits...he had some crooks use the robot to crack a bank. We don't know whether that actually happened or not. But he had them load a safe and the robot into a six-wheel trailer truck and start south. That ties in in some way, because those two kids who were killed told of seeing a trailer truck sunk in some quicksand."

"The story duplicated that too," Kathie said.

"Right. Now the question is this: did the writer send the truck into the swamp just because Epic had an idle set and wanted a swamp picture, or did he have some other reason for doing it?"

"I know how we could find out, Duke, darling."

'How?"

"By going back to Hollywood."

Duke didn't seem to hear her. "I've got a feeling the writer had a basic reason for the swamp locale. That's what's missing from the puzzle."

KATHIE reached up and gently pulled Duke's ear. Possibly, she thought to herself, somewhat dreamily, she had changed as Duke said. In the old days she'd never been interested in Duke's left ear. Now it seemed to be such a fine ear, a strong, masculine ear. Kathie said, "Duke, where is all this getting you? You're just throwing around pieces of a picture puzzle."

"Not exactly. Angel, I think I've got part of it figured out. The Prophet is mad—we know that. He's killer-mad. I think he killed the men in that truck—that he sunk it in the quicksand—that he got the robot to carry the money to a safe place for him—and that now he's protecting the money with all this hocus-pocus."

"But that doesn't make too much sense. Why doesn't he take the money and get out of here, if he's got it?"

"Honey, we're dealing with a madman—remember? They never act logical."

"You may be right about his having the robot."

"I think he *had* it, but I don't think it's working any more. I think he used it once to bust up the Carter house."

"We saw it the other night!"

"This Prophet, baby, is a smarter guy than we give him credit for being. He's got hidden talents. You know what I've got to do?"

"Kiss me."

Duke kissed her. "I've got to go further—"

Kathie lay back in his arms and rumpled his hair, murmured dreamily, "Without a marriage license, darling? I never believed it of you."

"We've got to find out where he's got that money hidden."

"Maybe there wasn't really any money. You're merely projecting."

"I think there was."

"How about in the church?"

"I doubt that. His religious fanaticism, even though it's only a part of his madness, wouldn't permit him to hide it there."

"I think you're just talking in order to kill time and stay around here. I think you actually like the place."

He grinned. "It isn't that I like this place more, but maybe I like some other place less." He kissed her. "Guess you better be getting back, or your mom'll give you another tanning."

Kathie blushed as she got to her feet. She postured, tightening the cloth of her dress over her hip. She indicated a small rip in the material. "Look there. See underneath? That's cloth from two flour sacks. I made some panties. Now a tanning isn't quite so embarrassing."

Duke laughed aloud. "Two flour sacks? Woman, you're sure spreading out."

"I am not! I never made a pair of pants before and I wasted a lot of material."

IT WAS Sunday morning and the swamp folk gathered at the church under the giant magnolia trees. They all came. None would dare stay away. Some were sick, but they came on the arms of others strong enough to help them. Every seat was filled.

Duke sat with the Lewits, surrounded by theoretical brothers and sisters he was getting to know—and to like.

After the congregation had been kept waiting for a half-hour, the Prophet strode in. He moved up the aisle staring straight ahead, like a Moses at the front of a conquering army. He reached the pulpit and turned, taking the Bible lying there in his great hands and raising it.

"Down on your knees!"

Like puppets, the congregation complied. Duke, his head lowered as were all the other heads in the place, stole a side and forward glance toward the pew of the Hays family— toward Kathie, kneeling demurely beside the shapeless Amazon who was supposed to be her mother. Duke's heart warmed at the sight of the slim girl in the tattered dress. He jerked his eyes back to the floor as the Prophet's voice thundered out:

"Oh Lord, we are sinners!"

The congregation responded. "Oh Lord, we are sinners."

"We deserve only your wrath."

The congregation agreed. They agreed also to other things that made Duke's skin crawl: agreed as the madman in the pulpit reviled them in flaming words—rotten words trimmed with blue fire.

Why do they take it? Duke asked himself. How this man had managed to cow and beat to the ground so many inherently strong and independent people was almost beyond conception.

Duke raised his eyes now, using the head in front as a blind, and studied the Prophet directly. It was the first time he'd gotten a really good look at the madman, and he found himself mentally cringing away—avoiding the impact of the power behind that face.

Several pieces of the puzzle clicked into place. Of course! He—

The Prophet started suddenly—like a sensitive, thoroughbred racehorse at an unaccustomed sound. His burning eyes came unerringly around to lock with those of Duke. He held Duke utterly helpless in a living gaze—like a bird trapped by the eyes of a snake. Duke felt hot perspiration well from his skin. He felt something shrivel and dry up inside his brain—withered and dried to powder by the blast furnace of those maniac's eyes.

HE SENSED a sneer of contempt riding the twin fire-beams into his brain—and he was free. Tossed aside as the Prophet released him—tossed down as a butcher would toss a stripped bone after cutting off the lean meat. Duke lowered his head and fought against a wave of nausea and weakness. And he knew that he must have lost consciousness for a moment, because the Prophet's booming voice came to him gradually, as though a loudspeaker's volume had been slowly increased.

"—and the Lord came to me in a cloud of fire and said, 'Tell my children to stay far from the wicked lands to the north, from the pine groves and the marshes and the swamp lands that border the far side of the Ogmulee River. For I am a jealous, vengeful God and will smite them in all my fury if they disobey you, my chosen servant'. This the Lord has told me in a dream, and it was a true dream. 'Stay away from the land I name, sayeth the Lord, because it is my land of vengeance!' "

The Prophet paused to survey his flock. Again his voice thundered out: "You—Morton Willis—stand up and face thy God!"

Duke looked far sidewise to see a thin, terrorized man come slowly to his feet. And all the time, in Duke's mind, a still voice was saying: *This can't be. It can't be.* But it was. A madman holding a churchful of strong men and women in groveling subservience.

"Morton Willis you broke God's commandment. You were hunting across the river yesterday."

"But—but, I didn't know. You didn't say nothing about—"

"The vengeance of God is all-inclusive. He quibbles not over a day or a month or an eon. You have broken His law!"

"Ye-yes. Reckon I did."

"You shall do penance."

"I'll do penance."

"For three days you and your family will stay within your house. You shall cover the windows and no one shall look out upon the night nor the day. If this is not done, the Beast shall—"

"It'll be done—it'll be done!"

There was such fear in the assurance that Duke felt sickened.

CHAPTER SEVEN

DUKE SAID, "The quicksand where the truck may have been sunk, and that old cabin you're talking about, are both the other side of the river?"

Franky nodded. "That's right. Over by Loon Marsh, where it's real wild."

"You must be wrong about the truck, though. How could a six-wheel trailer get in there without bogging down long before the quicksand? It would be impossible."

"No, it wouldn't. There's hard land—a long rocky ridge that runs past Big Foot Slough and among the pine hummocks. It all ain't marshy over there."

"I'd like to take a look."

Franky whistled. "You heard what the Prophet said on Sunday!" Franky didn't look particularly scared, however. Going against the Prophet would be too much of an adventure.

Duke noted this with satisfaction. "He wouldn't have to know."

"But what if he found out and sent The Beast after us?"

"We could run. I'll bet The Beast can't cross the river."

"I'll bet it can. It's got legs like trees. It could wade right across the Ogmulee."

"Maybe so, but we could stay out of its way. I'll bet you know some places to hide from it."

Franky said, "When do you want to go?"

"What's wrong with right now? It isn't more than ten o'clock."

Franky was suspicious. "You fixing to take that old Ginny Hays with you?"

Duke shook his head. "Nope. This trip is just for men."

"That's right," Franky scowled. "We don't want any old girls tagging along."

"Lead on, MacDuff!"

"Who?"

"Lead the way. I'm right behind you."

Duke followed Franky over a tortuous route that led three miles southward, and decided he was getting old. Or maybe it was too many cigarettes. Anyhow, he was thankful when Franky pulled up at a stagnant inlet and waded boldly into the water. He pushed in among some overhanging grass tufts and pulled out a lopsided, badly beaten up scow. "Bet the Beast couldn't ever find this."

"Looks like it needs some repairs. Will it get us across the river?"

"Sure will—after we bail it out."

They bailed it out and it repaid the kindness by taking them safely across the half-mile channel. Franky cached the boat again and started a new trek across even wilder country.

But the land got gradually higher and the going easier until the ridge came in sight. As they topped it, Duke could see the possibility of a truck making a safe way along its crest. Franky stopped and dropped to his knees. "See here? Rubber tire tracks—big ones. If a truck didn't make them, what did?"

"I think you've got something here." Duke could plainly follow the wide diamond tread through several stops of shallow sand.

A SENSE of impossibility—unreality—suddenly assailed him. How could a scriptwriter have taken any set of facts and extrapolated a sequence of events so stunningly accurate? So accurate that an almost true story was even now being shot on a swamp set in Hollywood. "That guy knew something." Duke muttered.

"What guy?"

"Never mind. Let's get to that patch of quicksand."

It was about a mile farther on where the ridge became a smooth, gentle slope across reasonably solid meadowland to end sharply in black, sinister marsh. Here, the big double treads were easily seen. There was a two-hundred-yard sweep of hard ground to the swamp edge. Duke saw how it had been done. Speed. He saw the big truck starting down the slope wide open picking up speed. It could have been hitting seventy at the swamp edge. Speed enough to send it end-over-end out into the black water if the front wheels stuck first.

When, Duke wondered, had the driver jumped? Or had there been a driver? He stood at the swamp edge and looked down into the black water. There would be little chance of ever retrieving the truck that lay, probably, under many feet of sucking sand. The truck or anything else caught in that awful mouth.

"You figuring on going in after it?" Franky grinned.

"Not today."

"Or any other day. Anything down in that sump is gone for good."

"Is the shack you were talking about very far from here?"

"About a mile up the line. You want to go look at it?"

"If you aren't afraid. I'm kind of curious."

"It's back this way."

They reversed their course and went back the way they'd come. After some twenty minutes of walking along the rocky ridge, Franky veered suddenly in-country, away from the river. He glanced over his shoulder toward the lowering sun. "Getting kind of late. We got to hurry or you won't see much."

"They may not like it at home—your being late."

"When Ma finds out I've been with you, she won't care."

Duke took the tribute in silence, his attention caught by a wide marsh they were skirting. Here, truly, was nature at her saddest. There was enough of the poet in Duke to envy the Master Artists who had done this scene.

For endless miles there stretched a melancholy waste of water reddened by the setting sun and dotted by myriad clusters of drooping cattails and grasses. Each tiny sound was magnified a thousandfold by the brooding silence. A frog croaked somewhere and the sound came echoing across the marsh to fade away in a dozen weakening echoes.

Out against the red sunset, a lone heron rose up on awkward wings to emit a sad cry and lumber off across the marsh to some rendezvous.

FRANKY stopped. Duke, preoccupied with the beauty about him, caught himself sharply.

"There it is."

Ahead was a clump of Georgia pine, scattered sparsely. In its heart stood a lone, bleak building—little more than a shack—weakened by years, its ridge pole sagging and tilted at a crazy angle.

"That's it," Franky said. "What do you think's in there?"

"I wish I knew."

"Nothing but a old abandoned shack. Why should the Prophet care whether us kids played in it or not?"

"I can't figure it out."

Franky, trying not to show his apprehension of the gathering darkness, looked swiftly about in a wide circle. "You think maybe the Prophet's hiding around here somewhere? Watching us maybe?"

"I doubt it. There's no place to hide."

"Plenty of trees over beyond. We have to go through them to get to the shallows, or else go back and get the scow."

"The place certainly looks deserted."

A thought struck Franky. "Maybe—could be the Prophet's on the inside a waitin' for us. Maybe he knew we were coming here and he's crouching in there—"

"How would he know?"

"The Prophet has ways of finding things out."

"We'll know if he's there—when I take a look."

"You're going in the shack?"

"We came all this way. We're going to find out one way or another."

"Th-then let's get over to it before we can't see nothing."

"You'd better wait for me."

"Uh-uh. If you go, I'm going too. I ain't no coward."

Duke smiled and tousled Franky's thick blonde hair. "That's my boy! Come on."

There appeared to be no danger whatever. An old shack—forgotten, deserted, miles from nowhere on the edge of a wild marshland. A shack with a false reputation for danger.

The door had not fallen away. In fact, the door seemed remarkably well preserved for so old a building. It was closed and the fit was snug.

Duke grasped the doorknob after a moment and listened. Nothing had sounded to frighten even a bird. Duke pushed open the door.

Only thick darkness met the eye. Darkness and silence. Duke put a foot over the doorsill.

BUT HE jerked it back quickly and whirled at Franky's scream of terror. Duke turned. Franky was pointing, but no indication of direction was necessary.

"The Beast," Franky screamed. "He set The Beast on us!"

And there it was, lumbering toward them from the marshes. A huge, terrifying monstrosity of full fifteen feet, with red rays flaring from crimson eye sockets.

"The Beast." Franky was already in panic-flight, across the open land toward the woods beyond. Duke got his legs moving and set out in pursuit. Behind the fleeing pair came the Prophet's instrument of vengeance.

"Franky!" Duke yelled. "Wait. It's all right. Don't be scared—"

It was like asking a person in a flaming house not to be burned. Franky ran with the speed of pure terror.

Duke's longer strides began to cut down the intervening distance. The speed of the thundering thing behind, however, was greater by far than that of Duke.

Duke caught up with Franky just on the edge of the woodland, and just as the monster was throwing rays of streaming red light over his shoulder. Duke reached out and brought Franky to the ground. "It's all right, kid! Take it easy. Lie still! Nothing's going to happen to you."

Then they seemed in the very maw of destruction—in the thunder and grind of a runaway locomotive.

But there was no agony save the agony of fear—no death—no ravening destruction. It seemed that the monster passed over them harmlessly, but not to travel on its maniacal way.

Rather to become a thing of silence—to fade and vanish, and become nothing.

"It's all over, Franky. There isn't any Beast. No Beast at all. See? You're still alive and in one piece. It didn't hurt you."

Franky was still sobbing out his terror as Duke held him close. Duke made no effort to hurry things, letting time take its course; letting Franky's fear die a natural death.

As they sat there a huge moon pushed up over the marsh, lighting the country all around—throwing its radiance until the lonely shack again stood out sharp and clear.

Franky at last found words. "There—there wasn't no Beast? But there had to be. I saw it!"

"Look, Franky. Where did it come from? Which way?"

"From the marsh."

"But it didn't come out of the marsh or we'd have seen it. It just appeared suddenly out on the level ground."

"It must have come from somewhere."

"It did, Franky. Out of your own mind."

The boy looked bewildered—found no words. Duke went on: "Franky, there are people who can put things into the minds of other people. Have you ever heard of hypnotism?"

"Isn't that when somebody makes you do things when you're asleep?"

"That's the idea. But there are stronger forms of hypnotism than that. And there are people who can do funny things along that line. Some crazy people especially. When a mind goes mad it sometimes gets stronger. False strength, maybe, but still strength. There was a Russian once—a man named Rasputin—who was crazy and yet had the ability to make people do things they didn't want to and even see things that didn't exist. The Prophet is that way. He has the power to make people see The Beast that isn't there."

FRANKY thought that over for a moment before he said, "Then did Mr. Carter just imagine his house got tromped on? I saw the place. It was a mess."

"There *was* a monster, Franky. It did wreck the Carter house. But I'm sure something happened to it. I've got a hunch it bogged down in the swamp some place. The tip-off was when I found out everybody sees a different kind of a

Beast. The one you see isn't the same as the one I see. Everybody at the landing sees a different one because each person has a different mind and imagination. The Prophet can make them see a Beast, but he can't make them all see the same one, because he's really forcing them to create their own Beasts out of their own imaginations."

Franky shook his head. "That's all pretty mixed up. I can't hardly make head or tail of it, but if you say so…" Franky's eyes went vague. Apparently his mind had conjured up another question. "Look, Tom. Suppose all you say is true. There's one thing I can't cypher out…why's the Prophet doing it? Why does he want to go around scaring people who never did him no harm?"

"That's a pretty deep question. Probably he thinks he's doing the right thing. His conception of God and God's law is a little twisted up. You can't blame him, because he's crazy, and crazy people aren't to be held accountable for their actions."

"You know, he wasn't always this way. It's just the last year or so. He used to be all right. He'd make fish poles and hooks for the kids, and he was all right. Then he began getting funny, making people afraid of him."

"He's got the people terrorized with this imaginary Beast. He probably got the idea from the real one."

"But why'd he set the Beast on us today? We weren't doing no harm."

"I think it was because he didn't want us to look into that shack. I've got a hunch we'll find the answer to a lot of things in there."

"You going to look?"

"That's right."

Franky stared apprehensively at the shack. It stood bleak and silent under the yellow moon—hostile now, forbidding.

"Maybe we better go home now and come back tomorrow. There ain't no hurry, is there?"

"No. But we've come a long way and I don't want to go home without getting what we came for. I think the Prophet is hiding a lot of money there. I want to find out."

"Money? What'd he want with money? It wouldn't do him no good."

"I think loving money is a part of his madness. Listen— you stay here where you can watch me, and I'll have a quick look into the house. It won't take a minute."

"Well—all right. But I'm going with you. We're together in this thing. I ain't any coward."

"Good boy. The place is obviously deserted. There's no danger whatever. Just think! If we find the money you'll be in line for a reward."

"How much?"

"Oh, maybe as much as a hundred dollars. Come on. Let's go inside."

THEY WALKED hand in hand toward the forlorn shack by the marsh; walked under a yellow moon that turned the world to day, glinted over the lonely water and accentuated the black, staring windows of the building.

As they came close their feet found a path, well worn but now grown over with meadow grass. A path made by feet long gone and now forgotten; a path made in happier days.

"Gosh!" Franky whispered. "I wonder what we'll find."

They were ten feet from the door when it opened— opened wide—and the huge figure of the Prophet stepped forth.

To Duke the sight was far more chilling than had been that of The Beast. Here was no figment of a man's imagination. Here was a towering pillar of mad strength. Here was a killer. Here was death.

Franky whimpered and cringed back. Duke, frozen in his tracks, felt somehow that retreat was useless.

The Prophet flung out his arms in a gesture too full of threat to be theatrical. His voice boomed up to the yellow moon. "Ye of the transgressor's band! Ye who disobey the command of the Lord God; Ye who are facing death!"

Duke kept his eyes on the huge maniac, reached back to touch Franky's shoulder. "Run, kid. Get the hell out of here. Hit for the river and home!"

It was Duke's last moment of respite. The Prophet, with a bull-roar of rage, charged full at him.

"Run, Franky!"

Duke would have been the first to concede himself to be no fighter. All his life he had avoided trouble rather than faced it. But never before had he looked death in the face. Never before had his life itself been at stake. His instinct rose to the occasion—at least partially.

It told him that once those great arms encircled him he would be through. They would crush his ribs, break his back. Once in the Prophet's embrace, he would not escape alive.

Nor could he possibly outrun the giant. So he did the thing his instinct told him to do. He struck out.

It was a good punch, a hard, straight right flush to the Prophet's mouth. Duke felt teeth snap under his knuckles; felt the blow recoil up his own arm into his shoulder.

It stopped the Prophet, sent him reeling backward. But Duke was not deceived. It had been mainly the surprise of the thing that had caught the Prophet off balance. He had not expected resistance.

The flowing white beard was stained with crimson as the Prophet reeled against the wall of the shack and came erect. He passed a hand across his month, wiping away the blood.

Here, Duke made a major mistake. He could have run; could probably have gotten enough of a head start to achieve the wooded area not too far away.

BUT THE success of the blow gave him a false courage. It had been so simple, possibly one more blow could do the trick. Maybe this mountainous maniac was not invincible. So Duke chose to stay and fight.

The Prophet came forward again. This time there was no roar of wrath, but the silence was even more frightening than the bellowed challenge. Out went the giant arms to enfold Duke in a death grip.

Again Duke slammed a jarring right fist into the wholly unprotected face; again the sound of flesh grinding against bone; again the Prophet staggered back.

But not so far this time. And he recovered quicker; came back to the attack sooner. Duke, flooded by a sense of desperation, aimed the third blow lower down. Swinging from the ankles, he sought to drive his fist, up to the wrist, into that sensitive spot just above the stomach. A powerful blow to the *solar plexus* could be an actual killer. It had caused more than one death.

Duke could as well have slammed his fist against a brick wall. He cried out from the pain and the bones of his hand snapped. The Prophet had a body of iron.

Duke sagged from the shock. Then the Prophet's arms went around him—found their hold. Duke stared into the eyes of death.

The pain in his bending spine was well nigh unbearable. But the Prophet chose not to end it quickly. The enemy must suffer. He applied the pressure as from an eyedropper— gradually. Slowly Duke's spine was bent into a backward bow.

A scream ripped Duke's ears. He realized it came from his own lips. But only one scream because, now, there was no air for his lungs. A scream would have been a luxury.

The pain was a crimson sea in which he floated. White-hot bubbles of agony seared his flesh. Until consciousness was blotted out. Until the crimson sea turned into a black ocean and there was nothing...

CHAPTER EIGHT

"TOM! —TOM! Wake up! You gotta wake up, Tom! I can't lug you no farther!"

Duke opened his eyes to see shadows—bars—across the yellow moon. Slowly he realized the bars were tree branches. "Franky? That you?"

"Uh-huh. It's me. You all right now, Tom? You feeling better now, Tom?"

"I—I guess so. What happened?"

"When the fight started I ran. I was that scared. I stopped in the trees and looked back and saw you and the Prophet wrestling. Then you let out a scream and I knew he had you. I had to do something, Tom, so I grabbed me a club and run back. The Prophet wasn't paying no attention to me so I hauled off and let him have a good one right across his head. He went down like an axed steer and I tried to wake you up. It was pretty hard, but I started dragging you and then you come to some and started kind of half walking. It was a little easier then, but I got plumb tuckered and had to put you down."

"Franky, you saved my life. You saved me from the Prophet."

"Think you can get up?"

"I think so. How far is the boat."

"Not far, but I ain't taking you home. You got to stay out of sight. I don't think I killed the Prophet, and now he'll really be gunning for you. You got to hide while I go home and scout around."

"It's all right. We'll go home to—"

"What's the matter?"

"I think it's my ribs. One of them's broken. It feels like a sharp point is digging in somewhere."

"I know a place, if you can walk another quarter mile."

"I can make it."

"All right—but real slow."

The place Franky knew was a hollowed-out embankment in the piney woods, a place made soft by many droppings of pine needles. Franky said, "That old Prophet won't find you here. You just get some sleep and I'll go home and see how things look. The Prophet'll probably come there looking for you. I'll sneak something to eat out in the morning. Don't make no sound."

"I'll be all right. Say—Franky, will you tell Ginny where I am?"

Franky's eyes fell. He spoke in a hurt voice. "You want that old girl knowing about it? Ain't I taking care of you all right?"

"Sure, Franky. I've changed my mind. Better not tell her—for a while anyway."

"See you in the morning."

Franky moved away like a shadow, and soon Duke was alone. He thought of Kathie. But he was glad Franky had objected to telling her. Better to leave her out of this until it took a turn one way or the other.

If Duke knew anything about psychology, the Prophet would be a raging demon of vengeance now. Probably, Duke thought, he had done the people at the landing a disservice with his snooping. The Prophet would come searching and his wrath would be terrible.

Duke thought of Kathie. She'd be wondering about him. No doubt he had done her a disservice too. Slowly, he drifted off to sleep.

"TOM! TOM! Wake up." The voice was soft, insistent. Duke opened his eyes.

"It's your mother, son. Wake up."

"Ma."

"What's happened, Tom? What did the Prophet do to you?"

Duke blinked gummy eyes. The faint light told him it was early dawn. "We had a little set-to, Ma. I'm all right." Duke saw Franky hovering uneasily in the background.

Franky said, "I didn't mean to tell. Tom, but Ma, she kind of worried it out of me. Then she made me bring her here."

"It's all right, kid."

"Franky said you were hurt in the chest. I brought some bandages. Can you sit up?"

Duke struggled to a sitting position. "It won't be bad when the stiffness is gone. Did the Prophet turn up at the landing?"

"No. Nobody's seen hide nor hair of him."

"He will. He's sure to come back there looking for me."

"Maybe I killed him," Franky said with it certain awe.

"Not a chance. You couldn't swing a club heavy enough to break that skull. He'll be along, and I've got to be at the landing when he gets there."

Mrs. Lewit's eyes were on Duke. He saw the puzzled look; the look he'd seen so often lately. He said, "Franky, take a little walk, will you? I want to talk to Ma."

"Sure—sure, Tom."

He watched in silence as Franky moved slowly, reluctantly, out of earshot. Then he turned his eyes back to the woman he had grown to love almost as a son loves a mother.

"Ma—you know I'm not your son, don't you?"

Her eyes were hard on his face. "Yes—yes, I think I do. You look the same. You act—almost the same. But there's something."

"Tom is a long way from here. In a place called Hollywood. I think. He'll probably be back to see you eventually."

"I—I don't understand. Why did he go away?"

"He doesn't know himself. He didn't go—he was taken away. Just as I was brought here. We changed places, just as Ginny changed places with a girl called Kathie."

"You mean Ginny Hays isn't—?"

"She isn't Ginny. Ginny, I think, is with Tom."

"That's good. They were in love with each other." Mrs. Lewit's eyes filled with something Duke had a hard time describing. Bitterness perhaps—and sadness. "They never had much chance in the swamp."

Duke marveled. "You're an amazing woman. No disbelief. And you take it so calmly—with such patience. Do you feel what I've told you is true?"

"I don't know. But I think maybe it is."

And Duke, who had gently patronized this woman, was suddenly ashamed of himself. Instead of giving her of his knowledge, he realized he should be seeking out hers. "Ma— why do you think it happened? I know it did happen, but I don't know why. Do you?"

"Prayer, maybe. I've prayed, and so have the other women of the landing; prayed to be rid of the scourge in our midst—the Prophet. We were helpless, and prayer was all we had. They say God moves in mysterious ways. Maybe you coming here was the only way."

"Maybe the Prophet will kill me, Ma."

There was a quiet strength in the woman—strength Duke was testing. She said, "I don't think so. I think, somehow, that this is the end of the Prophet." She looked down at Duke. "But, still, I don't want you to go back and face him."

"I've got to. I know that. I've got to be at the landing when he comes."

"If that's what your heart tells you."

"It does. The Prophet isn't what he appears to be to the people. He's a poor, tortured, misguided man. I think, in the end, we'll help him."

"Come, lean on my shoulder."

THE PEOPLE gathered silently, and Duke talked. A change came over his audience, but Duke realized he could take credit for only a small part of it. The change was wrought by his story rather than by his words.

He had met the Prophet and had fled. That, to them, was entirely understandable. No man could stand before the white-bearded maniac avenger. But through the long hours of the day Duke had waited at the landing for the Prophet to come for him. He had waited in vain, and in his waiting the people had found a hope that was, in reality, a strength.

The Prophet *should* have come. He should have charged into the landing long since, his eyes aflame with vengeance. He had not done this. Was he delaying because of fear? Or weakness?

Thus sprang their hope, while the sun moved deep in the west.

"Maybe he won't come."

"Maybe he's scared out."

"Maybe he's left the country."

"We'll wait a while longer," Duke said.

The sun sank beyond the edge of the brooding swamps. The Prophet had not arrived.

"Are we just going to sit here?"

There was defiance in the question. The first show of defiance Duke had seen. Without analyzing, he decided to capitalize on it. "We'll go after him. We'll go to the shack."

Soon torches blazed and the landing was lit from end to end. "We'll go up and wade the shallows!" someone called out, and soon a line of torches was winding through the swamp.

Duke had no great difficulty in keeping up because the line, of necessity, moved slowly. A full two hours passed before the torch parade broke out into the open land by the marsh and surrounded the lonely shack.

There had been shouts of defiance and encouragement during the march. Now all was quiet as courage ebbed before the unseen menace that had cowed them for so long. The circle closed in slowly.

Until it could tighten no more; until leadership was silently called for.

Duke took a torch from the closest man and moved toward the closed door of the shack. "Wait," he called. "All of you."

There was no dissent. Duke reached the door and his hand closed over the knob. Before he could open it, there was a rush of footsteps. He turned. Kathie.

"I'm going in with you. I won't let you go alone."

Duke grinned. "All right. I have a feeling there's nothing to fear inside. But stay behind me." He opened the door and walked inside.

THERE WAS a moment of darkness before the torch lit the single room, and during that moment Duke regretted his courage. During that moment he admitted to himself that he was not an inherently brave man, and that if he'd made a mistake this time he would die. The Prophet could still cow the people outside. He could kill Duke and no hand would be raised to fend him off. Their courage was as false as that of Duke himself.

Then the room was alive with torchlight and Duke's fear turned to a chill.

He and Kathie would always remember the sight that met their eyes. Stretched upon the floor, spread wide upon his back, by the Prophet—an unhappy madman, dead by his own hand. A warped and powerful brain come finally against solid agony too great to bear. The shotgun blast had left little of that brain.

But the Prophet was noted by Duke and Kathie only in passing. The center of interest was the figure on the rear wall. A figure crucified. A man bound wrist and ankle to the beams supporting the wall, starved, beaten, emaciated.

Dead.

And a terrible death it had been—a punishment far to great for any crime conceivable to any man—except the Prophet.

"Now I get it." Duke muttered. "Now that it's laid out in front of me, I get it."

Kathie shuddered and strove for words that wouldn't come.

"I did the old man an injustice. I said it was money. Maybe he was mad. But at least he kept his madness pure right to the end."

"His son?"

"Of course—his son. Call them in."

CHAPTER NINE

THERE WAS a new atmosphere at the landing. A brighter sun flashed down through the trees. The children shouted in their play. The people moved about with all tenseness gone.

Duke lay under a magnolia with Kathie seated beside him tickling his ear. "I went off base because that writer knew something I didn't. He evidently did a little research into that news story before he wrote the screen treatment. He found out one of the suspected bank mob came from the swamp country. That's why he wrote about the truck coming to the swamps. How was I to know the Prophet's son went bad?"

Kathie picked a blade of grass and tickled Duke's nose. "The writer didn't know that either."

"No, he didn't. That's why he didn't have the Prophet in his script. He had his mobster come down here and ditch the truck, which was exactly what happened in the real story that went a lot further. The Prophet's son, after getting in trouble with the mob and killing some of them, got away with the truck and came home to Dad."

"I wonder why he did that? I should think he'd have been ashamed."

"He did it because he was yellow. When the going got tough he came to his Dad for help."

Kathie shuddered. "He didn't know he was coming home to a maniac."

"He paid for his crimes. The Prophet saw to that. God I wonder how long he hung there—dying?"

"Let's not talk about it. Let's talk about us. We're going to leave here, aren't we?"

"I guess so. But we'll have to walk. We've got no money."

"We'll find the nearest town and wire for some."

"Anything you say, darling." Duke pulled her head down and kissed her.

They found a town, but they didn't wire for money. Just why, they never quite knew. It might have been the MAN WANTED sign in a gas station they came to. There was a cabin for the man, and it wasn't too hard—with help short— to wangle an advance for a marriage license and a week's provisions.

Then there was the old Ford the owner gave Duke. It needed a lot of work and there was no time to send wires.

Duke did a pretty good job on the car, and he liked the gas station. But he knew he couldn't stay there forever, with Kathie continually nipping at him.

Still he didn't want to wire Hollywood, so they compromised. They got in the Ford and started up the coast.

A hundred miles north another job got in the way. A bigger station needed a mechanic. Duke asked for the job and got it. Then there was nothing to do but stick around and find out if he had what it took to hold it down. Kathie was annoyed, but the lunch counter offered a chance to keep busy. She went to work as a waitress, but only to get enough money to reach Hollywood. Somehow, the idea of wiring for funds had been discarded.

"After all," Duke said, "who in Hollywood would want to send us any money—be glad to do it, I mean. Just think how you'd feel if we got turned down?"

THEY ACCUMULATED quite a bankroll before Kathie got them on the road again. This time they made New York City and went to a good hotel without feeling any pinch. They came in during the afternoon, took their time dressing and dining, and then went out and walked down Broadway. At 42nd Street, Kathie stopped dead and pointed. "Look!"

It was a huge marquee above which, in letters several feet high, were the words, *"The Spectre of Suicide Swamp."*

"Duke—it's a Broadway opening. Our picture!"

They pushed through the crowd and got to the inner ropes just as a limousine drove up.

"There they are—we are," Duke said. Somehow, he wasn't excited. It was almost as though he'd always known it would be like this.

Tom Lewit and Ginny Hays got out of the limousine and walked up the red carpet. Ginny was radiant. Tom was handsome. Ginny stopped, graciously, to bestow autographs. She stood not ten feet from Duke and Kathie.

"What can we do!" Kathie whispered. "They're—they're getting away with it! Shall we call a cop?"

"Don't be silly. You want to get put in the funny house?"

"Then there's—nothing we can do."

"I think there's a way."

"What is it?"

"Things won't snap back of their own accord—never again—but all you have to do is touch that girl. I'm sure of it. Touch her and something will happen to straighten things out."

Smiling, Ginny moved closer. Kathie's hand went out. Ginny pressed by. Kathie jerked her hand back quickly. Ginny went on into the theater.

"I—I couldn't," she whispered.

"Look at *him,*" Duke said. "The poor devil. I know how he feels."

"Duke—I just couldn't do it."

"Couldn't what?"

"Touch her."

"You didn't want to?"

"When it came right down to it, I guess I—I didn't want to."

"I didn't think you would."

"But Duke—do you think it would have worked?"

He grinned. "You know my hunches."

Kathie squeezed his arm. "I'm not used to you, even yet. Let's go back to the hotel."

So they did.

THE END

If you've enjoyed this book, you will not want to miss these terrific titles…

ARMCHAIR SCI-FI & HORROR DOUBLE NOVELS, $12.95 each

D-61 **THE MAN WHO STOPPED AT NOTHING** by Paul W. Fairman
TEN FROM INFINITY by Ivar Jorgensen

D-62 **WORLDS WITHIN** by Rog Phillips
THE SLAVE by C.M. Kornbluth

D-63 **SECRET OF THE BLACK PLANET** by Milton Lesser
THE OUTCASTS OF SOLAR III by Emmett McDowell

D-64 **WEB OF THE WORLDS** by Harry Harrison and Katherine MacLean
RULE GOLDEN by Damon Knight

D-65 **TEN TO THE STARS** by Raymond Z. Gallun
THE CONQUERORS by David H. Keller, M. D.

D-66 **THE HORDE FROM INFINITY** by Dwight V. Swain
THE DAY THE EARTH FROZE by Gerald Hatch

D-67 **THE WAR OF THE WORLDS** by H. G. Wells
THE TIME MACHINE by H. G. Wells

D-68 **STARCOMBERS** by Edmond Hamilton
THE YEAR WHEN STARDUST FELL by Raymond F. Jones

D-69 **HOCUS-POCUS UNIVERSE** by Jack Williamson
QUEEN OF THE PANTHER WORLD by Berkeley Livingston

D-70 **BATTERING RAMS OF SPACE** by Don Wilcox
DOOMSDAY WING by George H. Smith

ARMCHAIR SCIENCE FICTION & FANTASY CLASSICS, $12.95 each

C-19 **EMPIRE OF JEGGA**
by David V. Reed

C-20 **THE TOMORROW PEOPLE**
by Judith Merril

C-21 **THE MAN FROM YESTERDAY**
by Howard Browne as by Lee Francis

C-22 **THE TIME TRADERS**
by Andre Norton

C-23 **ISLANDS OF SPACE**
by John W. Campbell

C-24 **THE GALAXY PRIMES**
by E. E. "Doc" Smith

If you've enjoyed this book, you will not want to miss these terrific titles…

ARMCHAIR SCI-FI & HORROR DOUBLE NOVELS, $12.95 each

D-71 **THE DEEP END** by Gregory Luce
     TO WATCH BY NIGHT by Robert Moore Williams

D-72 **SWORDSMAN OF LOST TERRA** by Poul Anderson
     PLANET OF GHOSTS by David V. Reed

D-73 **MOON OF BATTLE** by J. J. Allerton
     THE MUTANT WEAPON by Murray Leinster

D-74 **OLD SPACEMEN NEVER DIE!** John Jakes
     RETURN TO EARTH by Bryan Berry

D-75 **THE THING FROM UNDERNEATH** by Milton Lesser
     OPERATION INTERSTELLAR by George O. Smith

D-76 **THE BURNING WORLD** by Algis Budrys
     FOREVER IS TOO LONG by Chester S. Geier

D-77 **THE COSMIC JUNKMAN** by Rog Phillips
     THE ULTIMATE WEAPON by John W. Campbell

D-78 **THE TIES OF EARTH** by James H. Schmitz
     CUE FOR QUIET by Thomas L. Sherred

D-79 **SECRET OF THE MARTIANS** by Paul W. Fairman
     THE VARIABLE MAN by Philip K. Dick

D-80 **THE GREEN GIRL** by Jack Williamson
     THE ROBOT PERIL by Don Wilcox

ARMCHAIR SCIENCE FICTION CLASSICS, $12.95 each

C-25 **THE STAR KINGS**
  b   y Edmond Hamilton

C-26 **NOT IN SOLITUDE**
     by Kenneth Gantz

C-32 **PROMETHEUS II**
     by S. J. Byrne

ARMCHAIR SCIENCE FICTION & HORROR GEMS SERIES, $12.95 each

G-7 **SCIENCE FICTION GEMS, Vol. Seven**
     Jack Sharkey and others

G-8 **HORROR GEMS, Vol. Eight**
     Seabury Quinn and others

If you've enjoyed this book, you will not want to miss these terrific titles…

SOMETHING STRANGE WAS GOING ON...

There was this doorway, see, to a place called Drendon. Drendon was full of things—hotsys and kwistians and sarks and wumbles. There were also furry fauns, sly satyrs, vampires, werewolves, witches and woodnymphs and the most unlikely collection of spells in any dimension.

And when you entered the forest of Drendon, and your girlfriend turned into a woodnymph, and her brother became a faun, and the dreadful parrot-beaked, cannibalistic Kwistian birds came to feast, you didn't waste precious time asking what's going on—

In short, it's a wild and woolly Jack Sharkey world where the title phrase is virtually the answer to any question!

CAST OF CHARACTERS

ALBERT HICKS
He was a librarian that felt life was passing him by—until he met some very interesting creatures from Drendon.

SUSAN/LORN
How did Albert's very boring, overly-proper girlfriend, become a tempting, winsome, lovely wood-goddess?

TIMOTHY/TIMTIK
This little ten-year old was no regular newspaper boy in Drendon—with cloven hooves and taloned fingers!

MAGGIE/MAGGOT
Transported into Drendon while cooking things in her kitchen—she simply became the Drendon equivalent of a witch.

PORKLE/KWIST
This big man had a park named after him, "Porkle Park." And there was a lot more to this "park" than most people realized.

COURTLAND/CORT
A sharp-beaked winged creature that seemed almost human— with the exception of his fondness for cooked woodnymph!

IT'S MAGIC,
YOU DOPE!

By
JACK SHARKEY

ARMCHAIR FICTION
PO Box 4369, Medford, Oregon   97501-0168

*For more information about Armchair Books and products, visit our
website at…*

www.armchairfiction.com

Or email us at…

armchairfiction@yahoo.com

CHAPTER ONE

IT was the same two guys. I spotted them standing down at the end of the dark street, just beyond the cone of light cast by the street lamp. They were pretending to be neighborhood people, carrying on a casual conversation on the corner, but I knew they were the same guys I'd seen standing outside the library when I'd left it a half hour before, in downtown Chicago.

I was quite curious, but lacked the nerve to approach them and ask what they wanted. They might want my wallet and watch, and then where'd I be? So I just slammed the door of my sedan, and started up the walk toward Susan's house, pretending I hadn't noticed them. I wished there were more people out on their porches, but the autumn evenings had been turning colder, and hardly anyone came out.

I rang the bell of the two-story bungalow where Susan lived with her folks, and was reassured to hear the sound of footsteps coming to answer the chimes. Mrs. Baker, Susan's mother, opened the door.

"Hello, Al," she said. "Susan'll be down in a minute. Here, let me take your hat." She rambled through some more mother-greeting-suitor talk, and I finally wound up in the living room, sitting in the center of the sofa, alone, while Mr. Baker, Susan's father, puffed at his pipe and tried to engage me in light conversation on the subject of burglary. Garvey Baker was the night watchman at the Marshall Field's store up near Lake Street in Oak Park. He was usually about to go out to work about the time I showed up to see Susan. It helped.

AS long as we were on the subject of crime, I mentioned those two guys who seemed to have followed me from the Loop. Mr. Baker laughed. "You've been reading too many mystery books," he said with an infuriatingly paternal smile.

"Yes, sir," I said, anxiously awaiting the moment when he would lift his gold watch from his vest pocket, say, "Well, better get down to the store before the thieves strip it bare," and go. Mrs. Baker came in with a tray.

"Thought you might like some cookies and lemonade," she explained, setting the tray down on the end table beside the sofa. I thanked her, and she laughed and went out into the kitchen again.

"Well," said Garvey Baker, getting ponderously to his feet, and glancing at that gold watch, "better get on up to the store before the thieves strip it bare." I was glad to hear the front door close behind him. Then a light patter of feet on the hall stairs announced the arrival of Miss Susan Baker, and I jumped gratefully to my feet.

"Al," she smiled, coming across the room to me, her hands outstretched to lightly grip mine.

"Hi, Susan," I said, taking hold of her fingertips for that brief moment before she'd deftly tug them free.

"Do you like my dress?" she said, pirouetting. "Pop got it at his discount. Isn't it adorable?"

I said it was, and she sat beside me on the sofa. Perhaps "beside" is too strong. It was a three-seater; she and I filled the one and three cushions.

"Your mother made lemonade for us," I said. "Here it is, on the tray."

"Oh, how nice!" said Susan, her eyes dancing. "Wasn't that nice of Mom, Al?"

I said it was, and we sat a while longer. Then, getting up a little courage, I turned to her and said, "Would you like some?"

"Oh, please," said Susan, brightly.

I arose and poured out two glasses of lemonade, gave one to her, and sat back with the other, on the two-cushion.

"Al—" said Susan. "Please." I moved back to the one-cushion.

"Cookie?" I asked.

"*Al!*" gasped Susan, her eyes round and startled.

"I mean, do you *want* a cookie?"

"Oh. No thank you. But thank you for asking me." She began to sip her lemonade. I began to sip mine. I searched my mind for a topic of conversation. (The Bakers had no TV.) I found one and made the most of it.

"Two men followed me from the library today."

"Goodness," said Susan. "Why?"

"I don't know," I said. "To rob me, maybe."

"A librarian?" Susan laughed lightly. "You barely make enough to support yourself, let alone support a wife…"

"Mr. Garson says I will get that ten percent increase at the end of November," I pointed out. "I will have been with the library five years."

"And then we can have our June wedding, as we planned," said Susan. "Won't it be nice?"

"Nice," oh, yes, I guess so.

"But what about your hours?" she said with a tiny pout. "You always come over so late, Al."

"You have to have seniority to get the early shift."

"That may take years," she sighed.

"I know," I said. "But at least I can sleep late in the mornings, after we're married."

"Al!" said Susan.

"Sorry," I said, not sure for what.

SUSAN flashed me a look of deep longing. "I think I will have that cookie, now, Al…" she murmured.

All at once, I wanted to scream.

"I said, I think I will have that cookie, now, Al," Susan repeated demurely.

I couldn't stand it any longer. Eschewing caution, I set my lemonade back on the tray, reached over and took Susan's and put it beside mine, then I slid onto the two-cushion and grabbed her by the upper arms. *"Susan—!"*

"Al!" Her voice was a panicky squeak. "Have you gone mad? Mother might come in!"

"I don't care," I grated. "I've got to talk to you about something more important than cookies or lemonade or my life at the library."

"Al, you're hurting me!" she said, tiny crystal tears twinkling upon her lower lashes. "How can you behave so horridly to me?"

"Susan," I groaned, "you're not even listening to me! Once— just this once—stop blathering all your usual inanities and give me your attention, please!"

"A gentleman," blathered Susan, "never uses fierce language like that in the presence of a girl he thinks of as a lady, so I can only assume that—"

"Stop!" My growl was so ferocious that some of the painted doll cuteness faded from her face, and a look of genuine adult apprehension overrode her features. She stared at me, blinking rapidly, then said she would listen if I'd only let go of her arms. I let go. She listened.

"Susan," I said, talking fast, and trying to put all the misery and frustration of my soul into words, "there must be something more than this. I mean, I should be the happiest man in the world, but I'm not. I don't know why. Here I am, with a steady job, chances for advancement and retirement, engaged to a lovely, young, intelligent girl, whose folks like and approve of me, with a raise in pay due in a few months, and my wedding date set for next June, and *it's driving me out of my mind!"*

"What is?" asked Susan, blinking stupidly.

"This! All of it. Cookies. Lemonade. You. I—I don't know. It's just that...Well, I keep having the feeling that life has much more to offer, that's all."

"What could it possibly?" she asked. "You love me, and I love you, and we will be married and live happily ever—"

"Stop!"

She stopped.

"Look, Susan—Honey—Darling... Oh, what's the use!"

Susan lowered her eyes and spoke in a hushed tone. "Are you trying to tell me you don't love me?"

I LOOKED at her, her long black lashes lying against her pale rose cheek, her lovely hair a golden aurora about her head, her trim little figure a pulse-maddening package in a royal blue dress with a lemon-colored belt...

Of *course* I loved her!

"I love you more every time I see you. But I still want to scream at you," I sighed. "I don't know why—Maybe because I constantly feel I'm not *reaching* you..."

"You know what Mom and Pop feel about—"

"Not like *that!* I mean conversationally. No, I don't mean that, either. It's like we don't *relate,* or *mesh,* or come in at the same terminal. Does that make sense?"

Susan looked into my eyes. "There's Another Woman, isn't there!" she declared. She hadn't understood a word I said. I stood up tall, glaring down at her.

"I wish there *were!*" I declared back at her. "Maybe life would have some excitement, then!"

"I suppose, Albert Hicks," said Susan, jumping up to face me, "you'd be happier if I did a *fan-dance* when you came over! Would *that* be exciting?"

"Darn tooting!" I snapped.

"Oh, Al," she whimpered, hiding her face in her hands. "That's an awful thing to suggest!"

"I didn't suggest it, I simply endorsed it!" I strode angrily into the front hall, grabbed my hat from the hall tree, and was just reaching for the doorknob when Susan came running after me.

"Don't go!" she said, catching me by the arm. "If—If you want a fan-dance, I'll—I'll do it. Even that. Anything, Al. Only— Don't go. Please don't go!"

I looked down into her earnest little face and melted. I took her gently into my arms and held her, slowly shaking my head. "Honey, honey—I didn't mean that about the dance. I just—I don't know. Maybe I need to get off someplace and think. I'm a little upset tonight. If I just drive around for awhile, maybe I can settle my mind a little. I'll see you later."

I kissed her lightly, then went out and shut the door behind me.

I FELT like a heel as I drove away from the curb, trying to get my mind back into a calm, orderly state. My own house was just around the block from Susan's, so I decided to drive the car there and leave it. I'd get more thinking done walking than driving. I pulled into my driveway and doused the headlights.

Just ahead of the nose of the car, and slightly to its left, I could see the bright yellow rectangles that were the kitchen windows of Susan's house. Now and then a shadow moved past them. Probably Mrs. Baker, making more cookies and lemonade. A smaller shadow trailed after the first one. That would be Timothy

Baker, Susan's younger brother. I'd met him relatively few times, since Mrs. Baker—bless her—felt that a boy of approximately ten years could get in the way of any even moderately romantic discussions between a girl and her fiancé.

I got out of the car and locked it, but just as I was about to walk back out toward the street to begin my meditative peregrinations, I remembered the six-pack of beer in my refrigerator and the remnants of a loaf of rye bread and some ham from Sunday's dinner. It took but a moment's thought to realize that they were just what I needed to take away the taste of cookies and lemonade. I abandoned my walking plans, and went into the house.

Relying on the light from Susan's kitchen, I made my way across my own kitchen in the dark and started hunting around for the bread. Just as I espied it on the cupboard shelf, a shadow flitted across the light, and I turned my head to see the silhouette of a man out in Susan's yard, messing around with something on the lawn.

With a small start, I recalled the two strangers who had followed me from the library. I couldn't tell in the dimness if this was one of them, but whoever he was, he had no business in Susan's yard.

I spun about and raced for my front door. I hurried to the corner, raced for Susan's street, and turned onto it, figuring to trap the guy between me and Susan's back fence. Halfway there, I saw the second man on the front lawn of her house, also fooling around with some kind of gadget. The thing glinted with metal and glass, and stood on a short tripod. Suddenly, the other man joined him, carrying his own counterpart of the gadget, and they jumped into a car and drove off.

Baffled by their conduct, I kept on toward Susan's, and turned to start up her front walk. My feet brushed autumn grass. I looked down. The path was gone. I looked up. So was Susan's house. Susan's had been the last in a row of houses before a small park. Now the park was twenty-five feet wider. Not even a hole where the foundation had been. And where the sofa I'd last seen Susan upon should have been, there stood a lofty elm, looking as though it had been rooted there for twenty years.

CHAPTER TWO

BACK in my own house, a few dazed moments later, I held off calling the police. I'd seen too many movies about people trying to convince policemen of the truth when the truth was slightly out of the ordinary; and this was anything but a slight extraordinariness. What I needed was someone to back up my story, and the likely person would be Garvey Baker.

Looking up the Marshall Field's number, I dialed quickly, and stood tapping my foot as the buzzing at the other end of the wire repeated without interruption. On the fifteenth buzz, someone picked up the phone.

"Watchman," said a voice.

"Mr. Baker?" I said. "This is Al."

"This ain't Mr. Baker. This is the watchman. Call back tomorra, maybe he'll be in then."

It wasn't even Garvey's voice. As I tried to explain my distress, the man hung up and left me with a dead line to talk to. I dropped the phone back into the cradle, more shaken than before I'd made the call. One more unlikelihood to tell the police. One that might buy me a jacket with buckles in the back, and not Ivy League, either.

There was one other way left—Or was there?

Feeling an uneasy tremor in my stomach, I reached out a slow hand for the phone book, and carefully checked through the Bs. There were seven Bakers listed. But not a Garvey, Susan, Timothy, or Maggie (Mrs. Baker's given name). And not one at the right address.

Susan's picture! Upstairs on my bureau! I raced up the stairs to look for it. The frame was there, and there was a picture in it, too. A picture of Annabel Simmons, the girl I'd dated before meeting Susan. I'd certainly not kept *her* picture... After a brain-racking moment, I remembered definitely that I *had* thrown it away. But here it was, as if it had never been gone, as though I were still going around with Annabel.

On a sudden unearthly hunch, I raced downstairs and dialed Annabel's number. In a few seconds, there was a soft, slightly husky voice awakening pangs of nostalgia in my ear. One would never believe we'd separated like outraged tigers a few months back, with Annabel vowing she'd rather go to the electric chair than ever see my face again.

"You—You're not mad, Annabel?" I said shakily.

"Mad? Mad, Albert? About what?"

"The fight. The fight we had."

"Fight?" Her bewilderment sounded genuine. "What fight are you talking about?"

"Look—" I persisted, evading the query. "When was—precisely, now—the very last time you saw me?"

"Oh—As precisely as I can recall, it was something in the neighborhood of fifteen minutes ago. You just now brought me home, Albert. Remember?"

"That's impossible," I groaned, and hung up.

IN approximately thirty seconds, the phone jangled sharply, and when I lifted it to my ear, it was Annabel again.

"Albert, are you all right?" she said. "Because if you're feeling under the weather or anything, I don't mind dropping over..."

"No," I said swiftly. "Don't come over."

"Why not?" she said, with a definite shading of suspicion in her tone. I vividly recalled Annabel's excitably jealous nature, then, and thought fast.

"Because it's too late, uh—honey—It wouldn't be right for you to come to a man's house all alone. It's past midnight."

"Silly," she said. "I'll bring Elizabeth, then." Elizabeth was Annabel's niece, who sometimes stayed with her when her parents were on vacation. "I'll pry the child loose from the Late Late Show and drag her along."

I was out of excuses. "Sure," I sighed. "Why not?"

My head was whirling as I hung up. Then I had my first flash of realistic inspiration. Suppose, instead of trying to figure *what* had happened, I thought about *why*. Never mind how the house was made to vanish; figure by whom. And I could guess that already.

THE man for whom the now expanded park beside Susan's house was named. Geoffrey Porkle. Porkle Park was only a few houseless lots, really. Barely a stretch of grass and trees. He had been trying, with little avail, to persuade the homeowners in the neighborhood to sell out to him, that he might further extend the confines of his pent-up park. The comfortably settled suburbanites had all refused. Garvey Baker, and I myself, had each been approached. I doubt if there was a casual passerby in Oak Park who had not been collared at one time by one of Porkle's representatives, with rabid urgings to sell out. So, in something that involved such a sudden extension of Porkle Park, Geoffrey Porkle was the natural suspect.

While I was still wondering what to do with my suspicions, the doorbell rang, and I went to let Annabel in. She entered, with her short blonde monster in tow, and began to remove her gloves. Elizabeth tilted back her curly golden head and gave a loud shriek. I was about to formulate some innocuous question that would clarify my curiosity about my unremembered recent association with Annabel without making her think I'd popped my cork when the doorbell rang again.

"Who can that be?" asked Annabel with green suspicion.

"Who *might* that be!" I corrected, my pre-library master's degree in English coming to the fore. "It could be anybody; it 'might' be relatively few people."

"Oh, shut up and answer the door," said Annabel, smoothing Elizabeth's hair. Elizabeth grunted like a pig, then gave another scream. I went to the door and opened it.

"Evening, Hicks," said Mr. Garson, my superior at the library, lumbering in. "I was driving by and saw your lights, and thought I'd drop in and see how you were doing on your report."

AT that moment, Elizabeth screamed again. Garson was visibly shaken. "Good grief, Hicks, what was *that!?*"

"That was Elizabeth," I said, gesturing him ahead of me and following him into the parlor. "She screams."

Annabel rose to her niece's defense immediately. "It's for her lungs," she said. "Her singing teacher says that a little screaming now and then develops lungpower."

As I made introductions, Elizabeth grunted like a pig.

"Lowers the voice," explained Annabel. "I want her to sing *Carmen* some day, don't I, sweetums! But it calls for a contralto."

"She—does this all the time?" asked Garson, his face a blend of fascination and revulsion.

"Only indoors," I said.

"Elizabeth can sing *The Song of the Flea* in Russian," said Annabel, with unpardonable pride. Elizabeth stuck her tongue out at Mr. Garson and made a vulgar sound.

"How nice," he murmured, looking nervous. "But isn't that a baritone number?"

I shook my head. "Bass. Anyone can sing *Carmen;* Lizzie has her sights on *Boris Goudanov.*"

"Albert!" Annabel was smiling, but her undertone was a hacksaw on broken glass. Garson cowered like a trapped rabbit.

"Perhaps," I said with evil genius, "Elizabeth could be persuaded to sing a few numbers for you while I finish that report, sir?"

Before I even completed the sentence, Annabel was moving toward my spinet, flexing her fingers, and Elizabeth was inflating her bony chest. "Hicks—" said Garson, trying to think of some way to avoid the impending menace of Elizabeth's lungs.

"Only be a short while, sir," I smiled, opening my study door and hurrying inside. I shut the door, locked it, then ducked out the connecting door to the kitchen and locked that, too. As I got into my sedan, even the walls of my house could not quite muffle the shrills and grunts that split the air of my living room.

* * *

PORKLE'S house was midway between my house and Marshall Field's store. There were lights on at the side window. I parked up the street, then hurried back on tiptoe.

The windowsill was just higher than my head, but by resting one shoe atop a garden hose faucet beneath it, I could raise myself high enough to see into the room.

Inside, a man sat at a desk, talking to a taller, thinner man, who was smiling to himself as he filled the bottom of a snifter with brandy. I couldn't be sure they were the two men I'd seen loitering earlier from their faces, but any doubts I might have had were dispelled by the presence of the two tripod-gadgets near the desk.

"You're *sure* there's no return from Drendon?" said the man at the desk.

"No, Geoffrey," said the other man to the would-be Park Czar. "I'm not at all sure. If people can be sent there, there's undoubtedly a way to get them back. How, I don't know, but the probability does exist."

"Damn it, Courtland," growled Porkle. "I wish you'd stop trying to be so inscrutable! Are we safe, or not!?"

Courtland, swirling his brandy in the snifter and inhaling its bouquet luxuriously, said, "Believe me, the odds are well with us. These vanishments—objects plus all record of their existence—have an opposite reaction, a sort of mental corollary in the minds of the vanishees."

"You mean they won't remember Oak Park? The U.S.? Earth?" said Porkle, his eyes widening. "But that's marvelous! Fat chance of returning if they don't recall—"

"But they *do* recall that there is an Earth, Geoffrey. Don't forget Drendon is a relative of Earth's, due to—"

"Spare me the details!" muttered Porkle, much to my annoyance. I'd been itching to find out what or where this mysterious Drendon was. "But," continued Porkle, "you said something to me about the unlikelihood of survival there."

"Their occupation while being transferred does, of course, influence their Drendon-shape, somewhat. But even a person who is adapted into Drendon-form will find that life there is fraught with dangers, even for the regular inhabitants."

I tried to recall what the Bakers might have been involved in when this odd translation occurred. Maggie Baker had been out in the kitchen, probably cooking. Timothy would have been tagging after her, asking kid-questions about her preparations, like a student of domestic science. Garvey Baker would have been at work watching the store. As to Susan, I didn't know. Last I saw of her, she'd been sitting mournfully on the sofa, looking lost and lorn, in the spot where the tree had materialized. I hoped earnestly that she hadn't become a Drendon-type weeping willow.

"You see," Courtland was continuing, "Drendon is an entity, as befits any enchanted woods. Drendon does not precisely *have* a tree; part of Drendon is a tree. And all the trees, like Drendon, are quite alive, and more or less intelligent according to age and species.

"Oh, you can't tell it at a glance, but just attempting to take an axe to one might bring on frightful results. And then, it has animals, too." His voice lowered here, and reminded me chillingly of one of those old-time horror-tale tellers on radio in the thirties. "Some animals slither in the gloom on nefarious missions of slimy terror, some bound about in gay abandon, frolicking on the sward in the hot glow of that ridiculous sun which only sets on certain occasions. Some you can go up to and kick without temerity; others you dare not even let know you're within shouting distance if you know what's healthy. And this latter sort are not only monstrous, they are well in the majority, and you can count it a day well spent if you narrowly escape death walking from the front door of your house to the mailbox. They prowl the forest incessantly, and are never sated!"

"Stop!" said Porkle, his plump face gray and greasy with sweat. He swabbed his thick features with a silken kerchief. "That's enough. I get the picture!"

"It's an intriguing place, really," said Courtland, disappointed in the other's lack of enthusiasm. "A mythophile's dream, Porkle, with its monsters, beasts, furry fauns, sly satyrs, vampires, werewolves, wyverns, centaurs and such. Always, day upon day, in this overgrown, vegetation-choked locale, every moment of life is precious, every life is in deadly peril, what with deadfalls, quicksands, pits, things that scream, things that slurp, things that impale you on their horns, things that crush you in their grasp, things that bite, things that stomp, and things that can do anything the other things can do, and much better."

"Please," said Porkle, weakly. "No more. I take your word for it. It's very unlikely we'll ever hear of the Bakers again, or that Hicks character."

THIS last phrase stymied me for a second, until I recalled that these two men had followed me to Susan's house. Then it started making sense. Susan's father had refused to sell; so had I. The plan might have been to kill two birds with one stone, getting me while I was inside Susan's house along with the family. But they hadn't known I'd leave the house so soon, or that I had left in fact. They still assumed that I had been translated into Drendon— wherever it was—with the others. Which gave me a slight leverage.

Dropping to the ground from my perch, I dusted the window-sill grit from my fingers and strolled around to the front door. A touch of the bell evoked muted chimes inside the house, and in a moment, the tall scientific half of the duo, Courtland, was opening the door to me. "Yes?" he said, scowling deeply. (It was, after all, nearly two in the morning.) "What is it? What do you want?"

"My name is Albert Hicks," I said, pleased to hear the quick intake of his breath. "And I want your scalp, if you don't mind."

"Hicks!" he echoed numbly.

"But how could you—?" Then a trace of his suave demeanor returned, and he said smoothly, "I'm afraid I don't follow you. But won't you come in?"

I kept my eyes on him as he shut the door behind me. Courtland wasn't the sort I trusted where I couldn't see him. He led the way toward the room in which I'd seen himself and Porkle discussing my supposed fate, and I went inside warily. At the desk, Porkle looked up blankly.

"Who—?" he began, but a wave of Courtland's hand silenced him.

"You were saying something about a scalp?" smiled Courtland, as I sat gingerly on the edge of a chair.

"Yes," I said, keeping my voice as politely sardonic as possible. "I think it's rude of people to shunt other people into strange woods without asking them first."

"What?" gasped Porkle, jumping to his feet. "Who is this guy, Courtland?"

"I'm Albert Hicks," I said grimly. "Lately of Drendon."

PORKLE'S face went chalky to the hairline, and he dropped back into his swivel chair with a soft squeal of alarm. I turned to

Courtland. "Doc, when you send people away like that, you ought to make sure it's for good. Your gimmick wore off in an hour, and we all popped right back where we belonged. Shame on you."

"You're lying," Courtland declared flatly, his eyes lusterless and deadly. "That cannot happen."

"But it has!" quailed Porkle. "Look! Here he is. If he didn't go there and back, then how does he *know* about Drendon?"

Courtland's shrewd eyes flicked about the room, and I felt a faint chill of panic as his glance came to rest upon the window, its lower edge slightly ajar. A mirthless smile up-tilted the corners of his thin mouth. "I think I understand," he said, stepping back from me and drawing a slim blue-black automatic from inside his suit jacket. I stared helplessly into the barrel of the gun, no longer feeling very clever, as Courtland reached for one of the tripod-things and touched a dial on its back. A soft throbbing hum began to issue from the odd construction atop the tripod, and in another instant the sound was received and echoed by the other machine, a few feet away.

Between the two things, the air began to shimmer and writhe, like air above a hot pavement in summertime. I didn't need a scientific education to know I was looking at the doorway to Drendon. Courtland motioned to me with the muzzle of his automatic.

"If you'll just step between the transmitters?" he said gently. Something in his tone told me that he didn't much care if I went through alive or dead. This gadget of his, discounting any other advantages it might have, was the ideal way to dispose of occasional corpses. If I didn't walk through that shimmering gateway, there was a good chance I'd be plugged through the head and simply dumped through.

I got to my feet and tried the only trump I seemed to have, Porkle's distrust of science. With a smile and a shrug, I stepped toward that pulsing blur as if I wasn't scared stiff, and said, "All right, if you insist. But I'll only reappear in an hour."

Even Courtland looked uneasy at my bluff, and his momentary expression of uncertainty was all the impetus Porkle needed to crack.

"You idiot!" he raged at Courtland, coming out from behind the desk. "I *told* you your stupid scheme was—!"

"Porkle!" Courtland yelped, spinning to face him. "Watch where you're—"

But Geoffrey Porkle's pudgy form was already a frozen statue of stupefaction in the grip of that eerie force between the tripods, and then, with a gentle *pop,* he was gone. And that's when I stepped forward and shoved the distracted Courtland right after him.

Caught off guard, he had only an instant to turn his malevolently contorted face toward mine, his lips forming a curse—Then he vanished.

AN instant later, the house did the same, and I was dropping down about five feet to the ground. My landing was cushioned by soft grass, and when I looked about, there was nothing left of Porkle's house but the two gadgets on their tripods, lying on the velvet lawn. I went over to them, but their humming had ceased. I lifted one and shook it. A rasping tinkle inside it told me that something had gone bust in the crash. However they'd functioned, they were beyond it now.

And there went my last chance of locating Susan.

Still dazed from the fall and my narrow escape, I got back to my car—the driveway was gone with the house, leaving my car in the midst of an open lawn—and drove wearily back homeward. I felt lost, and sick. I was completely out of schemes, now. No matter how I tried, my mind could supply no solution to the problem. Susan and her family were lost, and there didn't seem to be much anyone could do about it.

Porkle and Courtland were likewise lost, but that in itself was a small loss. I could only hope that whatever they'd become translated into in Drendon would not be as menacing to Susan as their Earth-counterparts had been.

If only there were someone I could tell, someone who'd believe me despite the way the facts looked. But the only one I'd ever felt that close to was Susan. And she already knew more of Drendon than I did.

It was only as I rolled the car back into my driveway that I heard the shrill gurgle and growl from within the house, and remembered Annabel, Garson and Elizabeth. Elizabeth was busily rendering—maybe 'rending' is a better word—*Old Man River,* at a pitch that made William Warfield's seem like a soprano.

As I tiptoed into the kitchen and once more let myself into my study, I had a momentary pang of regret about the callousness with which I'd shoved Courtland smack out of this world. "Well," I said to myself, sagging wearily against the paneling of the door to the living room, (awaiting the climax of Elizabeth's number, unable to forge the smile of required enjoyment on my face if I emerged while she was still at it) "it was him or me!"

Stubbornly trying to reinforce my decision with a jut of my lower lip, my English background came to mind, and I automatically self-corrected, "That is, 'he or I'."

Out of the darkness behind me, a voice asked, "What's the difference?"

"A pronominal object of the verb 'to be' always remains in the nominative case, rather than the objective, because—" I frowned. By all rights, I should have been completely alone in my study. I had the only key to either door, and they'd both been locked while I was gone.

"Because what?" the voice prompted.

"Because 'to be' expresses an equality rather than a result…" I said, slowly turning around. I saw no one, what with the blinds being down. I reached out a hand for the light switch, intensely curious…

"No, please!" said the voice.

For the first time, and with a sudden quiver in my stomach, I noted that it was a *female* voice. A rather pretty one. "Why not?" I asked.

"Because," said the voice, "I have no clothes on."

"You're joking," I replied, knowing somehow that she wasn't. My forehead went clammy at the thought, when I considered that my boss and Annabel were just beyond the door. The sturdy oak door suddenly assumed all the protective qualities of sawdust to my shaken mind.

"Well," said the voice, "dramatizing, maybe. But I'm certainly not clothed by your standards."

"You leave my standards out of this," I snapped. "Where do you get off prying into my standards?"

"I mean people's standards in this era." The voice had changed location, and now seemed to come from the vicinity of my unseen leather armchair.

"This—This era?" I asked, groping toward the chair.

"Yes," came the reply from the bookcase, halfway across the room.

I began to feel irritated. "Stop moving around like that!"

"I have to," said the soft, thrilling voice, "or you'll catch me." Her logic was beyond dispute.

"Well," I said, disgruntled, "if—if you'll stand still, I'll stand still!"

"All right. But if you move, I move."

I NODDED, then grunted at the foolishness of nodding into the dark, and seated myself carefully in the armchair. The situation was without precedent in my life. I wasn't quite sure how to proceed. Or even *if* to proceed.

"Now then—" I snapped on my lighter, going through the motions of igniting my cigarette, but actually trying to pierce the gloom by the dancing flame of the wick. "What are you doing here dressed like that? Or perhaps I should say *not*-dressed like that?"

"Right now, I'm observing you from the bookcase."

"In the dark?" I almost ignited the end of my nose. I hurriedly thrust the lighter into my pocket. Smoking could wait.

"Why not?" said the voice, and then the speaker laughed, and I suddenly found myself a boy again, on a hot day in July, running barefoot through warm grass toward a glittering cold creek. Then I was back again.

"Laugh again," I said.

"All right," said the voice. "Say something funny."

"I don't know anything funny," I admitted sadly.

"That's funny enough," said the voice, laughing again.

Once more I was on my way through the grass to the creek. And back again. "That's the damnedest thing. You won't believe this, but when you laugh it's as if—"

"You're out on the countryside, right?"

"Uh—Yes," I said, surprised. "Does this always happen when people hear you laugh?"

"Retention of childhood memories. Called nostalgia. You remember hearing me laugh as a child, and whatever you were doing at the time, it comes back when I laugh again. Simple."

I frowned, growing apprehensive. "See here, now, are you someone I knew as a child?" My slowly forming image of a curvy cutie was fading into oblivion. After all, she might be twice my age. I hated older women with girlish voices. Especially alone in the dark with me. Not dressed according to my standards.

"Honestly!" Exasperation colored her words. "I never saw you before in my life. When I say me, I mean we, but really mean me as a profession rather than as a person."

"Profession?" I choked. This had dire associations in my mind; more so with Annabel and Garson in the next room. I was cold all over. "What is your profession?"

"I'm a woodnymph," tinkled the voice.

CHAPTER THREE

I CONFESS I sat quite still for a long moment, thinking this over. Then I said slowly, still quite dizzy, "You're a woodnymph— like in the stories? Young, beautiful, diaphanous gown, hair like the color of autumn leaves, and all that?"

"Yes," said the voice, sweetly.

Completely nuts. I sighed to myself sadly. And such a nice voice, too. But nuts or not, she might *still* be young and beautiful. Would Annabel or Mr. Garson believe that she was nuts? It took me two seconds to answer that.

No. That was the likely conclusion. Of course, if I said, "Tell them who you are," and she said, "A woodnymph," they'd think she was nuts. But if I walked out of my study with a girl who wasn't "dressed according to my standards," I'd never have a chance to play quiz with them.

Then again, maybe she *wasn't* in anything wispy—She might be wadded into a Mother Hubbard and combat boots for all I knew. A nut wouldn't know the difference, would she?

"May I turn on the light?"

"Why?"

"I've never seen a...um...woodnymph before—"

"No one has," said the voice, with finality.

"Well—I wouldn't mind being the first man to see one," I hazarded.

"Who would!?" said the voice, and that strangely nostalgic laugh tinkled again. I had to forcibly wrench my emotions back from that warm grassy streamside field.

"I can't just talk to a voice. Do you have a name?"

"My name is Lorn," she said, in a voice that was a velvet caress. It made the backs of my knees itch.

"It's certainly a pretty name," I said sincerely.

"Naturally. All our names are pretty. Because all of us are pretty."

Curiosity was killing me. I began to wonder if I could edge toward the light without her noticing. She might just be kidding about seeing me in the dark. "This requires some thinking," I said, as a ruse to preclude the necessity of my speaking for a few moments. Carefully, I eased myself out of the chair and groped my way toward the light switch. My fingers touched it, and I whirled as the fluorescent ceiling light sputtered and popped on. The top of the bookcase was void of tenants.

However, in the center of the room, *something* was standing, watching me balefully from beneath lowered brows topped with bone-colored horns. From the waist upward, excluding those pointy, inch-long horns, it was a youth of about ten years, but from the waist down it seemed to be wearing dark brown angora tights. It smelt slightly.

"You're a woodnymph?" I gasped, disappointment mingling with shock at the sight. Woodnymph it might not be, but human being it could not be. For answer, I received a guttural growl from the thing.

And at the same moment, a suppressed giggle came from behind my armchair. "Lorn?" I queried, hopefully taking a step toward the chair.

THE thing in the center of the rug made a motion with its head that demonstrated forcefully the fact that those horns were more than ornamental. Its small cloven hooves pawed the carpet like those of an animal about to attack.

"Timtik!" said Lorn from behind the chair. "Don't gore him unless you have to. He's really rather nice."

"I don't trust humans!" rasped Timtik, his voice the kind of sound you hear over a tin can-and-string telephone. "You saw the way he tried to sneak a peek at you, Lorn!"

I was nonplussed. "Who or what *is* this thing, Lorn? He looks something like a satyr, but his size is too—" At this moment, a bit of lore regarding the behavior of woodnymphs and satyrs passed across my mind. Their almost symbiotic relationship was so firmly rooted in ancient mythologies that somehow I began to feel that if she was a woodnymph, and this was her current flame, and he was only four feet tall... Might not *she* also be...?

"Lorn—" I said haltingly. "Are you— Are you and he—um—" I stopped, dismayed.

"Nonsense," said Lorn. "Timtik is a faun, and that's not quite the same as a satyr. He and I are just good friends. Why, I don't even *have* a steady satyr!"

I felt ice in my stomach and my heart seemed to be pumping gelid sludge. "Then—You *do*...um...date satyrs?"

"Well, of course! Why not!"

I scratched my head. "I dunno. But in all the portraits I've seen, they look so—well—repulsive."

"Let me put it this way," said Lorn. "If *you* lived in a world peopled by, say, bald-headed women with bad teeth, what would *you* do?"

"Shoot myself," I said.

Lorn sighed. "I mean if you *did* go out with someone. You see, Albert, satyrs are all I've got. That's the reason I date them. Those stories you heard were just about the *bad* satyrs. Some of them are perfect gentlemen, and a few are even shy."

"How did you know my name?" I asked.

"I heard your wife mention it, Albert," answered Lorn.

"My wife?" I was momentarily perplexed. Then a small light flickered in my head. "Oh, you mean Annabel. She's not my wife. She's—" I glanced at the door, then lowered my voice. "She's not even much fun to have around for long. Much too bossy."

"I'm so glad!" Then Lorn's voice quickly extinguished the sparkle in its intonation and added, "But you *do* have a wife around, don't you?"

"No," I admitted, shaking my head. "At the moment, I have nary wife, nor fiancée, nor even a close friend of the opposite sex."

"Oh," said Lorn.

THERE was a pause of about ten seconds' duration, during which Timtik scratched idly at the thatch of fur on his haunch with talon-like fingernails.

"Oh, well, in *that* case—" Lorn said, and stood up into view from behind the armchair.

I sat down. On the floor. Hard. She stood there, smiling at me, deep blue eyes crinkling beneath flaming copper brows, long unruly coils of hair falling to her creamy shoulders like a sunrise—like a sunset—like an explosion in a ketchup factory! Her lips were soft, pink, and unpainted, and I could feel their moist warmth at ten feet. Those waves of flaming hair fell like coiling cataracts to her bare shoulders, and below that—Well—

I looked in wonder as I clambered back to my feet.

She'd been right. She had no clothes on at all by my standards, but she was not exactly bare, either. From her arching clavicles to her tiny toes she was swathed, or wrapped, or festooned, by a silky, satiny, gauzy, fluffy veil-type thing, its shades mingling emerald and viridian, like the color of moss on a bright but overcast day.

How it stayed up, on, or around, I had no idea.

"That's an unusual garment you're—uh—wearing, Lorn. How—how in the world do you keep it up?" I blurted.

"It's magic, you dope!" Timtik muttered, clomping his impatient hooves on the rug. He'd ceased his guard-stance once Lorn had risen up from behind the chair like the sun coming over a jungle valley at dawn—like a torch-haired South Seas volcano-goddess—like…I restrained myself from bursting into poetry. It was an effort.

"It's my diaphanous drapery," Lorn beamed, turning about to give me the complete vista. It dipped so low in back that I could have counted all her ribs if I'd wanted to put my hands on her bare back. And suddenly I wanted to, very much, but she'd already completed her rotation and my chance was gone.

"It never falls off?" I said, amazed. "Kind of looks as though if a gust of wind came prowling—"

Lorn shook her head decisively. "Not unless I wish it off."

Timtik began to show some interest in the conversation. "Lorn is the only one who knows the magic words that drop the drape. Maggot taught her when she wove it."

"*Who* taught her?" I'd been oddly stirred by the name.

"Maggot," said Timtik, impatiently. "She's a witch lives in Drendon."

"Drendon…" I echoed, savoring the word. And then realized, with a dizzy feeling in my brain, that I knew these two here before me in my study.

It was Susan Baker and her brother Timothy. And "Maggot" could only have rung that dull bell in my mind if it were Mrs. Maggie Baker, Susan's mother.

A LOT of things danced through my brain in a few short instants, even as my lips tried to make intelligent response to the faun's statement. Maggie Baker, switched into Drendon from cooking things in her kitchen—simply became the Drendon equivalent of a mixer, brewer, or concocter: a witch. And Susan, still in the throes of her unwonted urge to *do* me that fan-dance, sitting sad and—of course—*Lorn* in the spot where the tree had appeared, had become a tempting, winsome, lovely creature whose proper appellation would be wood-goddess, or tree goddess.

Not that I was sure yet. The face of Lorn might be the face of Susan, but where Susan's had always been reserved, vapid, and a bit lovably dopey, Lorn's was pert, peppery, and lovably dopey. The flame-colored hair had been a distraction, as had that "diaphanous drapery." But a sharp look now made me surer than ever that I was facing the girl I'd lost forever scant hours earlier. She was disguised somewhat, but all the differences seemed to be for the better.

And she treated me like a stranger.

I wondered if some word-associations might trigger her memory. "Drendon," I said carefully. "Why, that's the name of a forest, isn't it? Sort of contiguous with—um—Earth-Normal? Here, where only a little of it shows, we call it Porkle Park." I didn't know how much of what I said was true, but I had to see if they'd react at all.

Timtik reacted first. With disgust.

"Humans!" he spat. "Who could name something as lovely as a park something like 'Porkle'!?"

"I'm glad we live in Drendon," said Lorn. "It's a much prettier name."

"Then," I said, wonderingly, "it *is* contiguous with Porkle Park?"

"Only right here," Lorn said briskly. "Our homeland is tangent to the park here, but we live in an entirely different—what?" she asked Timtik quizzically.

"Dimension is the closest word the humans have for it," muttered the faun.

"You see, that's why we're here in the first place," said Lorn, smiling a blithe smile that any self-respecting temptress would have depleted her bank account to learn.

I fought a vertiginous impulse to leap the distance between us and cover her face with smoldering kisses, and quaked a little at the unfamiliarity of the feeling within myself. This wasn't like me. I was a librarian and a gentleman. And she was, after all, only a rag, a bone, a hank of hair... But what a rag! What a bone! What a hank of hair! I cleared my throat, and said puzzledly, "What made you come calling on *me?*"

For the first time since I'd seen him, Timtik lost some of his sullen impertinence. He actually looked embarrassed. "It's kind of my fault, Albert," he admitted, hanging his head. "I tried to hide the key from Lorn, and—"

"Timtik is a prankster, Albert," said Lorn. "He took the key from me to hold it for me (he said) because I didn't have any pockets—" (A bad choice of topic; my eyes were again drawn to those draperies of hers, and my breathing became slightly impaired.) "Albert—?" said Lorn, a little concerned. "Maybe I should leave. You don't look so well."

"I'm fine. I'm just not used to—to—I'm fine. Please go on."

WELL, once Timtik had the key, he tried to make me catch him to get it back, and you know how no one can outrun a faun, but he tripped, and I managed to lay hold of his hoof—" (I had to repress a shudder) "so he threw the key, and it came in here, and just as we'd sneaked inside to find it, you came in. That's all."

"All but one thing," I said. *"What* key?"

"The key to Drendon, stupid!" grunted the faun in his metallic rasp. "We can't get back to our dimension without it, and Lorn'll catch hell from Maggot for keeping me out this late as it is!"

"Me keeping *you* out!?" Her lovely face was alive with icy rancor. I watched her features with numb joy. She's beautiful when she's mad, I thought, and wished with biting regret that someone hadn't already coined that phrase. Then the happy thought occurred to me that perhaps the cliché hadn't yet penetrated her dimension.

"You're beautiful when you're angry," I ventured.

Lorn stopped harassing Timtik. "Why—Why, Albert! That's the loveliest thing anyone ever said to me. I'm so glad I showed myself to you."

"You're glad!" I said, my stomach doing cartwheels. "I've never been so happy in my life."

"Well, now that he knows why we're here, let's take the key and go," said Timtik, peering about the room.

"Go!?" I felt my world crumbling into—well—crumbs. I'd been somehow deluding myself that I was going to spend the rest of my life just looking at Lorn, just staring at and drinking in her loveliness, not eating, sleeping or anything, never leaving the room again. Just me and Lorn, and—well, maybe Timtik could've been bribed to leave us. But would a faun have any use for a quarter? Or an ice cream cone?

"We have to go, Albert," said Lorn, her face sweetly sad. "But I will remember you always, and all that sort of stuff. Now, where's that key?"

I felt she could have looked just a *little* more miserable about our parting, but Lorn was already down on her hands and knees, peering under furniture, and Timtik was clumping about making an awful racket, yelling, "Here key!"

Nothing happened, except to Lorn's expression. She became pale and apprehensive. "Call again!" she said.

Timtik, too, looked uneasy. "Here, key!" he shouted. Again nothing happened. Timtik looked genuinely scared. "The spell doesn't work, Lorn!"

"But it has to!" she said, rising gracefully from her ungainly crouch on the carpet. "If a spell works, it works, that's all. If the key can *hear* you, it *must* answer."

I felt a growing concern for their plight, despite my desire that they both remain until I could get them unbrainwashed and back into their proper identities—though I wasn't sure I wanted Susan to change all the way back...

"Maybe," I said helpfully, "magic won't work in this dimension?"

Timtik stopped clumping. "That's a horrible idea— Maybe— Hey, *Lorn!*"

She gave a tiny shriek, but her hands moved in time. That diaphanous drapery of hers hadn't sagged much, and only exposed a few extra inches of smooth pale flesh. But it was enough to turn my knees to water and bring the water to a boil. "I guess," I ventured not unhappily, "you're stuck in *this* dimension, huh?"

The resultant anguish on their faces made me feel *that* high. "Well, maybe—Maybe it's because *you* don't belong here that your magic didn't work. Maybe if *I* called—*Here, key!*"

"See me? See me?" squeaked a little voice. "Whee! Me! Me!"

"There she is!" said Timtik pointing.

I LOOKED atop the bookcase and saw what at first seemed to be a dry twig; then it wriggled, and I saw that it was alive after a fashion. Lorn and I sprang for it at the same moment. We crashed front to front, and somehow I found my arm around her waist, while my free hand scooped up the key. My hand scooped reflexively, because at the moment of contact between us, everything was forgotten but Lorn, Lorn, *Lorn!* And she certainly was staring at me as though something marvelous had occurred.

"Albert," she sighed, with wonder in her voice.

Timtik watched, aghast. "Lorn, he's from another dimension!" he warned.

At that moment, the key wriggled in my hand. I looked at it, and realized that I held the—well, the *key*—to Lorn's departure, and that without it…

I repressed an urge to chuckle, but could not repress the surge of just plain selfish desirous meanness that welled up inside me as I brought up my other hand behind Lorn and prepared to crumple and snap the key like the twig it most resembled… Fire lanced through my fingers! I almost dropped the thing, but the glow, which had momentarily heated the twig, faded as soon as I ceased twisting it.

Timtik went pale (to the waist). "Lorn! He tried to destroy the key! He did! And Maggot's counter-spell worked; I saw it. He doesn't want us to go!"

Lorn was looking into my face, sighing gently, her breath in my nostrils sweet and warm and moist as fresh-cut grass. "Who cares?" she said dreamily. "This beats satyrs all get-out!"

Timtik's face contorted tearfully. "But Lorn. Maggot will be expecting us, and you're supposed to be taking care of me, and I'll never get home again, and—" Here he broke down completely and blubbered salty tears into the hem of Lorn's diaphanous drapery, the horns coming dangerously near to snagging it. Lorn put her hand gently to my chest and pushed me back, with a reluctant smile. "He's right; I'll have to take him home."

"No, Lorn," I said. "Don't go. You must stay with me."

"Well, Albert—" Lorn looked perplexed. "I *want* to, of course, but I did promise Maggot I'd bring him home tonight. I'll be back. Honestly I will."

I fought for time, hoping to alter her decision. "But why did you come here in the first place, then? Merely to enchant me and then leave me a broken husk, seeking in vain for beauty I shall never view again?"

Timtik gagged. "Boy, is he corny!" He seemed quite recovered from his spate of tears. Lorn shot him a cold glance of deep reproach. "I think he's charming!" she said staunchly. Then to me, "I'd never heard of Earth, or anywhere outside Drendon, until Maggot decided to send Timtik out to spy on humans, to get experience. She needs someone to make the transition now and then, to keep her posted, especially on anything scientific. She likes to think she keeps Drendon up-to-date in its technology."

"I'm studying under her," said Timtik, proudly. "I'm an apprentice witch."

My knowledge of gender triumphed over strained credibility. "Warlock," I corrected. "Boys can't be witches."

"All right," Timtik muttered darkly. "Warlock, then."

"He had to see people," Lorn went on. "It's part of his training so that, someday, when he has to cast a spell on a human, he'll know how to make the doll."

The hair prickled on my neck. "Dolls? You mean voodoo?"

A light shone in Lorn's eyes. *"You* know *voodoo,* Albert?"

"Just the word," I admitted anticlimactically.

"It figures," Timtik muttered, again darkly.

"Well, anyhow—Maggot thought Timtik was too young to go alone, and she was mixing a batch of hell-brew to feed the Thrake, so the Kwistians couldn't get into our section of Drendon, and so she sent me. I'll do anything for excitement, and Maggot knows it, so she sent me to watch humans with him, and we were on our way back when he tossed the key in here—"

"Wait," I said. "If there are no humans in Drendon, why learn how to voodoo them?"

"Practice, you bonehead!" snarled the faun.

I bestowed my most withering glance upon his horny forehead. "People who live in glass houses—"

"—shouldn't take baths!" finished Lorn. "That's an oldie. Do you know this one: Too many cooks—"

"Make light work," finished Timtik.

I felt like a character on stage who'd forgotten to read his part of the script. They were talking my brain into a tangle. "Look, Lorn," I said, taking advantage of the speaking of her name to hold her closer, as if for emphasis, "if the key won't answer when *you* call, maybe it won't work to take you anywhere. Maybe it only works for me—"

"Well, I like that!" the key shrilled angrily. "I would too work for them, except that it was so warm and cozy in here that I got just a wee bit sleepy and dropped off just the teensiest bit and didn't hear them calling me, but I did hear you, so that's when I answered, so there!"

Timtik was intrigued. "If that's so, then why did Lorn's drapery start to sag?" A shocked expression widened his eyes. "Unless she *wanted* it to—!"

"I did not!" said Lorn, pink with indignation. "When it was intimated that spells might not work here, I simply tried my drape-dropping spell to test the theory. It worked perfectly. That's all. Of all the nerve, Timtik!" She was quite put out, and I was about to intercede to prevent any physical violence, when suddenly—

The faun froze in position, eyes alert, breath hushed. Lorn, too, had gone rigid, tense. I looked left and right. "What's wrong?" I said, feeling uneasy myself. "Is something—?"

AUNT ANNABEL!" came a familiar shriek behind me. "Albert has a LADY in there with no CLOTHES on!"

Too late I slapped my hand over the keyhole.

"Elizabeth," I said lamely. "She spies."

"No time to lose! Come on, Lorn!" said Timtik.

"Hicks!" came Garson's shocked voice through the oaken paneling. "What's going on in there! Open this door!" I couldn't tell from his tone if he wanted to stop the scandalous goings-on or take part in them.

"Oh, Albert," said Lorn, taking the key from my numb fingers. "I can't come back if there's going to be trouble. Maybe it's best if we never see each other again…"

Her beauty was unmarred, enhanced, really, by two crystal tears issuing over her rose-flushed cheeks. Her lovely eyes were cloudy, and my heart wrenched painfully to see them so. "No, Lorn," I pleaded. "Don't go—!"

My outstretched hand clutched the air she was just vacating, as she glided swiftly toward the window, soundless and deft on her small bare feet. Timtik had the window swiftly yawning wide against the night, and was helping her over the sill. I stood frozen, dazed at the abruptness of Elizabeth's yelp and the strange duo's precipitate departure. I watched the last trailing gossamer bit of the viridian drapery slither like a foaming green mist over the sill, then snapped out of my bewildered trance. I dove through the air, fingers out to grasp that last fleeing foot—

"Albert!" Annabel was shrieking. "Open this door at once! How *could* you! And in your own *home!*"

But even while Garson was cursing, and Annabel was alternately urging and egging him on and begging Elizabeth not to listen to him, and the hinges were screaming with the pounding strain, I was coming down toward the windowsill like a pouncing leopard after its prey, and my fingers were closing tightly over the wisp of veil remaining, and I was yelling loudly a single word—*"Lorn!"*

There was an abrupt, sharp click, a strange sort of tremor throughout my trunk and limbs and mind, and then my face smacked stunningly against hot, moist earth where it should have met the parquet flooring of my study.

CHAPTER FOUR

I LAY there, slightly stunned, for an instant, then managed, with a soft groan, to roll over on my back. I tried to catch my breath and get my mind in order. As my mind sent out fingers to test for broken limbs or at least a few frayed tendons, I heard the voices of Lorn and Timtik, and slitted my eyes to see them. I was prone at their feet, or rather, at her feet and his hooves. I lay where I was, and simply listened, for the moment.

"Pour water on him, Lorn," suggested Timtik.

"Do you have any?" Her voice was plaintive with worry about me. I liked that.

"No, but I think I can make some. Maggot showed me how," he said. Timtik proceeded to cross his fetlocks, fall down, swear, get up again, re-cross his fetlocks, fall down again, and swear again.

"That's a fascinating spell," Lorn enthused.

"Spell, nothing!" muttered the faun. "I can't even assume the primary position. Oh, for a pair of feet! Sometime *you* try standing with *your* fetlocks crossed!"

Lorn frowned prettily. "Maybe you could tell *me* what to do, and *I* could assume the primary position?"

Timtik rubbed his beardless chin between thumb and forefinger, carefully sheathing his talons as he did so. "Well—all spells are very secret, you know. I can't give them away; Maggot would be awfully angry."

Lorn nodded briskly. "Very well, then. I'll cross my legs, and you do the rest, and maybe if we hold hands it'll work. What do you think?"

Timtik pursed his lips. "Not a bad idea. Let's try."

Lorn carefully crossed her legs, gripping the faun's hand for a reason that seemed to be equal portions of necromancy and balance, and Timtik began his spell. It was quite a spell. His cabalistic incantation was punctuated with waving arms, and grunts and groans, sounding like a banshee in a beartrap. Suddenly, a tiny cloud, pink in color, began to materialize about two feet over my face.

Timtik frowned and howled some more. The cloud darkened and began to quiver. The faun emitted a savage curse, and the cloud sparked a bolt of lightning about three inches long.

Lorn whistled in appreciation. "It's working!"

"Quiet!" growled Timtik. "I'm not through yet!"

He began snapping his fingers, increased his howl, and moved his haunches in that motion Hawaiians call "around the island" when the hula is in full swing.

The cloud was quite black now, like a blob of inked cotton, and the lightning bolts were flashing on and off like flashbulbs at a Hollywood premiere. Suddenly there was a grinding noise, a little gasp, and the cloud exploded into nothingness. And at that same moment, I received about a cupful of water full in my upturned face.

I sat up gasping and sputtering. "That was cold!" I complained, wiping at my dripping features.

Timtik, crowing his delight, was dancing on the sunlit sward. "Oh what a witch *I'm* gonna make!"

"Warlock!" said Lorn, then looked to me for approval. I smiled my approval back at her. Who could disapprove of Lorn!

"All right—Warlock!" Timtik muttered. "But whatever I become, I'll be the best damned enchanter this forest has ever seen, that's for sure!"

I TOOK a deep breath of the warm fresh air and sighed, then looked around at the bright greenery of the forest that impinged upon the glade in which I'd landed. "It's certainly beautiful here," I said. "A guy could sit here and look at nature forever."

Timtik suddenly turned his gaze upon a dusty gray globe, about the size of an orange, burgeoning on the ground near my right hand. "No you couldn't, Albert," he said. "That's a hotsy!"

Lorn took a backward step such as a woman might do on hearing the word "bug." Her eyes widened. "You're right, Timtik! Let's go, quickly. Come on, Albert."

I looked again at the globe, which was now the size of a grapefruit. "A *hotsy!?* What does it do?"

Lorn and Timtik each grabbed an arm and hove me to my feet. "We'll explain later. Don't just sit there, it's almost *ripe!*"

I found myself stumbling along toward the encroaching edge or the woods with them. I shook their grips free of my arms, impatiently. "But what is a hotsy?" I looked back at it again. It was easy to see it. Already the size of a medicine ball, it was turning dull crimson. Then the grass about this ruddy spheroid began, abruptly, to smoke. Then it turned black and died. And still the hotsy grew, swollen and bloated, and radiating raw heat that I began to feel, a good sixty feet away. I no longer needed warnings from the woodnymph and faun. I turned on my heel and dashed after them (they hadn't halted their flight when I had).

Then, just as they were about to penetrate the first fringe of the woods, Lorn halted dead, and Timtik jumped backwards a good yard. "They're *coming!*" she cried, throwing herself flat on the earth. Timtik was pivoting about on one hoof, looking from the quivering globe to the forest and back again. Then I heard the sound. Off in the tanglewood, there was a hissing, buzzing, swishing, whizzing of angry noise. The sound was too much for Lorn. She jumped up again. "I'm afraid!" she whimpered to Timtik, "I can't stay here!"

"The other side of the hotsy, it's our only chance!" shrieked the faun, galloping off without her. I stood as he passed me, his head down and tiny hooves throwing up divots from the sod. Then Lorn rushed up to me, and right by me, yelling, "Run, Albert! *Run!*" I ran.

THE three of us, with Timtik's lead growing by the second, skirted the bulging diameter of the hotsy at a distance of ten feet, and even there my entire hotsy-side felt half-cooked before I got beyond it. The thing was almost ten feet high, now, and sagging horribly, like a huge scarlet-and-orange paper bag filled with wet mud. And just as we stumbled to a panting halt at the edge of woods bordering the opposite side of the glade, the hotsy was riven from within by its internal pressures, and splayed sluggishly open, disgorging a steaming red viscosity cluttered with small spheres. It looked like overgrown salmon roe, glowing with an incandescence that was nearly blinding. This gleaming glut of globes lay there for only an instant, and then the whizzing sound, which had been growing more piercing by the instant, reached a peak, and I cringed back, startled by the blue-white cloud of tiny flying things that came out of the other rim of the woods, at speeds well surpassing any bug I'd seen, ever.

Lorn clutched my arm, leaned her mouth to my ringing ear, and shouted, over the chaotic racket, *"Frost flies!"*

As the insects reached the goal of the globes, and crashed head-on, there came a keening screech, such as a warm coin makes on a block of dry ice, except that it would take all the coins in the U.S.A. on all the dry ice in the world to duplicate the volume of the shattering sound. The blue-white bugs glowed red, the globules shriveled into rime-coated raisins, and the erstwhile blast of heat became a sudden wintry chill in the air. As quickly as they'd come, the flies left, their reddish bodies turning blue-white again as they zoomed off and disappeared in a direction at right angles to the one they'd approached the glade at. The ensuing calm was downright soothing.

Lorn sagged against me and sighed. "That was very close. We were almost destroyed, you know." I hadn't known, of course, but I'd most certainly *suspected* something of the sort.

"Are those things as dangerous as they sound?"

"They live on heat. Any kind of heat. Body heat, for one," said Timtik. "And the hotsies live on cold. So they get along fine."

"They—they fly so *fast...*" I remarked, shivering.

"Have to," said Lorn. "To get from one hotsy to the next. They need the heat for enough pep to get from one hotsy to the other. They use it up fast. If they don't make it, they die. Not that anyone *cares.*"

"I guess a metabolism like that *would* keep you on the go," I agreed. Then, to change from an unpleasant topic, "By the way, where are we bound?"

"Well," said Lorn, "I have to take Timtik back to Maggot, first, then—" She gave me a sideways look.

"Then?" I said, my voice cracking.

Lorn shrugged, and gave me a friendly twitch in the ribs with her elbow. "We can maybe play charades or something."

Inside my collar, my neck did a brief imitation of a hotsy. "Uh—" I said intelligently.

Timtik tugged impatiently at Lorn's diaphanous drapery, then. "Let's go, Lorn. I'm getting hungry."

"All right, Timtik." Lorn took his hand, and I took hers, and we headed back across the glade, past the scene of the fly-hotsy encounter. In the circle of withered black grass, nothing remained, not even a wrinkled raisin. But my eyes stayed peeled for any more of those swift growing gray globes. It had been a close call, I began to realize, with delayed shock. One had a choice of running from the flies into that hellish heat, or from the heat into the deadly bullets of heat-hungry bugs.

As though sensing my thoughts over that scorched earth, Lorn said, "I saw Dalinda, another woodnymph, get caught in the middle, once. It was awful. She ran from the flies, and fell against the side of the hotsy, and as her front burnt up and turned black, the flies struck, and her back turned blue with spots of frostbite. It took more than five minutes until she was completely gone. The flies sat on her, and as the hotsy heated up a hunk of her they bit into it, and she screamed and kicked, and—"

"Lorn," I choked, feeling deathly ill, "I get the picture!"

"But don't you see what we missed, Albert!"

I saw, and nodded. "And I'm going to follow you and Timtik and do every single thing you say."

Timtik tugged Lorn's hand. "Come *on*, Lorn, huh? I'll be late for supper, and Maggot will whip me." Lorn nodded and picked up her pace. Together, the three of us entered the emerald gloom of the forest. The ground under my feet was springy as the base of a needle-floored pine forest, and the bushes were very strange.

As we'd near one in the gloaming, it seemed to fold back upon itself until we passed, then close up the gap behind us.

"Hey," I said, slowing my pace. "The way these things go shifting around, I'd never get out of here without help. Is the woods always so lively?"

Lorn smiled. "That's one of the handy things about being a woodnymph. The trees and shrubs and vines move aside for you. But don't worry, Albert. You'll have me with you on trips."

"If Maggot lets him make any," said Timtik, mysteriously. "She might not want a non-resident roaming around the woods."

"You're teasing," I said uneasily. "She wouldn't stop me."

"Of course not, Albert," said Lorn. "I'll even take you on a tour as soon as we get Timtik to Maggot's cave."

"She lives in a cave?" I asked, stepping around an idiotically grinning froggish thing that squatted lazily upon our path.

"Sometimes yes, sometimes no," Timtik explained. "Her dwelling changes with her moods."

Lorn tugged at me, as I lagged behind for another look at the froggish thing, which was now in the process of being consumed alive by another froggish thing, and looking quite rapturous about its grisly fate. "They're making love," said Lorn, pulling me along.

"But— It looks like the big one is *devouring* the little one!"

"Why not?" Lorn's voice was tinged with impatience, as a parent speaking to a beloved imbecile child. "Haven't you ever heard of being so deeply in love with a person you felt like just eating him up?"

"Well, sure. But if they *really* do it, how do they reproduce?"

"They don't," said Lorn with a shrug. "They never get the chance. One look and it's love, and the next thing you know, it's dinner."

"But," I persisted, peering back into the fronded gloom, trying to catch the finale of the catastrophe, "if that goes on, the species will dwindle!"

"Oh," said Lorn, matter-of-factly, "it has."

"Then why haven't the forest people set up a sort of—um—preservation program?"

Lorn looked at me. "Who'd want to preserve one of those?"

AT that moment, a mewling twang in the region of my upper trunk reminded me that I never had gotten around to making myself that ham sandwich back home. It seemed ages since I'd first thought of doing it. "Lorn," I said, "I'm getting hungry, too. Are there any restaurants, or— No, I guess that's out of the question. But is there any food available?"

Lorn paused, despite Timtik's impatient grumble. "I think Maggot should have enough to go around. I'd planned on joining her and Timtik for supper. You can probably sit in, too, if you don't mind a meal cooked by a witch."

"Well, if it's something familiar, I suppose I could manage to swallow—"

Lorn proceeded to move onward. "If you're that choosy, Albert, you're not as hungry as you think."

"But Lorn," I pleaded. "A witch's cooking sounds so—"

She had not paused, however, so I had to drop the subject and hurry to keep up with her before the shrubbery snapped back into my path. I came abreast of her, and she gripped my arm suddenly, making me go warm all over for the next five steps. Above us, then, something screamed, a raucous sort of scream, and a moment later, there came a crackling of branches, and something plunged to the path ahead of us with a sickening crunch.

I thought some magnificent bird had crashed, but only for a moment. As the bushes twisted out of our way, I saw that the broken wings, a good fifteen feet from tip to tip, were growing out of the back of a mannish creature, bronzed of flesh, right fist still clutching the haft of a slender, wicked-pointed brass trident. "A Kwistian," said Lorn. "That means we're getting near the Thrake."

"Thrake?" I stepped gingerly about the corpse. "What's that?"

"A blue thing about five inches long, and it does something no one understands to the wings of the Kwistians," said Timtik, kicking the corpse over on its back. The face was only semi-human, I saw with near-nausea. In lieu of nose and mouth, it sported a beak like a parrot's. And the eyes, human in size and shape, had no lids or lashes, just a nictitating membrane just now moving to cover the glazing yellow sclera. It was a mean face. Lorn shivered.

"Those beaks—Horrible. They eat people, you know."

Just about to touch the beak, I withdrew my hand in haste. "Eat people? Lorn, isn't there anything friendly in this forest?"

"Just me..." she said softly, closing one dark-lashed eye in a slow wink. Then she turned back to the path again. "But come on. I have to get Timtik home."

"People," I said thoughtfully as we moved onward, "should be rough on those beaks. You need teeth to get through thick muscle. They might give a sharp nip, or take off a finger or toe, but—"

"They—they cook their victims first," said Lorn, with a kind of uneasy twitch of her slim shoulders.

"In the *flame-pits!*" embellished Timtik, his eyes a-sparkle with excitement. *"Alive!"*

Lorn went ashy pale. "Timtik—Please!" At her words, he became suddenly subdued, and repentant.

I FELT some of their tension, and asked, "What is it, Lorn? For a girl who described death-by-hotsy a few minutes ago, you look almost ill."

Lorn smiled wanly. "It seems that the Kwistians prefer wood-nymphs on their menu. They don't always get us, of course, but they're always trying. Sometimes they get a lot at once, and eat them one at a time, fattening up the rest in cells in that dreadful Sark!"

"Where did you get this information?" I said, puzzled.

"I think the Thrake told Maggot," said Timtik. "No one knows how it stops the Kwistians from flying, but it does. Some people say it's really the soul of a maiden who died in a flame-pit, and this is how she gets her vengeance for her awful fate!"

"Gosh," I said, impressed, "it must be a handy thing for the woodnymphs, this Thrake."

"You said a mouthful," said Timtik.

"But," I asked, still at sea, "don't the Kwistians know by now not to fly anywhere near the Thrake?"

"They don't know where it's at," Lorn said. "They know only that it's in Maggot's hut. But she keeps her dwelling on the move, so they won't find it. The forest folk are all very glad to have Maggot around."

Timtik nodded proudly. "She's the oldest, wrinkledest, wisest witch there is. Everyone always says, 'If the monsters make you holler, Maggot has counter-spells, five for a dollar.'"

"Of course," the woodnymph interjected, brushing idly at her burnished tresses, where they'd fallen across her cheek, "no one knows where she lives, and if they did, no one uses dollars here."

"But the free word-of-mouth advertising helps her reputation considerably, and she always gets enough things in barter to keep her in health, so she can go on making her hell-brew for the Thrake."

I pretended to follow most of their dizzying conversation, and trailed along for about ten paces. Then I stopped dead. "Lorn—?"

"Yes?" Her eyes were inquisitive, and she paused.

"You don't know what this dwelling looks like, currently?"

The golden-red head shook lightly from side to side.

"And if you did know, it might still be anywhere in Drendon?" I added, while my stomach growled piteously. She nodded.

"Then," I said in annoyed perplexity, jamming my fists against my hips, "how do you know where we're *heading?*"

"I don't," she said brightly. "It's always this way, Albert. We just meander here and there, hoping she's outside gathering herbs or something. Though Timtik can spot her place nine times out of ten."

LORN turned back toward our path again, and I could only sigh and go tagging along after her. I couldn't think of an argument with such total illogicality. In a way, I kind of missed the Susan-side of Lorn. Susan wasn't so flashily seductive, but she had a brain on her shoulders, so to speak.

"Let's hurry," said Timtik, picking up the pace.

"It never takes too long," said Lorn to me. "Maggot sometimes senses our approach."

I eyed the clustering heavily vined growths through which we were wending our labyrinthine way, and said, in some doubt, "Through *this?*"

"She uses magic, you dope!"

Hot and hungry, and sore of foot, I had suddenly had enough of the faun's impudence. "Half-goat or not," I snapped, "you still have a behind I can paddle!" I lunged for him and my hands closed on the breeze of his departure. With a crow of delight, he was leaping away, gurgling his enjoyment. No one can catch a faun in full flight, barring a faunic mishap, and in the tanglewood we trod I couldn't have paced a whale on roller skates, but I was too mad to act with intelligence.

Lorn ran after me, as I crashed and plunged through the grasping shrubbery after Timtik. She shouted my name, and grabbed my sleeve just as I broke through an intricately tough tangle of the growths. I found myself swaying giddily on the brink of a short but steep embankment, and then Lorn came up too fast against me and we both went sprawling down the sunny slope through a welter of musky scented flowers, and slid for a short distance on some sort of glassy-topped substance.

When I clambered to my hands and knees, I saw that we were on a bright green glossy path, in the midst of thick purplish moss. The moss spread out in all directions, as broad as the surface of a mountain lake, but quite still. Then I noticed that—although I could have sworn we'd slid from the base of the embankment—there was nothing but more moss between us and the edge of the woods, a good broadjump away.

Lorn sat up, looked about, then gave a frightened whimper.

"What is it?" I stared at her, apprehensive. Gone was the self-composure she'd heretofore exhibited. She was squealing and moaning, and biting her lower lip in terror, and wringing her hands. "Albert—" she said weakly, "we're in the mossfields of Sark!"

"The what?"

"They surround the castle. Sark is the castle where the Kwistians dwell. That's where this path leads, and there's no getting back."

I looked at the edge of the path behind us, cut off as smoothly as with a knife, and took a step back from the edge to get a running start for the jump that might take me to the embankment. A distance of path equal to my pace shimmered, faded and vanished. Behind us, the path was self-destructive. We could only go forward. To the castle where the parrot-beaked flying cannibals were waiting. I was debating the usefulness of sitting down beside Lorn and joining her in a good long cry, when I remembered the faun. "Where's Timtik?" I said, glancing about. "If he's still near the brink, he can tell Maggot, can't he?"

Lorn's face lighted with the first trace of hope I'd seen since our skid onto the green path. "Of course!" she said. "We can wait here till she figures out some way to rescue us."

"Timtik!" we yelled together. "TIMTIK!"

THE all-enshrouding green growths at the edge of the woods remained unbroken. It was as though Timtik had never been with us at all. The sun beat down upon us, stark and hot. And a few inches at the end of the path made an impatient disappearance, forcing us to move backward, and the instant we did so, even more path evaporated. We were a good thirty feet from the embankment's nearest point.

"Is that moss as dangerous as it looks?" I said, its alien purple hue having repelled any thoughts I'd had of trying to tread upon it. "What's under it—Monsters? Quicksand?"

"No one knows," said Lorn, her voice panicky. "But it's supposed to be death to fall into it. Don't leave me!"

I hesitated, then took a step onto the soft velvet stuff. It gave, parted, and I oozed downward into black muddy bog to the knees as I swiftly grabbed for the edge of the path. Then, just as Lorn gripped my arms, the soft wet feel of the mud changed, as something slithered in the thick slime, and then sharp burning pain grated on my flesh like razor-scrapes, and I was yelping as Lorn managed to drag me back onto the path.

I looked down. My legs were spotted with pinkish burns, and a few ugly white blisters; my trousers, shoes and socks were gone wherever the mud had flowed. I had slightly less pants left than go into a pair of Bermuda shorts.

"It's no use, Albert," Lorn sighed. "We'll have to either go onward to the castle of Sark, or stay here and fall into that stuff when the path vanishes again."

"Well—" I said uncertainly, "the moss is *sure* death... I guess the castle's our best bet, if only because it'll put off our destruction until we can get help from Maggot, maybe—"

"I hope," said Lorn, lovely beyond my wildest dreams, "Timtik gets to Maggot in time."

"And," I added with a weak smile, "that Maggot gets to us in time."

CHAPTER FIVE

Now, shortly before this time (albeit I didn't learn of it in detail until much later from Maggot—who can apparently find out *anything* she has a mind to) there were things afoot that were going to have extraordinary, if not downright dire effects on my fate. It seems that, at the moment Lorn and I were asprawl on the edge of that weird green path, still confused from our tumble down the embankment, things were happening at that ancient cannibal stronghold, the castle of Sark...

*   *   *

The green buzzer flashed and crackled.

Cort, drowsing in the sunlight by the great stone casement of his laboratory, clacked his beak in annoyance and peered at the panel of lights. As his eye ascertained the source of the noise, his insouciance fell away from him like a cloak, and he hurried over to the panel, his long, cruelly taloned index finger punching the Stop button. The buzzing and flashing ceased instantly, and the core of a dull crystal disc upon a squat stone tripod began to coruscate with jabs of cold blue light. Cort passed a hand commandingly above its surface, peered into its depths, and the face of Kwist, the winged emperor, swam into sharp focus.

"Well?" snarled Kwist, evilly.

"Woodnymph," said Cort. "Just now hit the path."

Kwist wiped a bit of spittle off his beaktip. "How soon is she expected?"

"Give her about an hour," said Cort, after a quick mental calculation.

"I'll have the flame-pits stoked up," said the emperor, with a blissful glow in his bright yellow eyes. His image faded swiftly, and the crystal went dull and opaque.

Cort rubbed his hands together gleefully, and hummed tunelessly as he moved to the casement to survey the vista of the purple mossfields. The vista from that high vantage point was a broad one indeed. Not only due to the giddy height of the casement, but also to a salient feature of this strange dimension that made it exceedingly alien to the ordinary topography of Earth—

* * *

"There's no horizon!" I gasped.

Lorn shook her head. "No, there isn't. Drendon is a perfect plane surface."

I looked with wonder at the sight I'd just become aware of, the sight I'd been unable to detect in the depths of the forest. Land, moss-covered to the rim of the distant forest, rolled back in all directions from where I stood, until it merged by perspective into a solid dark color, which still continued onward and onward. "That's impossible," I said. "It has to *end,* doesn't it?"

LORN shrugged. "Who knows? Maybe it does, maybe it doesn't. No one has ever been ambitious enough to walk far enough to see."

"But if this place is a plane, how can it be contiguous with Earth?" I asked, scratching my head.

"Well," said the woodnymph, scowling as she searched her mind for a solution, "it's—it's as though your planet were an orange, and our land were a table on which the orange lay. At the point where the orange touched the table, the two would have a common point of existence."

I suddenly got the picture. "And Porkle Park is the contact point! The gateway to your dimension!"

"Right," said Lorn. "By now, we're probably miles from the park, and centuries from your era."

"Centuries…?" I felt suddenly cold inside.

"Yes. The farther we get from the park, the farther from that moment when we left Earth. We have no time here as you do there. Your time depends on *when,* ours on *where."*

I PUZZLED this out slowly. If it were true, it meant that there were an infinity of contact points with Earth, each at a different age of Earth's existence… "Um— What time is it now?"

Lorn frowned, glanced about her, and seemed to be calculating. "Well, Albert, in this direction it's about late eighteenth century, your time. If we had a key, we could arrive on the Earth that touched Drendon at this point, during the French Revolution, I believe."

"That's better than the flame-pits, isn't it? And I can speak a little French— *'Voulez-vous'—"* No, maybe *she* could speak a little French, too. "How," I went on, "did Drendon happen to contact Earth in the first place?"

"It didn't come to Earth. It almost went *from* it. Remember that orange I mentioned?" I remembered. "Well, it's as though our dimension had once been the skin of that orange. But at the Edict of Banishment, it spread away, leaving Earth except at one point. It's always touched the Earth since then, but always at a different time, and a new point."

"What was this Edict of Banishment?" I asked.

"Merlin did it," said Lorn. "With his semi-scientific thaumaturgics. It was at King Arthur's request. Don't you know your own history?"

"History? But Arthur is a legend, a myth…"

"Is Drendon a myth?" asked the woodnymph.

I looked at the unsetting sun, the horizonless vista, the purple moss and the green path. "I guess not," I had to admit. Even minus those clues, Timtik's hooves were proof enough.

"Well then!" said Lorn. "So he banished Drendon—"

"Why?" I asked.

"The Kwistians, naturally!" she said irritably. "They were spoiling all his knight's fun. It was hard enough slaying dragons and things without having flying men always pricking your horse's flanks with their tridents, and sometimes swiping your lance, or carrying off the maiden you'd ridden for leagues to rescue. So Arthur banished them. Merlin made a powerful spell, and sent the Kwistians and their ilk away from Earth, leaving only one contact-point, in case they should become better behaved, or that Arthur should change his mind. He planned on checking every so often."

"You say 'planned' as though he flubbed up," I observed, completely fascinated. "What went wrong?"

"The scheme backfired. The dragons went with the Kwistians, and so did the other so-called mythological entities of Earth, and the knights were left with nothing to fight. So they got lazy, and then Lancelot started giving Guinevere the eye, and things kind of went to pot. Arthur decided to switch back, fast, then. It's better to have a dragon in the garden than a paramour on the porch. But Merlin couldn't do it. In banishing Drendon, he'd weakened himself more than he'd planned—he was part-monster himself, you recall—and in his weak human condition, he couldn't pull a rabbit out of a hat, let alone a whole dimension back from limbo."

"Funny," I remarked, "but I don't remember any mention of flying cannibals in the Arthurian Legend. Dragons, yes; them, no."

"Well, of course not, Albert!" Lorn said scornfully. "When they were officially banished, their names were struck from the rosters of creatures. It was forbidden to even *mention* them, let alone write their history. So here we are, in Drendon." She passed a hand before her face, and a lot of her Susan-self shone through her features for a confused moment. "Anyone who—who enters here—has to *attune,* or perish."

"Attune?" I asked, although "perish" was the word that bothered me.

To fit with things here, like—like me and Timtik." She held her lovely face between her hands, and closed her eyes tightly, trying to evoke an elusive memory. Then she shook her head and dropped her hands. "The trouble is," she said with a friendly glance, "the timelessness here gets at your memory, and you find it hard to think of anything that might have happened—*before…*"

"Then why haven't *I* changed?" I asked. "I'm here…"

"Oh," she said nonchalantly, "you will. It just takes a while to readjust to environment. If the change were a swift one, Timtik and I would have reverted to some sort of Earth-creatures when we showed up at your house. But we weren't out that long."

"Well why didn't you *stay,* for pete's sake!" I moaned, just realizing the opportunity I'd muffed back in my study.

Lorn was incredulous. "And leave Maggot here alone? She'd go out of her mind without us."

"Why couldn't she leave with you, then?" I inquired reasonably.

"Because of the Thrake, silly! She can't leave it and she can't take it away."

I shook my head, dizzily aware that she was getting me onto one of those conversational merry-go-rounds again. "I give up. This is too much natural history in one dose. Look, Lorn, why don't you and I scoot out of here to the French Revolution? We'll be safer among the *jacquerie* than with flying cannibals. And Maggot can probably reach us sooner or later…"

"But I have the key to *your* time, not that one." She held it up for my inspection. "This only works at one point in Drendon, the spot where it touches Porkle Park." I looked at the little thing, which resembled an undernourished mandrake root, and an idea glimmered into life.

"Lorn…that thing can talk, right? Well, *it's* light enough to travel *over* the moss. We could send a message to Maggot!"

"What message?" Lorn sighed. *"Goodbye?"*

I grimaced in exasperation. "Lorn, how can you be so intellectual in your speech sometimes, and then revert to downright idiocy?"

"Rote," said Lorn. "I sound bright when I'm quoting information I've gotten from Maggot, but it's all rote. I can recite, but I can't figure very well. All I just told you about Drendon was memorized fact. I couldn't *explain* any of it."

"That's crazy—" I protested. "If you know you *don't* know…"

"Who," said Lorn stubbornly, "discovered America?"

"Columbus," I retorted automatically, before I had a chance to wonder why she'd asked.

"How did he travel?" she went inexplicably on.

"By boat. The Nina, the Pinta, and—"

"Can *you* sail a boat?"

"Well, no…" I admitted.

"Furl a sail?"

"No…"

"Chart a course?"

"No."

"Command an expedition? Speak Italian and Spanish?"

"No," I said, my replies growing softer by the second.

"Columbus could!" said Lorn, as though she'd made a point. I stood there on that strange green path, staring into her face for a long moment. Then my frustrated soul wrenched a cry of misery from my heart.

"So what!" I shrieked.

"Albert," said Lorn, with weary patience, "can't you see that your position is exactly like mine? You know Columbus discovered America by boat after getting money from the Spanish queen and you let it go at that. You couldn't explain *how* he sailed to the west, or *what* he said to cozen the queen, or *where* they got the lumber for the ships, or *why* he picked that time to make his trip, could you?"

"No," I said. "I guess not. But—"

"So," she interrupted triumphantly, "how do you expect me to understand precisely how Drendon came to be when you—an adult male of supposedly average intelligence—cannot even explain the discovery of America!?"

I STOOD there, completely stripped of erudition, feeling intellectually naked. What, after all, did anyone know about anything, when you got right down to it? Taking discretion as the better part of valor, I changed the subject violently back to where it had been a few moments before. "Lorn, *about* this key—"

"What about it?" she said brightly.

I almost shouted, then controlled my vexation and said softly, "If we send this key-twig thing to Maggot with a message, then she can save us, can't she?"

Lorn wrinkled her brow. "I don't know, Albert. But I suppose it is worth a try—" She set the key upon the path, where it stood expectantly on its skimpy root-legs. "Key, can you take a message to Maggot?"

The key squeaked delightedly. "Yes. What message?"

"Help!" said Lorn.

"Isn't that rather brief?" I asked.

Lorn shrugged. "We'll be lucky if the key remembers *that*. Her brains can't be much bigger than a grain of sand."

"Help?" giggled the key, scurrying about in an eager dance of impatience. "Help? Is that right?"

"Perfect," said Lorn. "Now, hurry!"

With a shrill snicker of mirth, the key danced away from us over the lavender moss-tufts, screaming "Help!" at every bound.

"There!" I said, happy that the moss didn't suck it into that corrosive mud with its slithery occupants, "I guess we're all set, now. When Maggot gets the key and hears the message, she'll know we're in trouble, and—"

"How?" said Lorn, looking suddenly pleased.

A numb apprehensiveness touched my heart. "Lorn— This key— It's the only one to the woods, isn't it?"

Lorn stepped back from me, apparently frightened by my cold intensity. "No. Maggot will give them to any reliable person who wants a peep at the Earth people...Why? Is it important?"

I smacked the palm of my hand to my brow. *"Important?* Lorn, how the hell will Maggot know who *sent* the message?"

"I don't know. I didn't think of that."

I turned and stared futilely in the direction the key had gone. It was no longer visible, but I could hear a wispy treble repeating, "Help! Help! Help!" in the dim distance.

I turned and glared at Lorn, my hands clenching— Then, seeing her eyes fill with fright, I melted, and simply reached out and pulled her to me. She tensed as I touched her, then slipped her own arms about me and relaxed against my chest, sniffing softly. "I'm sorry," she said. "I *told* you I wasn't very bright!"

Holding her there in my arms, warm, soft and helpless, I couldn't stay even a little angry. "Lorn, Lorn…" I sighed. "I don't know, I just don't know!" I chuckled with helpless hysteria at the stupidity of what had just happened. "You're such a lovable dope!" I kissed her behind the ear. "And I'm nuts about you."

Lorn sighed and snuggled closer. Then something occurred to me. I looked back at the edge of the green path. It was clear up to my heels, but had advanced no further. "Lorn," I said elatedly, "we've been here for many minutes, and the path hasn't dissolved any further!"

She looked. "Is it broken?" she queried hopefully.

"I don't believe so. It's psychological! It wants to scare us into moving, but doesn't want us falling into the mossfields. By standing still, we call its bluff!"

"Wonderful," said Lorn clapping her hands and doing a small dance of delight on that fatal brink before I grabbed her again. "So what shall we do?" she asked.

"Stay right here," I replied. "Maybe Timtik will get to Maggot with news of us, or she'll figure out where the key came from. But it's better than walking." I held her tighter. "Much better than walking."

"Will we be rescued soon?" asked Lorn, cuddling near me, her flaming hair wafting a scent of fresh blossoms to my nearby nose.

"I sincerely hope not."

CHAPTER SIX

TWO hours!" growled Kwist, standing arms akimbo in the archway of Cort's laboratory. Cort, jerked awake by the words, took a second to orient himself, and then realized that it was indeed later than he'd expected. Hiding his own puzzlement, he said testily, "So?"

"So where's the woodnymph? I'm as empty as—as your head!" the emperor grunted. "And while we're at it, how come no 'Your Imperial Majesty' in your responses, eh? I thought we had that out the other day!"

"We did, Kwist, and I won the toss, remember?" Cort deliberately turned his back on the emperor and stalked to his lab table, his huge white wings rustling in fury.

"Ha!" shrieked Kwist. "You used some of that stinking magic of yours to win. You *never* lose a toss!"

"All the more fool you for bothering to call the toss."

Kwist strode to his vizier and spun him about with a snarl. Then he took a quick backward step as Cort's sparking yellow eyes flashed ominously. "Don't you ever do that again, Kwist! Let's get it straight who's running things around here. You wouldn't last *that* long—" he flipped thumb and forefinger with a sharp crack "—without my science and wizardry to back you. I'm the power behind your throne, and the sooner you stop pretending otherwise, the better for all of us!"

Kwist seethed in impotent rage. "All right—maybe I can't run the empire alone, but listen here, you have certain responsibilities, whether you like it or not, and the primary one at the moment is the getting of *food* for the rest of us! And I simply wish to know, WHERE IS IT!?" His anger was a physical pain, setting his great wing-muscles quivering.

Cort, albeit the brighter, was the weaker of the two, almost in inverse ratio. He frowned, uneasily, at the visible tension in the other's tall powerful frame. "I don't know," he replied desultorily. "Let me look at the indicator board."

He waved a hand through a bank of lights on the wall, and a large blank panel glowed into topographic life, a map of the mossfields. From the black square at its base, marking the location of Castle Sark, a thin green ribbon ran erratically up the board. Its upper extremity, within the heart of the mossfields, lay motionless.

"Damn that woodnymph! She's staying put!" snapped Cort. "I thought those creatures were too dumb to reason out the path's operation."

"Are you sure it *is* a woodnymph?" asked the emperor.

Cort quirked a feathery eyebrow. "Certainly. If any other creature fell into the mossfields, it would sink and be destroyed. Only a woodnymph can activate the path. Once activated, of course, it will take any amount of traffic that cares to join her in her fate, but there must be at *least* one woodnymph present to trigger the path's initiation."

"Well," said the monarch, impatiently, "what do we do about her? Let her loaf while we starve?"

Cort looked coldly at the emperor. "You're the ruler around here; pull some rank on your Imperial Guards, and send a couple of them out after her."

Kwist, about to challenge the other's impertinent attitude, decided it could wait until his hunger was assuaged. He simply nodded. "All right, Cort." Then he had an afterthought. His physical advantage was of no use when Cort used wizardry or science against him. Might as well make harmony among the upper echelons—"And," he said with bad grace, "I'm sorry I shouted at you like that. Lost my head."

"Ha ha," Cort said mirthlessly. Kwist turned a bit pink, but spun about and strode away without further argument, vanishing through the great stone archway. Cort listened to the monarch's voice raging in a distant corridor and then the air in the courtyard below his open casement was thumped by great pinions. In another moment, two graceful Imperial Guards, tridents poised deftly, soared up into the open sky and sailed swiftly out over the path snaking through the mossfields, seeking their prey...

*   *   *

LET'S lie down," said Lorn, adding, as my eyes bulged a bit. "I'm tired of just standing here." My voice wouldn't quite work, so I nodded bravely and slowly lay back onto the shimmering green pathway. Lorn flopped gracefully beside me, and we lay there in silence. Then...

"The path is cold and hard, Albert," said Lorn. "May I rest my head upon your strong warm shoulder?"

"Oh...Why not!" I croaked, nervously.

Her head, with its glorious tresses, snuggled down against my right biceps and pectoral. There was a lull. Then—

"May I slip my arms about you?" she asked gently.

While I tried to think of a reply that wouldn't abet the adolescent squeak that was starting to possess my larynx, she went ahead and did it anyhow. Another lull. Then—

"May I give you a fond kiss?" asked Lorn.

I tried to come up with an answer, pursed my lips in deep thought, and then her soft warm mouth was pressing lightly down upon mine, and if I had felt about one percent happier, my hair would have caught fire.

"Comfy?" Lorn whispered, returning her head to my shoulder.

"Uh-huh," I grunted, after swallowing three times in succession.

"Ssh!" Lorn held a finger to my lips. "Don't talk. It spoils it."

"I won't," I promised.

"Now," she sighed, "let's have a nap, and maybe when we waken, Maggot will be here, and we'll be rescued."

"Good thinking," I mumbled. The sun was warm and soothing, and I felt I had been awake an awfully long time. Even Lorn's presence didn't alleviate the weariness in my body, more used to sitting in a chair while I pored over dusty tomes than pushing its way through a tanglewood, I closed my eyes, sighed and relaxed.

When I was still hovering on the border of sleep, I felt Lorn stir. I guess she'd grown tired of leaning on me, once my attention had lagged. Not to mention the sharp stubble sprouting on my face, undoubtedly irritating to a woodnymph's tender skin. I peeked up at her, but she was only standing with a hand shading her eyes, peering out over the fields in the direction the key had taken. Then my fatigue caught up with me, and I dozed off…

* * *

Blue water foamed on baked sand, and white froth boiled about my waist, while surging seas tugged strongly against my legs. I was watching her, there on the shore. Rosemarie, my first love. I was ten, and she was seven. I waved to her, shouted her name, and then she saw me, and immediately pretended she didn't, until I plowed my way against the resisting water to the shore. She turned then, shyly, and gazed serenely at me with warm brown eyes. Her smile was gentle, mature for her years. I returned her gaze, unashamed, she blushed and lowered her eyes.

Then those selfsame eyes opened very wide, and her mouth followed suit. "Your knees!" she said, backing away and pointing. "Albert! You're knock-kneed!" A giggle broke from her, and then she was joined by a covey of girls her own age.

"Albert is a knock-knee, Albert is a knock-knee!" They sang it loudly, and gestured at me, and one imitated my stance as she crossed her eyes and stuck out her pink tongue.

I turned about and plunged once more into the concealing waves of ocean, striking out for the horizon, my face stinging hot with agonized mortification. I wanted to drown, to die, to get a chill, to never see them or anyone again. Then I got a mouthful of water, and it gagged me, and I sputtered and turned back. Drowning was much too unpleasant a termination. But I would never speak to Rosemarie again. Never...!

*   *   *

THE taste of salt was strong in my mouth as I came awake, but as the hot flicker of the burning sun dappled my closed eyelids with lemon and orange flashes, the taste faded along with the mental image from my childhood, and I realized that it had been, after all, only a painfully traumatic dream-memory. I lay there a moment, eyes shut, thinking. Thinking about Lorn, with whom—Susan-side or no Susan-side—I was suddenly very much in love, the very least reason for which being that although the moss had eroded my trousers to the thighs, exposing to her eyes my secret shame, she'd never said a word, cast a glance, smothered a smile. My heart thumped cheerily in my chest, percolating with passion.

"Lorn—" I said, sitting up on the path and blinking my eyes into focus. *"Albert...Albert...!"* carried her voice.

I got my vision functioning and stared. About thirty feet down the path, Lorn was running frantically toward me, her face alight with happiness. For a moment, I couldn't see how our situation was any different than it had been, then I followed her line of sight and saw the short, straining figure moving toward us through the moss.

Timtik, balancing precariously upon the upper curve of a vaguely saurian-shaped log, was shoving strenuously into the deep black bog beneath the moss with a long hardwood pole, and actually making progress toward us in that muck. Behind him, twisting into the distance, lay his wake, where the thick black ooze had not yet been recovered by the furry purple growth. His progress must have been about one foot per stroke of that pole, and the strain was showing in his face. His upper body, the non-goatish part, was a perfect scintilla of shiny sweat.

"Hi!" he croaked weakly, in that tin-telephone voice, as the nose of the log nuzzled the end of the path near my heels. "You dopes could've stopped walking about a mile back, couldn't you?" he grunted. "This is hard work."

"Oh, Timtik," Lorn said compassionately, "you look nearly dead."

"Don't worry," he said in his grumpy way. "On the return trip, Albert can do the work. This is my contribution to this rescue. Let *his* muscles sprain for awhile."

Lorn had run to the edge of the path, and was about to step aboard the log, but Timtik waved her back. "Hold it, dopey!" he snarled. "Let Albert get aboard first. Soon's *you* step off, the path'll vanish, and I'm not up to tugging Albert out of the moss."

"Thank you," I said sincerely, hurrying forward and stepping carefully onto the rough cylinder. Balance, I could see at once, was going to be somewhat of a problem. I was actually grateful when he handed me the end of the pole. Poling might be work, but it'd keep me upright. I hung on tightly, as Timtik sheathed his claws and assisted Lorn gracefully onto the corrugated bark surface. The instant her rearward foot left the path, the entire green serpentine hissed like a drop of ginger ale on a hot griddle, and shimmered quietly out of existence.

Lorn took a seat near the shoreward end of the log, leaning comfortably back against the upthrust of a short stumpy limb. How she managed comfort with her bare back against that rough surface, I don't know; I guess her being a woodnymph had something to do with it. She was quite at home with anything wooden.

Timtik lay gently down upon the logtop on his back and lazily crossed his fetlocks. "Pole away, Albert," he smiled, and shut his eyes.

I SHOVED with the pole, aiming the shoreward end of the log by means of Timtik's still visible wake in the bog, and we started moving. My stroke was just a bit better than his, if only because I had longer arms, and we started sliding slowly over the muck at about three feet per effort. After ten hearty shoves, my back and shoulders started mumbling polite protests. After twenty, they were murmuring uneasily, and after twenty-five they were starting to whimper. And Lorn and Timtik let me struggle alone.

"Hard work," I said between tight lips, shaking my head to flick away the sweat droplets from my eyebrows.

"What did you think it would be?" asked the faun, with an unpleasantly contented smile.

I opened my mouth to reply, but Lorn, sensing a hum of antagonism in our tones, interrupted deftly, "Timtik, tell us what happened since we last saw you. Why didn't you answer when we called?"

"Didn't hear you," he said simply. "And of course, I never expected *you* to go near the mossfields; I forgot you had old Fumblefoot along."

"Now look—!" I muttered angrily.

"Please tell us what happened," said Lorn, swiftly.

"Oh, all right," said the faun, with easy nonchalance. "Right after Albert started chasing me, I located Maggot..."

As his metallic voice droned onward, I managed to cut down slightly on my stroke. If they noticed, they were nice enough not to mention it. And I listened in interest to his tale...

IN the shadowy thickets of Drendon, beside a sluggish swampy morass of dank fetid earth, lurked a blob. It gave a quiver now and then, its off-pink color deepening to red, then back to off-pink. Every so often it hissed and seemed to shrug. To most of the forest folk, it had the outward appearance of a Wumbl. A Wumbl, to the uninitiated, was a protoplasmic atavism. Very like an amoeba, it differed mainly in size. It stood about eight feet high (when it was standing), but attained a mean horizontal diameter of about thirty feet when it flattened out to expand its pseudopods and flow along the ground after food. Worse still, it took on the color of the ground over which it slithered, and unless a traveler were quite careful about where he set his foot, he might suddenly find himself ingested whole into that loathsome body, encased abruptly in tough, rubbery walls filled with a viscous jelly which would then begin to ooze digestive juices all over him. Wumbls were very unpleasant creatures.

But, as noted, this thing had a Wumbl's *outward* appearance. Actually, it was not any such thing, but just seemed to be, as camouflage from prying eyes. No one who spotted a Wumbl ever paused to check its authenticity. Wumbls could move faster than whippets when aroused, and they were aroused by anything that looked even a little bit edible, and they ate anything at all, so—

Well, it was at this particular thing that Timtik ran, full tilt, just after avoiding my clutching fingers. Had he been an elephant, he might possibly had stood to defeat a Wumbl, for his tusks could rip a gaping hole in the hideous body and let the viscous matter burst out, sure death for a one-celled creature. But Timtik's horns were barely long enough to be worthy of the name, and he would be helpless against such a monstrosity.

But rather than cease his precipitate pace, he only moved the faster when he espied it. "Ho, Maggot!" he cried, dashing up to the side of the awful thing. There was a moment's quivering hesitation in the Wumbloid, then a rectangular slab appeared in its side, and swung outward on creaky hinges.

"Come in, Timtik," said Maggot the witch. Timtik sprang lithely through the gap, and the gap sealed over immediately. Maggot looked up at the faun from over a steaming cauldron of noisome stuff, her coarse gray hair dank from the rising fumes, her eyes bleary from lack of sleep. "You're late," she chided as she stirred the mess. "Sit down and have your supper."

"Lorn's in love with a *human!*" said Timtik, glad to be the primal purveyor of the latest scandal.

"Do tell," Maggot muttered toothlessly. Well, not quite tooth-lessly; she had upper and lower canines yet, and when she yawned, they resembled nothing so much as stalactites and stalagmites in a greasy red cavern. The upper canines protruded over her lower lip when her mouth was closed, and were horribly yellow and rotted. Timtik often wondered if she ever bathed, but he'd thought the topic too delicate to mention to one of her finer feelings. He glanced toward a heap of cobwebby odds and ends on a dusty wooden shelf over the fireplace.

"How's the Thrake?" he inquired.

MAGGOT mumbled scornfully, "If anything had happened to it, would I be wasting my time with this hell-brew?" A muted squeal came from the shelf. "Patience, patience!" grumbled the witch, throwing a fistful of dandelion fluff into the stew. "I have to let it simmer a bit."

The squeal repeated, more shrilly, but a bit weakly.

Maggot shrugged and stuck a dipper into the cauldron, drawing off a slimy clot of hell-brew. It steamed and stank, and Timtik averted his nose. With no ceremony, Maggot deposited the dripping glup on the shelf. "There," she said. "That'll hold you for awhile."

From out of the heap of refuse cluttered upon the shelf, a tiny blue tentacle snaked. It hovered over the mess, prodded it to make sure it was all it should be, and then a small blue thing popped out its tiny head and sniffed the rancid aroma. It nodded as though pleased, and with a squeal of delight, pounced upon the hell-brew and began to slup it up with repulsive enjoyment, grunting and gurgling with slowly sated hunger pangs. Timtik suddenly didn't feel much like eating.

"You haven't touched your food," said Maggot. "Little queasy about the tummy? Well, old Maggot'll fix that up." From beside the gobbling Thrake she took a small copper flask and twisted out the cork. "Here, drink."

Timtik took it carefully, then shut his eyes and swallowed a manly mouthful of it. His eyes widened, and blurred with moisture. "Hey, that's good!" he exclaimed, wiping his lips with the back of his hand. "What is it?"

Maggot smiled a secret smile. "It's called '90 proof', dearie."

"It makes my ears burn," said Timtik, holding his slightly pointed extrusions.

"It's supposed to," Maggot crooned, running a claw-like hand through his hair. Her eyes flicked the entrance. "But where's Lorn?" she asked. "Not hungry?"

Timtik paused in his dinner and frowned. "I wonder... She may have gone back, but—I didn't think she'd go without saying goodbye, at least..."

"Back? *Back?*" Maggot's eyes were suddenly hot red and protruding from their sockets as she leaned over the faun like a hungry hawk. "Back where?"

Timtik shrank down in his chair, thoroughly frightened. "To Earth. She was going back with Albert..."

"With?" grated Maggot, her canines clacking and sparking in her fury. "He's HERE? In DRENDON?"

TIMTIK nodded mutely, sliding down in his chair until his shoulder blades touched the seat. Maggot hung over him a moment more, then cracked her palms together. "A human," she murmured thoughtfully. "Here in Drendon...Hmmm."

"We didn't *mean* to bring him, Maggot..." Timtik had never seen her so aroused before, except once when he'd curiously tried to touch the Thrake. She'd blasted him clear across the room with a bolt of red lightning, and he'd tingled for days. "You see," he said carefully, "Albert grabbed Lorn's drapery just as she was turning the key, and suddenly he popped into Drendon along with us. He almost materialized on a hotsy, and the frost-flies came and—"

Maggot was suddenly all over him, prodding, prying, feeling, sensing. "Frost-flies! Oh, my little baby faun, they didn't hurt you? Didn't touch you? You're all right?" Her sudden concern was a relief after her anger, albeit Timtik writhed under her touch, which was clammy and repulsive upon his flesh.

He kept answering "No, Maggot," over and over, till she stopped her anxious tactile inspection. Maggot was, in her witch-like way, harsh-appearing on its surface, quite fond of the little creature, and her hot dry eyes would shed their first tears if anything happened to rob her of her beloved apprentice.

"You're sure—?" she said, reluctantly releasing him.

"I'm fine," Timtik insisted. "I led Albert and Lorn to the other side of the hotsy from the frost-flies, and we weren't even touched." Maggot plopped into a chair and sagged.

"What a scare you gave me, Tikky. My poor old heart can't take that sort of thing."

Timtik laughed hoarsely. "Your poor old heart is as strong as solid oak. You did it with a spell. You told me you did it."

Maggot sniffed and wiped a grimy forefinger across her nostrils. "Well, it's the principle of the thing, Tikky. If my heart *were* weak, it'd surely have stopped... But where is Lorn?" she said, peering out through the wall of the "Wumbl," which was, of course, quite transparent to her eyes. Timtik shifted uneasily. "She was right behind me," he mused, "and when Albert tried to spank me—"

"Spank YOU?" Maggot reared up. "A mere human DARED to—"

"It was my fault," Timtik admitted. "I goaded him into it, because I got mad at Lorn for paying so much attention to him."

"Oh," said Maggot, unrearing a trifle. "Oh," she said, relaxing. Then she shrugged. "Well, if you had it coming... You say he *tried* to? What stopped him?"

"I ducked, and he fell, and I ran here, and—" The faun paused. "You don't think he got hurt? Maybe he fell into a Wumbl or something."

Maggot shook her head. "Nonsense. Lorn could have saved him from that fate. Any tree would be happy to slash the Wumbl's membrane for a woodnymph—unless this was out in the *open?*"

Timtik shook his head. "No, it was in the deep woods, just between here and the mossfields." He stopped speaking, chilled with a terrible thought. Maggot had the same thought.

"My crystal, quickly!" she shrieked.

Timtik bounded across the room to a great casket of a trunk, and began rummaging within it. Over his shoulder flew the contents as he groped away. A shredded bit of cloth-of-gold, a bottle of grave mold, clumps of leaves from the gray ivy vine, two used mandrake roots, a wax doll bristling with pins, a box of assorted rare earths, liquid herb juices, some bat squeezings, and an old dog-eared copy of *Moby Dick*. No crystal. Timtik turned to face the witch. "It's gone!"

135

MAGGOT slapped her forehead. "What an idiot I am! Of course! I lent it to my cousin Hortense, yesterweek, for the Black Carnival…"

"Help!" said a small voice outside the entrance. Maggot hissed a mystic word, and the door opened. In clambered the forest key, struggling across the high sill. "Help!" it giggled dutifully.

"That might be Lorn's key!" said Timtik. "Come to tell us what happened to her!"

"Nonsense. Nymphs aren't that brainy. She'd never think to send a message—"

"But maybe Albert thought of it," suggested the faun.

"Hmmm," Maggot murmured. "Could be."

"Help!" the key re-giggled. "This is fun. I've never been in an adventure before."

"Who sent you?" demanded Timtik.

"Help?" the key said hopefully. Lorn's estimation of its brain-size was more generous than she knew.

"Where is Lorn, and Albert the human!?" asked Maggot, transfixing the key with a steely gaze.

"Help?" it offered despondently. "Is that right?"

Timtik scowled. "This is getting us nowhere."

"Wait," said Maggot. "I'll check the serial number in the sign-out book." She waddled grossly over to a thick ledger on the table and peered myopically at the page that opened to her automatically as she approached. "Lorn's signed out for key number X-54. What's this key's number?"

Timtik picked it up, turned it over, shook it, then scratched his head deftly with an extended claw. "It's rubbed out, mostly. I can hardly see it at all."

"Key!" Maggot accused harshly. "You've been scratching!"

The key sniveled piteously. "But I *itched!*"

Timtik pondered the matter. "Maybe I could retrace my steps, and see if Lorn fell off the edge of the woods?"

"Too long!" muttered the witch. "The Kwistians might be feasting on Lorn's spareribs before you found your way back to the same spot. No, this calls for swift measures." The key whimpered a little. Maggot threw it a piece of pickled ham, and it carried its prize off to a corner and began to munch contentedly.

"EEEEE!" said a voice from the shelf.

"The Thrake!" groaned Maggot. "I got so engrossed, I forgot to feed it again. It eats every fifteen minutes lately. I spend all my time making this hellbrew to keep it alive, and all I get for my pains is hunger-tantrums!" The Thrake squealed again.

MAGGOT scooped up a fistful of mess from the cauldron and threw it on the shelf. The Thrake quieted. Maggot wiped off her fingers on her dress, leaving clinging bits of the stuff still between her knuckly fingers. Now, where were we?" she asked.

Timtik jumped up, suddenly joyous. "Maggot!" he said, "Don't you have a Finders-Weepers spell on the crystal?"

"Of course!" Maggot snapped her fingers and looked annoyed at her own lack of hindsight. "Just let me remember the words… Hmmm…" She dipped into a pocket of her voluminous dress, and pulled forth a pinch of blue powder, which she flung into the flames licking the scorched sides of the cauldron. A brilliant tongue of blue flame shot up, and as it splashed hotly off the ceiling, Maggot chanted:

"Flame get hotter than a pistol;
Bring me back my peeking-crystal!"

There was a hum, a twang, and a crackling snap, and the crystal appeared in the air between Maggot and the faun. Both grabbed it before it could shatter on the floor. Maggot picked up her spectacles from the table, got them on upside-down, cursed virulently, righted them, and peered into the crystal.

"Oh my!" she said. Timtik, straining his eyes at the sphere, could detect nothing but cloudy swirlings. He was still three lessons away from crystal gazing. It was one of the more advanced courses, hard to master. "Well, my stars!" said Maggot. "They're all right. They *did* strike the path, but Albert has enough sense not to go any farther, so they'll be safe until that Cort sends someone to find what the delay is."

"But *where* are they?" shouted the faun. "What part of the mossfields? I can hurry right out there, and—"

"I could bring them back by spell," said the witch. "It's only fifteen minutes work to assemble the paraphernalia, and—"

The Thrake, its shelf once again cleared of hell-brew, started quizzical little whines of hunger. "Damn," said Maggot. "This just isn't my day! Tell you what, Tikky—You start out looking for them, and in the meantime, I'll try to rig a pickup spell on them. If you get there first, fine. If not, I'll pick them up sooner or later."

Timtik was dancing up and down with impatience. "Tell *me* how to do the spell, and *I'll* get them!" he cried.

Maggot hesitated, then reached for some more of the blue powder. "Well, I suppose it'd be all—No!" She replaced the powder with decision. "You're too young to learn how to get anything you want. It'd be dangerous to know at your age. I'm sorry, Tikky, but you'll have to go by boat or something over the bog."

"Oh, all right," the faun mumbled, scuffing one hoof. "But it's a lot of work, when a few magic words could—"

"That's enough, Tikky!" said the witch. She had that red-lightning tone in her voice. Timtik stopped complaining, made his goodbyes, and, after ascertaining the approximate location of his quarry, hurried out into the forest...

"—and here I am," he finished, yawning lazily.

I'd stopped counting my strokes by now. After the one hundred mark, the less accurately my muscles knew of their labors, the better. "Maggot sounds charming," I said. Timtik peered up at me from beneath furry brows.

"I wouldn't be sarcastic in front of her, if I were you!"

"Now, look—" I said, but was interrupted by a sharp cry.

"Look!" gasped Lorn, pointing off behind me.

I turned my head, but the sunlight was in my eyes and made seeing difficult. Then I saw the dark shadows undulating along swiftly over the purple surface of the moss, and high in the sky above them, I caught the glint of a polished brass trident.

"Kwistians!" rasped Timtik, springing upright. "Pole, Albert! Pole!"

I shoved and grunted and strained, but our progress was like that of a turtle fleeing a flock of eagles. In another moment, I heard the thump of immense wings on the hot bright air, and the whistling of the cannibals' rapid passage. I turned about, yanking out the pole from the muck as the only handy weapon to fend off a murderous swoop of the downrushing creatures.

Even as I raised my mud-dripping weapon skyward, I knew I'd made a fatal error. The tugging of the pole had unbalanced me, and my quick grab for the upright stump against which Lorn had been lolling was an even worse mistake. The entire log began to turn slowly on its longitudinal axis, and the three of us started to topple, woodnymph, faun and myself, tottering back toward the deadly bog beneath the purple moss.

I expected to be impaled like an olive on one of those tridents even before I struck the moss, so close were our airborne adversaries, but they had plans only for Lorn.

She shrieked in fright as the tall bronzed Kwistians, their magnificent pinions spread wide to slow their descent, reached out—each with his tridentless hand—to clutch her arms as she semaphored for balance. And even as they neared her, Timtik-in mid-air on his way into the bog—waved his fingers in a strange way at her, and shouted a weird, short phrase that buzzed like angry bees through the air.

Then the Kwistians had Lorn by the arms and were soaring skyward with their catch, and—and Lorn was still beside me and Timtik, in mid-fall on that twisting log, as the cannibals swooped off with the other her in their grasp...

All this had happened within a moment of my yanking the pole from the bog, in one bewildering, rushing speck of time. Then my back struck the yielding moss, and black ooze started to close over my face, and—

Reality shifted, vanished, and reappeared.

Lorn, Timtik and myself were standing inside a small, musty hut, and I found myself staring into a wizened fanged face, that under its wild grizzled hair could only be—"Maggot?" I said, dazed.

"Howdy-do!" said the witch. She glanced at me, her eyes giving a shrewd once-over. Then she smiled, as though in approval, and said, "You're knock-kneed!"

I blushed in shame.

CHAPTER SEVEN

AFTER I had—thanks to a healthy swig from that copper flask—recovered somewhat from the shock of my abrupt transition, I had a few moments of queasy dread about this grizzled creature with whom I was temporarily entombed in the entrails of the false Wumbl. I suppose that Maggot was not at all bad looking, as witches go, but her appearance clung too tightly to the traits demanded by protocol to suit my esthetic senses.

Had she wanted, she said, she could have been young looking, and rather pretty, but she took great pride in her witchiness, tradition being a powerful spur in any union, and there was also the notorious prestige involved in aiming for the title of Most Dreadful. Not that Maggot was yet the ghastliest sight available, but she was always in there pitching, taking ugly-pills, wart-sustainer, skin wrinkler, hair-grayer, breath-fetidation capsules, and all the latest creams and lotions from the nearest Black Apothecary Shoppe, to keep abreast of the latest fashions in hideousness.

However, this was her say-so, that she was far from being the worst sight in Drendon. So far as I was concerned, she was the ugliest, most raucous, smelliest, slimiest creature I'd ever beheld in my life, and I'd seen some corkers.

"Another piece of pie?" asked Maggot, holding out a crisply crusted wedge of peach-choked pastry.

"Yes, thank you," I said, wiping my lips on the embroidered linen napkin, and extending my plate with an effort—the plate was solid gold, and quite weighty for all its delicately sculptured filigrees. I had to admit she was a damned nice, almost genteel hostess, if a bit horrible to view. Maggot beamed as I slowly forked the wedge in wolf-size bites down my gullet and subdued the minor temblor of a sated belch.

"All through?" she crooned, and at my nod snapped her fingers, and whispered a certain syllable. My dishes and utensils vanished with a sparking crack. I confess I jumped a little. It was still hard to accept sorcery, even given the other odd goings-on in this dimension. Neither Lorn nor Timtik batted an eye. But I figured if they could believe in Drendon, they could believe anything.

The Thrake chose that moment to squeal, in a sort of crowing sigh unlike its hunger-plaint. "Hot dog!" said Maggot, drawing a transverse line through four upright ones on the rough oaken wall. "That's the fifth today!"

"Fifth what?" I asked.

"Another Kwistian knocked out of the sky," said Lorn.

"Thrake kind of gloats each time it crimps their wings," mumbled Timtik, absorbed in his third helping of pie.

I eyed the tiny blue horror with misgivings. "How does it do it?"

Maggot pursued her lips and nodded her head sagely. "There's many a one in Drendon Wood wishes he knew the answer to *that!*" she said, throwing weeds into the cauldron.

"I take it," I said respectfully, "it's a secret?"

"One I shall carry to my grave," said the witch. "Can't have those Kwistians zooming around here day and night, hooting and hollering, and spearing poor forest folk on their tridents. Makes for unrest."

I recalled the pair that nearly impaled me back on that log, and shuddered. "Hope the thing doesn't wear out," I said, looking at the voracious Thrake, slupping up mess from the shelf.

"What's night?" asked Timtik, looking toward Maggot. "You just said 'night'…"

"That's when the sun goes down," said Maggot. "Like it was when you and Lorn went on your little tour to Earth."

"Oh," said Timtik, returning to his pie. "I thought it was black there all the time."

I RAISED an inquiring eyebrow. "No night here at all?" I said.

"Only on special occasions," said Maggot, swirling the gluey roiling mess in the cauldron with a long wooden spoon.

"Such as?"

"Such as the sun going down. That's always a special occasion."

I thought this over. The logic seemed a bit circuitous. "How's that again?" I murmured.

Maggot eased up on her hellbrew stirring for a moment. "You see, we use the same sun you do, but we don't revolve on our axis, so it's always noon, here. The only time it gets dark is during an eclipse."

"Makes for short nights," I remarked.

Maggot shivered. "The shorter the better. When night falls here, the Thrake sleeps, and all hell breaks loose. Kwistians zooming around, killing off creatures for the fun of it, or carrying them off alive for their flame-pits..."

Her statement reminded me of something that had been bugging me since before our arrival, but my attempts at speech had hitherto been shushed by the witch, as she ordered us all to eat first, talk later. As an abstracted wave of her gnarled hand caused three delicate alabaster demitasses to appear before Lorn, Timtik and myself, I assumed it was the hour for after-dinner chatting, and cleared my throat.

Maggot raised a fuzzy gray eyebrow at me, and her luminous glittering eye fixed me with more absolute attention than I really wanted. "Yes, Albert," she said, as if with resignation. "Now you can tell me whatever it is that's been troubling you since your arrival."

"It's—" I fumbled awkwardly for a starting point, then blurted, "it's about that *other* Lorn, Maggot..."

"Other Lorn?" she said, dropping the spoon into the cauldron, handle and all. "What other Lorn?"

"It's okay," said Timtik, with ill-concealed pride. *"I* did that!"

"Did what?" snapped the witch, in a voice so terrible that the three of us nearly turned to stone. "Tikky... You didn't use the Scapegoat Spell?"

The faun, his monumental aplomb fading, murmured, "Why—Sure I did. Just like you taught me. I made a duplicate of Lorn, to confuse the Kwistians. You said the spell was handy to baffle an enemy, to make him take a false image of a person instead of the real person..."

"Fool!" shrieked the witch, her eyes crackling with red sparks. "That spell is never to be used on *others!"*

"But—" faltered Timtik, very pale and afraid.

"On yourself, fine!" howled Maggot, jabbing a forefinger at his chest. "Because even after the bifurcation, *you* know which is you and which is your false self, and can let the false self be captured with impunity. But on another—!" she rasped furiously. *"Which* Lorn did they *take?"*

Timtik's eyes, already wide and apprehensive, turned to Lorn pleadingly. "Lorn—?" he said. "This is you, isn't it?"

"Of course it is," said the woodnymph, after a swift glance downward to see if she were still present. "I know it is..."

"How?" spat Maggot. "A Scapegoat Image believes itself to be real, too. But there is a terrible difference between the true creature and the false."

"What difference?" I asked, with an almost clairvoyant intuition of the terrible truth.

"Either one," said the witch, beginning to pace the floor of the hut, her voluminous garments swirling in her wake, "will pass any test of existence one cares to make upon it... But—If the *true* self perishes, then so does the *false!"*

"You mean," I said numbly, "that if the Kwistians have the false Lorn, and destroy her, *this* Lorn will continue on alive and healthy, but if they've taken the *true* one..."

"She will die in the flame-pits, and this one will simply pop into nothingness," said the witch.

"Oh, dear!" said Lorn. "What can we do to find out which is which?"

MAGGOT regarded her with a smile of irony. "We can sit here and wait, and if you *don't* vanish, you are the real Lorn."

"But if the other Lorn is real—!" gasped the woodnymph.

"Exactly!" Maggot said savagely. "Death for both! So waiting is out of the question. Since we are *not* sure, we must act as though that *is* the true Lorn who was taken, and proceed accordingly. That other Lorn is in terrible danger. Every second brings her closer to flaming death!"

If true, why had we sat calmly eating pie!? I trembled with frustrated rage. "We've got to *do* something! Can't you bring the other Lorn here as you brought *us?* Then maybe Timtik can kind of—um—*merge* the two, again…"

Maggot nodded kindly. "A good thought, Albert. But you see, although such a merger is possible, it cannot be done unless the other image is present, and I am afraid that Cort, the wizard, has a neutralizer enchantment on Sark. My magic won't work in Sark from so great a range. If I were *there,* of course—But that's impossible. I cannot leave the Thrake. The forest folk count on me."

"But your house moves," I insisted. "Can't you—"

"It won't go near the castle," explained Lorn sadly. "Cort has the forest bugged with proximity alarms that shoot thunderbolts if the Thrake gets within range."

"But," I said to Maggot, "you've got to do something!"

"*I* can do nothing," she said pointedly. Then, she, Timtik and Lorn turned their heads slowly until their eyes rested on my face. I felt uneasy under their unblinking gazes. "I can *help*…" said the witch, "but I can't go in person. We need someone who is willing to risk his life, to face terrible danger, to dare the journey to Sark…"

"Me," I realized, my stomach hollow and cold and sinking. "You want *me* to go?"

Timtik and Lorn nodded eagerly, hopefully. Maggot watched me through slitted eyes, her bated breath keeping her nostrils aflare. "Yes," she hissed softly. "You are the logical one. Timtik is too young, too little. Lorn is too weak, too stupid. I am too valuable right here. Whom else have we to send? You're our only hope."

I looked at Lorn—if this *was* Lorn—with her deep blue eyes, copper brows, flaming hair… Could I *chance* her being the true Lorn? Could I stake her young life on odds no better than a coin-flip? I took a deep breath, faced Maggot, and gave a short, mute nod.

"You'll go?" said Timtik, half-rising from his place. Maggot clenched her gnarled fingers till the blood-throb showed in her old white knuckles. Lorn sat tensely, her beautiful eyes locked in half-hope, half-despair, upon my face.

"I'll go," I said.

BUT why not?" whined Timtik, irritably stamping his pointed cloven hooves.

Maggot was at her wit's end. "No!" she rasped, nearly in tears, her voice suddenly as old as her appearance. "You can't go with him, it's too dangerous!"

"But Albert doesn't know the forest. He doesn't realize the dangers; he almost got killed by that hotsy!" Timtik rationalized, tugging at her copious skirt.

Maggot sat down and held her head in her hands. "But Tikky, you're all I've got… If anything happened to you—"

"But it won't!" Timtik sobbed furiously. "I know all the spells you've taught me, and even without them, there's nothing in Drendon can catch me when I run full speed. And you're giving Albert some protective spells, and you can watch us through the crystal and help us out. Please, Maggot, please!?"

Maggot gave a hopeless shake of her gray head, and smiled wryly at me. "I suppose I'd be annoyed if he *didn't* feel this way. I've raised him to be considerate of others, and kind, and I guess he's learnt his lessons too well…" She looked at Timtik. "Very well," she said, wiping at the tip of her nose and sniffling miserably.

And I found, abruptly, that I had become fond of the ugly old creature. "Look—" I said clumsily, "I don't think I need to tell you I'll try my best to look out for him…"

Maggot's withered hand pressed shakily down upon mine. "I know you will, Albert," she sighed. "You're a good man. And Lorn will be a help, too, if she doesn't do something imbecilically fatal, as is sometimes her wont."

She went to her cavernous trunk, still sniffling. "I wish it were possible to give you a map, but it would be no use in Drendon. The forest layout changes constantly."

"Tribes move about," Lorn amplified, "animals change their water-holes, trees decide to ungrow and turn back into seeds—A map a minute wouldn't keep you up to date."

Maggot, rummaging through the trunk, grunted happily and set something on the floor beside her with a clink. I thought it looked suspiciously like a bottle of *Schlitz*. "It is," said Maggot, before I could word my query.

Then she took out a crisp piece of pasteboard and tossed it onto the floor beside the bottle. I squinted curiously at the printing upon it. Maggot again answered my unspoken question over her shoulder. "Commuter's ticket: Long Island Railroad."

The pile grew; to the ticket and the beer were added a spool of thread, a tube of depilatory cream, and a solid gold molar, roots and all. Then Maggot lifted out something quite heavy from the bottom recesses of the trunk, and set it on the floor with a grunt. It was an ancient Spanish-style cuirass, dull gray, and rather thick, with heavy leathern straps to anchor it upon the wearer's breast.

Maggot stood up and dusted her palms together. "There!"

Realization suddenly flashed upon me. "Those?" I choked, waggling a forefinger at the heap. *"Those* are the spells?" I felt a sudden letdown, like the time I had—at the tender age of six— received a new suit for Christmas when I'd been praying for a bicycle.

"Certainly," said Maggot. "Hold on while I get you a wallet for them."

From a stumpy peg on the wall, she lifted down a dusty leather wallet, the old-style wallet, the kind worn with a long shoulder strap, and is about the size of a fishing creel. She, lifted its upper flap and began to drop the first five items into it, one by incomprehensible one. The beer, the ticket, the tube of cream, the spool of thread, and that molar. As she did so, she chuckled.

I CAME forward and slowly took the filled wallet from her. "Maggot—" I didn't quite know what to say, but once again she was ready with an answer to unspoken questions.

"You Earth people!" she snorted in disgust. "What did you expect, Albert? I have to make do with whatever is on hand, don't I? These items happened to pop through into Drendon, so they're as good as anything. Remember, a spell is judged not by its trigger, but by its effect! I suppose *you* were expecting mystic powders, distillations of ogre sweat, magic wands—?"

I felt silly, but I nodded. "Something like that."

"Mark me well, Earthman," said Maggot. "These spells will work when you need them. Have no doubts on that!"

Timtik was jumping up and down impatiently, and Lorn seemed to be starting a slow fidget. "Let's hurry," said the faun. "That other Lorn may be on the brink of the flame-pit right now!"

"Hush, Tikky," said Maggot. "Albert, you three will have to get there before those Kwistians arrive at Sark with the other Lorn. This—" She placed the cuirass upon my breast, fastening the straps tightly with a magic word, "you must not remove until it is time." She halted my question with an upraised finger. "You will know it, when the time comes. I promise you."

"But the spells…" I worried aloud.

"Use one for each peril," Maggot advised. "It really doesn't matter which is used for which, much, but now and then one will adapt better than another."

"But how do I set them off? What do I do? Or say?"

"You'll figure it out," said the witch. "The usage may not always be the same, so I won't burden you with instructions that could be subject to change in certain circumstances. They will serve you well, though. Really."

I was staggering slightly under the weight of the metal breastplate. Timtik clutched my hand and tugged me toward the door, which opened of its own accord to permit the two of us to emerge into the sunlight. Lorn and Maggot trailed after us, but Maggot halted in the doorway. "This thing must be made out of lead," I remarked uncomfortably.

Maggot smiled gently. "It is, Albert," she said, waving farewell.

"But—" I said. The door resealed, and Maggot was gone inside the hidden recesses of the false Wumbl. Already I was sweltering in the heavy armor, as the sun beat down through the overhanging fronds and leaves of the thicket.

I looked helplessly at Timtik and Lorn, who were awaiting me at the edge of the woods. "But why is it made out of *lead?*" I asked them. "Why not iron or steel?"

Timtik shrugged. "In case we meet a radioactive dragon, you dope!"

Lorn and Timtik entered the forest, and I followed uneasily after them. "How thoughtful of Maggot—" I mumbled, going frozen-hearted despite the external heat.

"You never know," said Timtik, darkly.

CHAPTER EIGHT

THE forest of Drendon is a large one, spreading for a mile upon mile, toward where a horizon should be, but never is. It can match the actual antiquity of Earth, and easily surpass that planet's recorded history by many centuries. Forever new, forever old, always moving outward into the vast chaotic wastes that marked its perimeter, taming the unknown with infiltrating soil, burgeoning shrubbery, creeping trees, and a living population of beasts and horrors that moved with the woods.

Into this treacherous entity, only slightly aware of the danger, I was marching, my only protection and hope of further life a childlike faun and lovely but not too bright woodnymph, plus a wallet full of spells none of us could be sure of employing correctly in the face of imminent disaster.

"But isn't the castle over that way, more toward the mossfields?" I asked, keeping carefully apace of Lorn.

Timtik, ahead of us in the sun-spattered underbrush, shook his head. "It is, but if we are to make it to Sark before those two Kwistians get there with that other Lorn, we have to take the long way around. They have a start of nearly a half an hour on us, and it will take them another half hour to finally arrive at the castle."

"I don't get it," I protested. "If they're flying, in a straight line, and we're walking, on a long curve through this tanglewood, they'll be there hours before we will!"

"No," said Lorn. "You see, Albert, according to Maggot's calculations, we should arrive there at the same time they do, if not shortly before. Time is a little different in our dimension.

"How so?" I said, dubiously.

"Well," said Timtik, skirting a green mound of a rough basketball-shape in his path, "you live on a curved surface, where the shortest distance between two points is a straight line. So, conversely, we live on a plane surface, where the shortest distance is a curve.

"Don't think of Drendon as a simple plane; think of it as a Mercator projection of a globe of the world—remember what Lorn told you about the orange-peel—and you'll see at once that certain apparent distances are actually much shorter than some longer-looking ones. Remember that the entire top edge of a Mercator map represents a single point, the pole; so that whole edge has no length at all in actuality, see?"

"I—I think so—" I said, trying to equate the comparison with my limited knowledge of Drendon. "But—" I started, as my forward foot stepped squarely onto that rotund green mound. Instantly, off in the depths of the forest, a whistle blew two sharp hoots, a gong reverberated brazenly, and a chorus of bloodthirsty shrieks began to sound, louder by the moment.

LORN muttered a ladylike-curse at me, and Timtik whirled, his face blank with surprise. "Albert—!" he croaked in his tinny voice, "Did you step on the *Snitch?*"

"That little green thing?" I said, having hastily withdrawn my foot.

"Odds bodkins!" muttered the faun. "The whole Thrang nation will be alerted. Come on, we'll have to run for it!"

I felt quite frustrated. "I thought you were going to be my guide!" I complained as Lorn and I ran up abreast of the faun, who was impeding his fleet pace to accommodate us.

"Albert," said Lorn, trotting easily beside me. "Timtik can't think of everything! He simply forgot you'd never seen a Snitch before."

"Shut up, you two, and run!" grumbled the faun, diving head-long over a wide stretch of vinous growths which a moment later caught me on the instep and sent me sprawling into Lorn and knocking her down with me.

In another moment, the forest seemed to fall in on us. I could hear Timtik's shriek of dismay as he, too, was swept up in the disaster I'd triggered. A heavy jungle of writhing vines and twigs was interlacing rapidly in all directions, sewing the three of us up like dressing inside a turkey.

"What happened?" I gasped.

Timtik's voice in the leafy tangle was low with disgust. "You kicked a Snatch!"

DRUMS were beating frenziedly as the bearers toted the ball of tight foliage into the center of the compound. Through the thick leaves and stalks of the Snatch, I had been unable to see our captors clearly, but from the noise they were making, I wasn't sure I wanted to. Timtik, whom I could make out only dimly beside me in the tangled green fronded interior, wasn't even speaking to me.

"But Timtik," I pled, "how could I have known? I thought you were diving over the Snatch to make better time. How was I to know *it* was in cahoots with the Thrangs, too? You know I didn't mean to drop the wallet; that Snatch kind of shook me up, and I just naturally got uncoordinated for the moment..."

"Oh... Damn it all," Timtik muttered wearily. "I guess you're right. If I only had some genie powder, I could magick it back to us. *If* I knew the spell-chant."

As I nodded sympathetically, the Snatch suddenly fell to the ground and snapped open flat, as swiftly as a popping corn kernel, giving me my first view of our captors. One look was a lifetime's worth. I gave a terrified moan and kicked down hard on the surface of the flattened Snatch with my heel. It resnapped shut instantly, and there was a concerted howl of annoyance from the Thrangs outside.

"Nice thinking, Albert!" said Timtik, openly admiring.

"Are we safe now?" Lorn hoped brightly.

"Till it opens again," I muttered. "Get your hooves ready, Timtik!"

There came a muttering thunder of voices outside, as though the Thrangs were discussing the novelty of the situation. And inside, a sudden groan escaped Timtik, and he smacked his palm to his forehead.

"Lorn, you crazy creature—!" he said. "You're a woodnymph, and this thing is vinous. *Tell* it to stay shut!"

"Oh," said Lorn. "That's right!" She lifted a tendril of ferny frond to her lips and whispered polite instructions, like an empress giving dinner directions to the palace chef. "All set," she said brightly.

Outside, the mumbling ceased at that moment, and I figured the Thrangs were going to give it the old college try, because they hefted us up again. I tensed, awaiting the fall. To be sure, they could keep dropping the thing till they brained us, but it seemed a nicer fate than being brained by them in person.

I REALIZED something was up when the Snatch remained aloft, swaying gently. We were taken someplace else.

"We're lucky they didn't think of poking a spear into this basket to get us," I said. "We'd never be able to dodge."

"Oh, they don't want us *dead,* Albert," said Lorn. "That's what's so horrible about capture by the Thrangs."

"They want us as *pets!*" explained the faun.

"Pets?" I moaned. "But the Thrangs— It looked to me like they were built on the order of mushrooms with frayed tops. Every tentacle on that topside is ridged with spiky things like ten--penny nails! Why, if one of them fondled a pet, it'd either be crushed to death in their grasp, or impaled on one of those horny growths…"

"That's what makes it ghastly," sighed Timtik. "They are so damned friendly that they treat pets with the utmost gentleness. Sometimes the pets linger on for weeks."

"Killed with kindness!" I remarked ruefully, then broke off with a gasp as I caught the glint of sunlight on something ripply beneath the Snatch— "Lorn!" I yelped, with what turned out to be damned lucky intuition. "R*everse* your orders to this thing, and quick!"

Even as she bent to the front and did so, Timtik—who hadn't seen what I had—gave a cry of fright as the Snatch was released again… And did *not* hit the ground. It must have been a fifty-foot drop into that lake. An instant after the Snatch opened to Lorn's remanded order, we were all up to our eyebrows in icy water, gurgling our way back to breathing level.

The lake was small, about ten feet deep, ringed by a solid escarpment of sheer cliffs. Cheering Thrangs ringed the surrounding brink. I trod water valiantly with my companions, wondering what came next.

Then a heavy vine, with plenty of shoots to grasp, came un-coiling down the cliffside. Timtik was having a difficult time tread-ing with his skimpy hooves.

Lorn and I grasped his hair and heaved his face above the surface again. Liquid spouted from Timtik's nose in a frothy gush, and his eyes were glassy. "Thanks," he gurgled.

Then something tightened under my armpits, and I realized the Thrang's insidious scheme. The end of that tossed vine had swum, eel-like, about us in the water, and was now a firm noose, the other end in the tentacles of strong Thrangs. With numb shock, I found we were being lifted from the water, then bumping and banging our way up the face of the cliff toward the yowling Thrang nation.

"Albert," gasped Timtik, still spouting water, "I have a plan. Lorn and I will delay the Thrangs, and your job is to run back into the woods and find the wallet of spells!"

Before I could ask how, we were on the rim of the cliff. There wasn't a moment to spare. The Thrangs had grown even fonder during their brief frustration, and were at that moment dropping the end of the vine and surging forward as we tugged ourselves free of the now limp looped end.

"Run, Albert!" yelled Timtik. "This won't hold them long!"

"*What* won't?" I squeaked, looking in vain for an open spot between those converging ranks of tentacled affection. Then I saw that Lorn, with crossed legs, was holding Timtik's hand, as he howled mystic words at the sky. It was his thunderstorm spell, and he was giving it his thaumaturgic all.

THE lumbering, spiky, seven-foot tall Thrangs were only a yard short of tentacle-grab. I backed from them, figuring that at worst we three could leap from the cliff and take our chances in the lake again...

Thunder bammed! Lightning crashed and showered hissing sparks! A torrent of drenching rain poured to the ground.

The Thrangs reacted instantly. With delight.

With a happy cheer, they swung their tentacles till the spikes meshed overhead like a zipper's teeth, and their tubular bodies stiffened and stretched upward, the downpour now starting to fill their tulip-shaped tops formed by the meshed tentacles. They were having the Thrang equivalent of a binge.

While Timtik's magic held the field, I did a quick slalom-run between the towering bodies of the Thrangs.

Then the rain ceased. I looked back to see Timtik keel over wearily. I stopped dead, and turned back, instantly. I grabbed him up in my arms and with Lorn beside me, I raced back through those tall slurping ranks toward the forest rim. "How long will it take them to drink that water?" I panted.

"Not long…" the faun gasped weakly. "Hurry…"

Luckily, the Snatch had occupied an area about ten feet square. Not yet overgrown, the wallet was easy to spot in the semi-barren center. I set Timtik back upon his own two hooves again and grabbed it up. At the same instant, the Thrangs started to howl once more, in the distance. The binge was over. I turned the wallet upside-down and shook it.

Out fluttered the commuters' ticket. Nothing else.

"Where's the rest of the things?" wailed Lorn. "I don't even see the sealing-flap!"

"It must be a sign!" urged Timtik. "Use it!"

"How!?" I gibbered, waving the ticket.

The crash of Thrang bodies entering heavy shrubbery sent an icy ramrod up my spine.

I've got to *think!"* I snarled, my hands trembling. "Ticket…railroad…ride…commute…poker game…smoking car…conductor…punch…" My heart contracted sharply. "PUNCH!" I yelled.

The Thrangs crashed into the clearing behind us.

"Albert!" squealed Lorn, flinging her arms about my neck.

Then my eyes lighted on Timtik's forehead, and the twin horns thereon. "To ride, you got to get the ticket punched!" I hollered, ramming the piece of pasteboard upon the tiny point of his left horn. A neat disc of paper popped out like a conservative's confetti, then—while Lorn still clung to me, I grabbed Timtik up into my arms, and yelled, "Hang on!"

Steel tracks whizzed across the clearing—Metal screamed and squealed—A hot, sulphurous blast of gases flashed into our faces as something chugged past, its tall metal sides a dynamic blue of hurtling tonnage—

Then the world jerked wildly and turned upside down as a tugging wrench shot along my frame, a numbing yank that I felt from head to foot...

The last thing I saw of the Thrangs was a row of stupefied faces as the three of us whizzed swiftly away, the train's mail-pickup hook neatly snagged in the collar strap of my lead cuirass, beside a long car painted with the legend "Long Island Railroad." And as we went, the tracks vanished neatly behind us.

CHAPTER NINE

THE little gray-haired man cowered miserably at the far corner of the lurching car, his ears deaf to the clatter of metal wheels beneath him, his eyes blind to all but the sight of his unexpected visitors. There was an adenoidal gape to his jaw, and his breathing was perfunctory at best, coming in short, fast gasps.

"Are you taking your little boy to the city for some treatments?" he finally managed. The mail car attendant appeared, with his greenish pallor, quite genuinely ill.

Timtik said, obligingly, "I'm a faun, not a boy. That's why I have goat legs and horns."

The man clamped his eyes tightly shut.

And a pretty sight we were to the man, I imagine. Lorn looking like a gorgeous hussy in a green negligee. Timtik with his weird endowments and me looking like an escapee from a Norse saga, with my metal breastplate, leather wallet slung by its strap across shoulder and chest, face sun burnt where it wasn't covered with coarse stubble, and legs bare and still slightly raw in spots from that brief sojourn beneath the moss.

"I don't understand," the man moaned piteously, all at once. "We were just about to pull in at Valley Stream, Long Island. I've never seen this woods before on my route..."

I felt a twinge of pity for the man. Perhaps if I could explain— or would he believe me? While I tugged at this tough mental knot, Timtik suddenly tensed and tugged at my fingers.

"Albert! The spell's ending!" he shouted, pointing to the wall against which the attendant crouched. As Lorn gasped in delight, I saw that it was indeed ending. The wall slowly grew translucent, then smokily transparent, like a sheet of ice amid a blast of steam. At that moment, the engineer applied the brakes.

The three of us, caught unprepared for the sudden stop, staggered forward and then plunged toward the floor of the car simultaneous with a loudspeaker over the door blaring, "Valley Stream!"

FOR a fleeting moment I saw the high concrete-and-steel platform, and row upon row of cottages, then the floor rushed up at my face with a rapidity that caused me to release myself from Timtik's grip on my fingers, and to throw my arms protectively before my eyes...

The faun and I thumped heavily into hot, sandy earth, and rolled from the brunt of the impact. I sat up and dusted sand from my eyes and stubbly whiskers and mouth, looking stupidly about me. There was an echo of squealing brakes hovering upon the warm, still air then it faded to silence. The train was gone. We were once more in the forest of Drendon.

We walked for about a mile, finding this stretch of woods less densely overgrown than the part where we'd begun our journey. Going was relatively easy, what with wider lanes between the trees, and less briary shrubbery to dodge, close on Lorn's bush-controlling heels.

The average distance between the trees began to stay at pretty much of a constant, but I suddenly realized that the *character* of the trees was changing. Boughs no longer nodded politely as Lorn went by, and the terrain, too, was undergoing a topographical metamorphosis.

I halted suddenly. Lorn and Timtik did so at the same moment. Timtik moved nearer to me, his tiny hand finding its way into mine. Lorn edged to my other side, gripped my arm, and the three of us stood quite still, downright unsettled inside...

Where the forest we'd started in had been choked with thick vegetation and sodded with rich loam, this section had neither fern nor bush upon the earth. The ground was of hard-baked clay and slate-like rock. I noticed that the trees, which in the prior woods had been rich chocolate-color on bole and branch, were gray-black and starkly barren of even the tiniest trace of foliage. I pressed an exploratory finger against the trunk of a dull black elm. The surface was cold, hard, and slippery-smooth. "I think they're petrified," I said.

Then, in the distance, lost in outlying clumps of gnarled dead trees, a mournful howl sounded, rising, then chopping off in a short series of angry barks.

Timtik embraced my right leg. "So am I!"

THE sun still shone, but its light was no longer warm yellow; a chilly blue-white, almost like moonlight, bathed us. And the sky had sickly gray clouds lying long and emaciated against its paler gray skein. The howl sounded again. It sounded closer.

I clutched at the wallet of spells where it hung athwart my hip. I was going to be *sure* I didn't drop it this time.

A gray gauzy cloud slithered deftly in front of the sun, and the cold grew bitter as the atmosphere darkened to sudden frosty twilight. A swift darting form bounded from behind a tree not ten paces from where we stood, and vanished behind a thick black boulder. *"What was that!?"* we said in unison, taking simultaneous backward steps like a soft-shoe trio. The howl repeated.

"He's trying to scare us," faltered Lorn.

"He's doing a fine job," quavered Timtik.

I found myself frantically shaking the upended wallet, trying to jar loose a new spell. Nothing came out. The wallet wouldn't even open to my fingers.

A flicker of movement outside the direct line of my vision caused me to jerk my head up sharply, my eyes alert, my breathing raspy.

"He moved again!" said Lorn. "He's closer, behind that big oak. It looks like a man—Sort of..."

"He's got a furry face, and funny teeth," appended the faun.

The truth dawned upon me, icily. "I think I know what it is," I said, pointing at the sun, which shone a bleak silver-white through the gray finger-like clouds. "That's supposed to look like a full moon, because during the full moon, the—" I swallowed, and my dry throat received the saliva like a load of dust. "The werewolves," I finished, unsuccessfully trying to keep blind terror out of my voice. "Men by day, beasts by night. I saw it once in a movie."

"Are they vulnerable to anything?"

"To anything silver—" I said plumbing my memory.

"Do you have anything silver on you?" asked Lorn.

"Only the fillings in my teeth."

Timtik, considering this, said sincerely, "Well, you better take the first bite!"

"Look," I said, in my cowardly way, "as long as we know which way it's coming from, why don't we run the *other* way?"

"Run?" said Timtik, as the loudest howl yet arose from behind the oak. "I can't even *move!*"

WITH a lithe spring, the beast appeared. Landing in a menacing crouch before us, beady eyes glittering hungrily, sharp yellow fangs slavering and dripping froth, its thick deadly claws flexing on humanoid hands matted with lusterless gray fur. It looked decidedly unfriendly. But the item that drew my attention was its vest. Across the lower part of it arced a short gold watchchain. I knew that vest and chain.

I was staring at the Drendon-form of Garvey Baker, Susan's father. This, then, was the enchanted version of a night watchman. I'd never been able to reason with Garvey Baker in his Earth-form; in his Drendon-form, I wasn't even going to *try.*

"Guh-*raaaah!*" said the beast, snarling deep in its thick furry throat. It took a shuffling step forward. We took a shuffling step backward. "Guh-*rowww!*" it said, taking a scuttling step to the left. We instantly took a step to the right.

Two gambits made, no men lost on either side. Werewolf and trembling trio eyed each other warily. I shook the wallet once more, but still nothing came forth. The sudden motion made the werewolf cringe back for an instant. I noted the motion with sudden hope. Perhaps this was a timid werewolf, a craven? I pried Timtik from my leg, shoved Lorn gently away from my side, and took a careful step toward it, then waved my arms suddenly, and yelled *"Boo!"*

The werewolf sprang upright from its menacing crouch, threw back its head, and gave vent to a barking howl of hate that made the ground tremble. That did it.

As one person, Lorn, Timtik and I leapt past the momentarily preoccupied monster and ran hell-for-leather toward the thicker woods ahead. I ventured a glance backward as we fled, and was horrified to see that the thing had dropped to all fours and was bounding after us, ten feet at a jump.

"Run, run!" shrilled Lorn. We were barely into the clump of dead trees when the werewolf was at its edge, and capture and death seemed momentary. I shoved Lorn to my left and Timtik to my right, and then grabbed at a low-hanging petrified branch and swung my feet high.

My timing had been lucky. The pouncing grayish form met only empty air in its dive, and then the furry head met the stone bole of a thick oak with a pleasant smack. The beast-man sat on the ground, shaking its head and growling. We had a brief respite of danger.

"Up here, quick!" I cried, clambering further into my tree haven. Timtik sprang for my extended hand and I swung him onto a fork in the limb. Lorn shinnied up near the trunk and joined Timtik and myself. The werewolf, regaining its feet, looked around for us, its heavy jawed head snapping left and right in a terrible manner. Overhead, I shivered in silent anticipation of the chill moment when it would espy us in our arboreal sanctuary. It did so, finally, with a sudden backward step and satisfied yelp.

It roared, leaped to the base of the tree, and clutched recklessly at the branches.

"Climb!" I urged my companions, hopelessly. We were in a petrified crabapple tree and these don't grow too tall. They tend to burgeon more outward than upward, and this one was no exception. And below us, the monster was placing first one foot, then the other, beginning his ascent.

THERE was not, however, much farther we could travel. Soon, the three of us were perched helpless on the highest branch that would bear our combined weights, watching the relentless approach of the ghastly creature. Would he kill us? Maybe eat us? Or just chew on us till we screamed for mercy?

Anything was better than sitting dully and waiting for those fangs. I decided to say something. Anything.

"Look here," I extemporized, "you're making a terrible mistake."

The hideous face hesitated, scant feet below my bare toes. The beast-man smiled toothily. "I don't think so."

"Oh, yes you are," I said, thinking up objections as I talked, anything to forestall his arrival. "You are—um—an ordinary run-of-the-forest man by day, right?"

"So they tell me," said the creature, not halting its upward climb.

"Well," I said, trying to sound authoritative, "you're going to look pretty silly when I tell you, but it's *daytime!*"

For the first time, a quirk of doubt appeared above the monster's shaggy eyebrows. "But the full moon up there—"

"Ha ha," I said, a forced laugh that didn't quite come off as planned.

"What's so funny, huh?" snarled the thing, champing its wicked fangs, blue-white froth running from the wide savage mouth. I manfully repressed an urge to scream.

"That's not the moon," I said in a calm little croak. "It's the sun. The day's just a bit overcast with clouds."

"Just a minute," said the beast-man. "If that wasn't the moon, I wouldn't look like a wolf. Who you trying to kid?"

I stared into that grizzled face, my brain whirling—and had the answer. I knew at last why the bag of spells hadn't opened before: The werewolf's thinking hadn't been conditioned. The flap opened to my touch, this time. I dipped a hand inside and withdrew the proper item, holding it in my clenched fist.

"Enough of this foolishness!" cried the monster, springing upward, jaws wide for that first horrendous bite—

There was no time to twist off the cap. I just gave a hearty squeeze. Then an even heartier one.

With a soggy pop, the soft metal was riven asunder, and the contents spewed full in the face of the werewolf.

The effect was—well—magical. Though, by its outer dimensions, the tube could not have held more than a few ounces of caustic paste, under the influence of the spell the volume was greater than could have been contained in a milk truck.

The werewolf, clotted with tons of waxy white depilatory cream, crashed soggily back to the ground, and lay there kicking and screaming for the five minutes it took the goo to do its work. Lorn clutched my shoulder and whispered tremulously in my ear, "What did you do to him?"

"Gave him the full beauty treatment," I said. "He'll be bald as a peeled onion in a moment."

"But," said Lorn, "can't he eat us, furry or not?"

"We'll soon find out."

In a moment we had our answer. The spell hadn't stopped with fur. With the sundering of the tube, the gray clouds went soughing away, the breeze sighed with springtime fragrances, the sun turned golden yellow and bright, and even the rocky ground took on a cheerful reflected glow.

I glanced at the spiky twigs of our tree, half-expecting them to be suddenly laden with gay pink blossoms. However, there's a limit even to magic. The trees remained as stark and lifeless as before.

AS we entered the next green section of woods to which the werewolf had guided us, he remained behind on a squat boulder, waving us a fond farewell. We waved back at our deluded "normal man," then hurried out of his sight into the shrubbery. "Now," I said, "let's make tracks."

Timtik shuddered. "That was definitely a close call."

"And we lost some time, too," I said, "up in that tree. We have miles of forest ahead of us, and only three spells left in the wallet!"

"How do *you* know how much forest there is?" asked Lorn.

"Just guessing," I lied. I already knew something my companions didn't. If that spot where we'd seen the hotsy represented the Earth-locale of my house, and this petrified place the Drendon-site of Oak Park's Marshall Field's store, where Garvey Baker had night-watched, then I had a pretty good idea where we'd meet up with Emperor Kwist and his wizard-scientist-vizier Cort. Right in the relative spot where I'd managed to translate Geoffrey Porkle, his crony Courtland, and his house, into Drendon.

In a sort of haunted, nightmarish way, things were making very good sense.

CHAPTER TEN

WE were moving across a waist-deep field of green and straw-colored ferns, when a puzzling memory came back to me.

"Um...I've been wondering about something," I said. "How come this lead breastplate I'm wearing didn't hold me down at the bottom of that lake, back in Thrang country?"

Lorn shrugged lightly and continued her graceful progress through the ferns. "It probably floated and helped hold you up," she theorized, "instead of weighting you down."

"Lead doesn't float," I protested. "It sinks like—like lead!"

"It's magic, you dope!" snapped Timtik, up ahead of us. I decided to drop the matter. None of my queries seemed to get beyond that all-purpose explanation of the faun's.

The land broke free of the ferns, abruptly, and we found ourselves on a wide, greenish-gray plain, the ground soft, moist, and springy to the step. Timtik, however, instead of picking up his pace, cut his speed in half, as did Lorn. Each of them watched the ground for a split second before treading upon it. Having grown considerably wiser in the ways of Drendon, after the incidents with the hotsy, the Snitch, and the Snatch, I was instantly alerted.

"What now?" I said, afraid to step until I knew what it was I had to avoid stepping on.

"Cheesers," said Timtik, pointing to slightly darker green patches on the ground. "They always live on soil like this. Makes them hard to see."

"Cheesers?" I said. "Those wettish-looking blobs?"

Timtik nodded his curly horned head. "Right. Make sure you don't step on one. They're really fierce.

"What do they do?" I asked.

"They grow," Lorn explained. "You step on one, and it cleaves to your skin, and starts to get bigger and bigger until you're covered completely. They get at your bloodstream; take out all the sugar."

I looked solemnly at a pulsating blob. It seemed to be not so much one thing as a horde of smaller things, banded together for a common purpose. "They act like a mess of ants without a village," I observed.

"The Centaurs use them for their orgies," said Timtik.

"They're a surly bunch," he explained, looking right and left, uneasily, pricking up his pointed ears. "They live around here, and if they catch anyone passing through, they—Well, they fatten up the Cheesers on them, then stick the remains into a vat, add some kind of wet grain, and—"

"I've got it!" I said suddenly. "These things are molds; yeast plants I should've recognized that sickly-sharp smell. And the Centaurs use them to make moonshine!"

"*Hey!*" said the faun, freezing.

I didn't hear anything for a second, then my legs felt the shuddering of the earth, a steady ratchet of dull vibration. Somewhere off across the field, I could hear shouts. The Centaurs.

"Run, Albert!" cautioned Timtik, spurting forward.

"Hurry," pled Lorn, doing the same.

"Right," I yelped, dashing after them, but keeping one cautious eye groundward lest I turn into some lurking yeast plant's blueplate special.

"*Yuh*-hoo! *Yip*-pee!" came from the edge of the plain.

I GLANCED that way, and was momentarily stopped with surprise. A broad stampede of creatures was galloping my way, at an angle that would soon intersect my line of flight if I didn't start up again and make for the woods. Once there, Lorn's tree-talk could impede pursuers. But out in the open—I shuddered and ran. Lorn and Timtik were already at the first fringe of trees, not even looking back for me.

The thundering hooves were deafening. I ran in panicky flight toward the woods. One look at the Centaurs convinced me they meant trouble. From the chest of the equine body upwards they had the semblance of a man's upper torso. But there was no sharp line of demarcation.

Their arms alone spoiled the illusion of simple malformed horses. They had hands, and the hands had rough hempen lariats, carried at the ready.

"Hurry!" came Timtik's voice, far off ahead of me. I pounded the soft turf with my bare feet in a frantic dash away from those quadrupedal horrors. The hedges of the woods loomed greenly before me. Thirty yards away, twenty-five, twenty—

Then, with a whirring swish, the lariat dropped whip-like about my throat and yanked me to a sprawling, choking halt. The line tugged, taut, brutally tight, and I felt my eyes start from their sockets. I saw Timtik burst from the woods, coming back to me. He'd be massacred. There was only one chance open to me. Even as I toppled, I grabbed the wallet of spells from my shoulder, gave them a quick spin by the strap, and let them fly in a swift arc toward the faun.

"*Scram!*" I yelled, as the rope grew tourniquet-tight, and the world turned dull crimson before my eyes, then flowed into icy blackness...

CONSCIOUSNESS returned slowly, painfully. I tried to recall where I was, what had happened. My neck was raw, but the noose, my swimming mind knew gratefully, had been removed.

I was still prone upon the earth—not, praise God, in the clammy clutch of any Cheesers—but an experimental try at moving showed me that I was bound tightly at wrists and ankles. I opened my eyes cautiously, and saw the huge sweaty flanks of the Centaurs a few yards from where I lay.

They were busy about a vat, a huge vat, of stained wood, onto which one of them—the chief brewer, I expect—was constantly climbing via a sort of roughhewn ramp. The yeast-smell was sickeningly strong, and I noticed that other of the Centaurs were carrying quivering Cheesers, safely upon some sort of fiber mats, up to the lip of the enormous vat, and dropping them in with a soggy thump.

The vat creaked and groaned at the seams, as from heavy movement within. The Cheesers were hungry. I eased my head from the earth, careful not to attract any attention, and tried to increase the range of my vision, ignoring the aching clamor of my neck muscles.

I was still well clear of the green forest rim, I saw with regret. Even could I have slipped my bonds, I'd never have been able to get within the comparative safety of the underbrush ahead of those swift monsters. There was nothing to do but lie back and await what might come. I hoped Timtik would think of something...

Then I was struck by an unfamiliar feeling.

I'd sensed upon awakening that something had changed, but hadn't until that moment been able to isolate the sensation. It was the cool-feeling freedom of my upper torso that brought the truth home to me.

The lead cuirass had been removed.

How, I had no idea. The best I'd been able to do with it was shift it for scratching when I itched, which was often; it seemed months since my last bath. I'd thought that removing the spell-attached breastplate was impossible. But here it was, off.

Curious, I tried to recall Maggot's exact information about the cuirass, and why it would not leave my body by my own efforts. "This," she'd said, "you must not take off till it's time. You will know when the time comes."

So the removal of the cuirass was definitely something to take into my consideration. I thought the thing out, step by step. If it were not to be removed until "the time," and it *had* been removed, spell or no spell, then *this* must be the time. Mustn't it?

I RAISED my head to see if it were within sight. It lay almost beside me on the soft earth, the straps hanging limply, the buckles undone. "There it is," I thought. *"Now* what?"

A short whispered colloquy between two of the nearer Centaurs drew me back from my meditations. But they were not discussing me. One of them was pointing with a tilt of his head at the forest rim, and I didn't like the cruel smile on the face of the other when he glanced that way. As the two of them surreptitiously slipped up to their companions and passed the word along, I finally got to see the object of their amused discussion, which had been blocked to me by their bodies.

A tree was coming toward us, stealthily, easing along on its thick splayed roots, and pausing every so often in its motion, as a cat pauses while sneaking up on a bird.

"Lorn!" I groaned to myself, shutting my eyes. Lorn, with her influential tree-talk! Her entrance was about as subtle as a tidal wave. I re-opened my eyes and looked hopelessly up into the foliage, and soon espied the greener-than-green shimmer of her "diaphanous drapery," and a flicker of sunlight on coral tresses. The nut! The wonderful, lovable nut! To come to my rescue in a tree, of all things. But I wished she'd chosen a sturdy oak, instead of her present vehicle. It was a silvery aspen, not much thicker across the trunk than a man's arm. The Centaurs could—

Even as I thought it, the Centaurs *did*.

A phalanx of them suddenly sprang into a gallop and sur-rounded the tree, cutting off its retreat. Then, with flailing forelegs, they reared up and kicked mercilessly at the slender growth, their hands grappling for its roots and yanking them upward to knock it off balance—And then Lorn came sprawling out through the leaves, the branches trying in vain to ease her fall as she plummeted to the ground, and lay still, face downward.

As the Centaurs surrounded her there, I struggled in vain to sit up, to break free of my hempen bonds. And then I heard light hoofbeats behind me, and Timtik came dashing up carrying the bag of spells. He dropped the bag to the ground, and said urgently, "Roll on your face, quick!"

"But Lorn—!" I choked out.

"A deceptive maneuver!" he growled, trying to push me over on my face when I didn't move. "She's only doing it so I can get the spells to you!"

"But can't you and she—" I said, rolling over.

"No, damn it!" he interpolated. "The spells won't come out of the wallet for us. That's the way Maggot set the wallet up. It's a one-man bag of tricks."

I felt his fingers struggling with the tough knots, and felt the first thrill of hope since my capture—Then heavy hoofbeats sounded, and I yelled, "Run!" about ten seconds too late. I felt him snatched off the ground behind me, and, as I rolled over, his squirming body was being borne back to the cluster about Lorn, in the muscular arms of a raven-black Centaur, who was laughing gustily over his prize. And the bag of spells was still with Timtik.

WE'RE done for..." I realized dully. "Nothing can help us now..." Then my eye was again caught by the bulky cuirass. Its color seemed changed. Instead of the leaden gray surface, it was light-colored, almost shiny. And squarely in the center of the breastplate, where there'd been no such thing before, scintillated a blinding diamond, the size of a postage stamp, set into a tight steel ring.

At an earlier period of my life, pre-Drendon, I'd have simply stared. Or admired and then forgotten it. But I knew better, after meeting this unearthly dimension. As if possessed by a cognoscentic power, one look at that diamond stud *told* me what it was for.

Activation, of course.

The Centaurs had forgotten about me for a time. They were too busy dragging Lorn from her tree and bringing her and Timtik toward that hulking wooden vat full of Cheesers. I didn't have time to think, only to act.

I arched my back and flipped myself sideways toward the armor, which was glowing whiter and more brilliant by the second. My coordination was luckily perfect; I landed with my back squarely atop the front of the breastplate, the cut surface of the diamond directly under my questing fingers.

"Hey," cried a voice. "What's *he* doing?!"

The leader of the Centaurs, a thick-bodied roan, had turned his long, bucktoothed face toward me, and was coming my way at a quick canter.

I pressed the jewel, hard.

ALL at once, my wrists and ankles were free, and I fell back to the ground with a thump. I'd felt something growing out of the base of the cuirass as I'd jabbed the diamond, something that had changed the entire shape of the cuirass into a slim, elongated shape that had severed my bonds with one smooth slice as it came into being. There was something cylindrical forcing itself into my right hand, and I gripped it tightly as I sprang to my feet to face the oncoming monster. The Centaur started to increase his speed, then braked to an abrupt halt as I brought my hand from behind my back.

Set snugly in my fist, the squarish diamond coruscating madly where the crosspiece traversed the handle and blade, was a four-foot silver sword.

The Centaur looked at me, warily. Beside the vat, the others, too had stopped moving. All stared wide-eyed at the wicked glinting of my magical weapon. The leader hesitated, still shaken, then his face-hardened, and he grinned. "It's only a close range weapon!" he thundered. "Get him from where you are!"

The others, glad somebody had thought of *something,* began whirling their dangerous lariats, and hurling the looped hemp toward me. For an instant, my vista was made up of nothing but whizzing, spinning rope.

One sweeping stroke of the blade fixed that. Its flashing edge met the tough hemp like an acetylene torch on a strand of cobweb. In frayed, useless clumps, the severed loops fell away.

None of the Centaurs wanted to meet a weapon like that at close quarters. Nor were any foolhardy enough to bother casting another loop. On the other hand, while I could defend myself, now, I lacked the speed and agility I'd need to get Lorn and Timtik before they could be tossed into the vat of hungry yeast-plants. It looked like an impasse. One which was abruptly resolved in a terrified yell.

"Wumbls!" shrieked a Centaur, pointing.

From the perimeter of the plain, as we all held our breaths, came a bone-chilling sloshing sound. I looked toward the source. Something was moving over the ground toward us, something that could not be seen due to near-transparency, but off whose taut-skinned surface the sun glinted in yellow warning. The herd of hungry protoplasm was converging on the fat, slithering over the ground swifter than water from a ruptured dam. There was a scared, frozen, timeless moment. Then—

Timtik, jerking free from his momentarily numb captor, raced over the ground toward me, waving the bag of spells. I grabbed it from him, slung the strap across my shoulder, and dipped a hand past the dodging flap to come up with the next spell. The label read, *"Schlitz Brewing Company, Milwaukee."*

"Come on!" I snapped at Timtik, and grabbed Lorn with my free arm. The Wumbls were nearly upon us. The Centaurs were breaking into sporadic gallops, fitfully stopping, turning, terrified as the half-seen glistening enemy slid swiftly inward from all sides.

"AN opener!" I shouted to Timtik, over the tumult of hooves and cries of hoarse fear. The leader of the Centaurs reared up nearby, his face strained and terrified. I shot the sword-blade out before him, and he struck the flat of the blade like he'd run into a cement wall. And as he staggered, dazed, I jammed the stem of the bottle into his tooth-happy mouth, and twisted the edge of the cap against those protruding incisors. It popped off better than with a standard opener.

Then I yelled to Timtik, and he leapt obediently up into Lorn's arms, as I flung the opened bottle into the heart of the onrushing Wumbl herd. As Lorn grabbed Timtik, I grabbed her. My back to the vat, I held her one-armed, and extended the magic blade for what good it might do against that army of ambulant slosh.

But there was no need for swordplay.

Like warm champagne from a shaken flask, golden sparkles of foam and liquid were gushing from the mouth of the bottle. Gushing like a Niagara over the slithering bodies. Rolling like an ocean over the plain, like a monstrous carbonated tidal wave. A surge of frothy lager rose beneath us, up to my armpits before it lifted me clear of the ground with Lorn and Timtik snugly beside me, and carried us on a wave-crest at dizzy speed toward the swaying green boughs of the thick woods ahead.

The comber broke, scattering us onto a springy clump of bushes and high grass, then receded, leaving us high and anything but dry, and smelling like Saturday night in skid row.

When we looked back, nothing could be seen save a sea of heaving, foaming, frothing, seething golden lager. The vat, the Centaurs, the Cheesers and the Wumbls had all long since been swirled beneath the thundering amber waves of Schlitz.

CHAPTER ELEVEN

ABOUT ten acres of lush forest later, moving faster than was comfortable to make up for the lost time, my ears detected the familiar "ching-ching" of a bicycle bell. We stopped, looking about us, and the cheery little "ching-ching" sounded again. Then from a small copse of tree, a strange figure appeared, pedaling energetically along on a small Schwinn; a mannish creature, two feet tall, with a white beard that came dangerously close to tangling in his wheel spokes. He wore a bright orange doublet, belted with a wide strip of black leather, and joined sturdily in front with a silver buckle four inches on a side. But, most intriguing was his regulation Western Union cap.

"Telegram for Albert Hicks!" he declared, braking.

"I'm Albert Hicks," I said.

"Whoosh," said the dwarf, clutching the cap between thumb and forefinger by the visor while he wiped at his dripping brow with the same hand. "Thought I'd never find you. I've been pedaling through the bushes for half an hour!"

"Sorry," I said lamely. "May I have the telegram?"

"What? Oh. Sure. Here 'tis!" He poked around inside his cap and withdrew a slightly damp yellow envelope, which he presented with a flourish. Tearing the envelope open, I noticed he was still loitering before me, whistling tunelessly between his teeth.

"Oh," I said, embarrassed.

I fumbled in my pants pocket and came up with a dime, which I handed to the dwarf. He bit down on the edge of it, snorted at me, and pedaled off huffily into the green shadows of the forest. Timtik was by now dancing up and down in impatience.

"Who's it *from*, for corn's sake!" he exclaimed.

The telegram was a thick one, and I had to flip to the final page to check the signature. "Maggot," I said.

"Hurry up," wailed the faun, "and *read* it!"

I cleared my throat and began:

Dear Albert,

I'm sorry to interrupt your itinerary, but there are a few things you should know before going onward. Too bad about your delay with those damn Centaurs, but at least you've got the silver sword, now (isn't it a honey!?), so the interval wasn't a total loss. But unfortunately, the time lag during your captivity was long enough for the Kwistians to arrive at Sark with the other Lorn.

But don't give up hope. Things could be worse—Don't ask me how; I'm busy making hellbrew. The thing I wanted to warn you about is Cort. He's already questioned the two Kwistians who brought the other Lorn back, and found out about you being here in Drendon.

Cort is upset because he feels you might be bringing the Thrake to the castle, with some sort of magical safeguard for it against his booby traps, so he's posted a special guard near the main entrance to watch for you when you arrive. This means that you and Timtik and Lorn (if it *is* Lorn) will have to detour slightly, and come at the castle from the side. Sorry for the inconvenience. Hurry, keep cool, and do your best. I'm sure everything will turn out splendidly. (Well—Fairly sure.)

Give my best to Timtik and Lorn (if that *is* Lorn with you), and whatever you do—and this is *most* important!—don't let the Tinklings get under your skin!

Sincerely,
Maggot

P.S. Try and get back before mealtime. I'm baking a cake.

THAT's it," I said, folding the message and tucking it into my shirt pocket. "What did she mean by 'Tinklings'?"

"Search me," said Timtik. "Must be some danger that's indigenous to the Sark area. But no one ever comes here unless they have to. Especially woodnymphs."

"Don't remind me!" said Lorn, shuddering. She bounded bravely from her leafy bower, however, and strode off into the shrubbery. Timtik and I raced to keep up. As I watched her relentless progress ahead of us, a rather bothersome thought came to me, and I expressed it to Timtik.

"I've been noticing something," I said, so Lorn wouldn't hear me. His pointed ears perked forward, curiously. "Your thundershower spell doesn't last long. And that train-ride was only five minutes before it wore out. And that werewolf was refuzzing before we got out of sight. And I'm willing to bet that those drowned Centaurs are lying on a dry field right now, with shriveled Wumbls and an empty bottle. Look at ourselves: Not so much as a whiff of the hops left, and ten minutes ago we were reeking."

Timtik, skipping nimbly through the grass, grinned. "Your sword can't wear out, if that's what's worrying you. Those alternate copper and ivory bands around the handle represent the balance of positive and negative power. "The edge of the blade is *out*going power, the flat is *in*coming. One exerts force, one absorbs it. It can't wear out. Use of the edge drains the flat, and makes it more absorbent; use of the flat sucks power to strengthen the edge."

"Damn it," I said, "you can't have it *both* ways!"

Timtik's nostrils flared, and it seemed momentarily that he was about to blow up with a loud bang. Then he controlled himself, and muttered, "It's magic, you dope!"

"Why didn't you say that in the *first* place!" I snapped. Then added, *"However—!"* so fiercely that the faun skidded to a halt and stood staring at me.

"Now what?" he said.

"The possibly short-lived sword was not my point," I said.

His face twisted into an expression of martyred patience. "Which spell bugs you, then?"

"The Scapegoat Spell, that's which!" I growled. "How long before *that* wears off, and one of the two Lorns vanishes?"

The mockery left Timtik's face and he went a little pale. "Jeepers, Albert—I don't know! In actual time, an *hour,* but—"

"I know. We've been short-circuiting time by taking the long way around, so you have no idea how much real time's gone."

"If we have the real Lorn with *us,*" he said, hopefully, "Maggot'd send word as soon as the Scapegoat Image vanished from the castle, and we could turn around and go right home." He looked suddenly uncomfortable. "But, if *our* Lorn vanishes, we'd know the real one was on the brink of the flame—*Urk!*"

A SWATCH of thorn bush had sung through the air and smacked loudly against his bare chest. "Tangle, Albert," he muttered, stepping back and brushing at himself. I stepped up beside him, slashing the silver blade through the barbed jumble. It fell into a heap of loose fibers.

"This is the handiest thing!" I enthused, staring in admiration at the blade, its shining surface unsullied by its contact with the thick, moist growths. "With a gadget like this, we hardly need—" My eyes met Timtik's. "...Lorn!"

The back-snapping bush's significance hit us. Our foliage-control was gone as though she'd never existed.

"Lorn?" Timtik called out frantically. "Lorn!"

I joined in yelling her name, but my heart wasn't in it, and neither was his. We knew the truth. The real Lorn was in the castle, prisoner of the Kwistians. And we had yet to reach the side wall.

"Come on, faun!" I said, racing forward through the forest, my silver blade flashing.

*　*　*

The mist seeped up from nowhere.

We'd come hurrying out of a thicket, and about halfway across an open stretch of smooth ground, we'd waded into a blanket of billowing vapor at ankle depth. As we moved onward, the air became woven with grayish windings of fog, and soon I couldn't see even the top of Timtik's head, although the faun walked right beside me, his hand in mine lest we become separated.

"Keep your eyes turned upward just a little," Timtik said softly; something about dense fog makes people whisper. "The fog's thinnest at the top."

"Okay," I said, "but what am I watching for?"

"The winged towers of Sark. The towers spread out into great stone wings in a position of flight. Kwist had them gilded, or something. They look pretty fancy in the sunlight."

As suddenly as it had begun, the mist dispersed, dwindling into white clumps, which melted, into the air with careless rapidity. The sunlight was blinding as it reflected from the great gold-and-stone winged towers of the castle of Sark, just outside the copse in which we stood. A mere two hundred yards across a stretch of purple moss.

"Odds bodkins," murmured the faun. "That open stretch by the moss is the place we just crossed! The mist must have been Maggot's doing! Otherwise, we'd be full of tridents right now!"

"How do we cross the moss?" I said, uneasily.

"We'll face that problem when we come to it," said Timtik. "Come on, now, follow me quickly. And Albert, for corn's sake lower that sword! The way it gleams, you'd be less conspicuous carrying carillon bells!"

"Sorry," I said. "Which way from here?"

"To the side. And tiptoe till we're away from the main wall. Kwistians have sharp ears."

ACCIDENTS will happen. The closest scrutiny can be kept on the most important thing by the most careful guard of the highest integrity, and still things can go wrong. So with Maggot.

As she later informed me, when relating the harrowing details, it was just one of those unavoidable things that make a mockery of care and caution, and the last thing she'd have wanted to see occur.

Dandelions, as plentiful as they may be in any spot where no control is put upon growing things, like to take their own sweet time about seeding. And, as you may recall; the fluff from a dandelion ready to burst into a white spray of tasseled seeds was a necessary ingredient for the hell-brew. Maggot, as can any cook who forgets to check her stores, ran out of this vital ingredient.

Just outside her hut dandelions grew a-plenty. But there was not one that was not bright, moist and yellow. Useless for hell-brew.

But Maggot had a simple spell for aging things, a byproduct of the spell she used to keep her haggard looks down-to-par.

And so, laden with an armload of yellow dandelions, she entered her hut, went to her worktable, and began chanting the spell that would age the yellow into fluffy white. Her plump back was turned to the cluttered shelf over the steaming cauldron of hell-brew, on which squirmed the always-ravenous Thrake. The all-necessary Thrake.

And that tiny blue animal grew abruptly tired of waiting for Maggot to cater to it, and tried—by the insufficient power of its puny tentacles—to flip itself from the rim of the shelf to the rim of the cauldron which held its bubbling, gluey food.

It missed the rim by an inch, certainly no more. Maggot heard its shrill, hapless squeal as it dropped directly into the scorching tendrils of fire beneath the cauldron. But by this time its cry of discomfort had been long overused, so—

"Patience, patience," crooned the witch, cackling softly. She turned her head toward the shelf... "Just another few moments, my pretty. As soon as I add these to the brew, I'll—"

Her rheumy red eyes rested upon the unwontedly still clutter of ort and cobwebs. It seemed terribly motionless. Suddenly afraid, the old witch flung the fluff into the cauldron, more to free her hands than anything else, and began to claw through the mess on the shelf, her voice rising in panic. "Thrake? Where are you? Don't play hide-and-seek with poor old Maggot! Where are you hiding? Come out now. I've put your fluff in the hell-brew, and—"

Her eyes, flicking searchingly over the shelf and its vicinity, noted a dangling bit of old hellbrew pendant on the lip of the shelf. With a cry of clairvoyant horror, she crouched and pawed the flame-baked earth directly beneath.

The remains of the Thrake were barely identifiable.

"Hell's bells!" she gasped. "There goes a life of single minded devotion, up in smoke!" But instead of sitting down and mourning the deceased, her always-practical mind considered the bright side. "Well, I'm no longer tied down," she mused, pulling at her limp nether lip with a gnarled finger. "So I may as well see what I can do to help Albert—*in person!*" Gleefully, she grabbed a black faggot-broom from a dusty corner. "I could use a change of scenery!"

With the grating howl that is the trademark of the traveling witch, she whipped a long black cloak from a peg on the rough wooden wall, tossed it across her shoulders, sat upon the broom-stick and went roaring out through a gap in the obediently dodging wall.

WHAT'S that tinkling sound?" I said to Timtik.

His ears pricked up. "I dunno. It's up ahead of us, I think, right on our way to the side wall of the castle. Do you think it's what Maggot warned us about?"

"Wouldn't be a bit surprised," I said, pulling the telegram from my shirt and consulting it. "She said that we shouldn't let the Tinklings get under our skin...You think the sound's hypnotic, or what?"

"One way to find out," said the faun.

We hurried forward, and suddenly the forest began to change. A strange dappling of light fell over us, unlike the normal green-gold pied effect of sunlight through leaves. Bits and pieces of geometric glows danced in rainbow profusion on the tree trunks, on our bodies and faces.

"You don't think it was a misspelling?" I said. "What if she meant 'Twinklings'?!"

"Couldn't have," said the faun. "Listen..."

I stopped crunching through the underbrush, and heard the sounds, much louder, in an erratic tempo almost in harmonic counterpoint to the coruscations of colored light. "You're right," I said.

Then we were in an open space, and for the first time saw what lay ahead. Acre upon acre of trees, short shrubs, and twisting vines, ranging in tones from palest pink to bloodiest crimson, from luminous turquoise to lambent purple, from metallic orange to crystalline yellow to sparkling emerald. A small portion of the woods, done up in splendid Easter Parade tones, and every twig, every tendril, every leaf, constructed in the most delicate symmetry and fragile filigree—of glass.

I had to shut my eyes and shake my head a moment before proceeding into that chromatic tangle. Then, sword in hand, I followed Timtik in a swift dash toward the glass forest...

...Wind was worming through the leaves. They flicked out of its path with a sound like muted bells, exquisitely toned. The sound was eerily charming, and atonically harmonious, and I rather enjoyed it for the first few paces.

Then my flesh began to prickle. A muscle started jumping under my left eye. The insistent noise of the leaves grew in intensity, and as we drew near the center of the region, a raw discomfort began abrading my flesh. The music of the tinkling leaves was musical no longer. It was as maddening as being locked in an echo chamber with a million Good Humor trucks, each in a different key.

"Timtik—!" I said. I stopped walking. My voice was hoarse with tension. I screwed up my face and pulled my elbows tightly up against my ribs.

AS if encouraged by my words, the wind became livelier, and the clangor arose in shrill gaiety. My body shook, went into a nervous shiver, horrible little thrills rushed down my spine, through my limbs. My ears rang, and felt like they were drawing away from the noise into my skull. I opened my clenched eyelids to try and see the path out of the flashing chaos, the pandemonic noise, and saw nothing but sparkle and glint and flash. In all directions. Blinding, confusing. Then the babble of glass began to sound like conversation, like the multi-phonic sound you hear at a crowded cocktail party.

"Tink?" sang a leaf.

"Kinkink-kang!" came the response.

"Jang-jing, jing-clang!" interrupted a third.

Other voices joined them.

"Stop!" I called, my voice ripping brutally from my lungs, my eyes rammed shut, heels of my hands clamped futilely against my ears. Something was growing inside me. It burned in my veins, plucked at muscle and bone, ate at my brain…

Directly before me, a fabulous pink-and-green glass rosebush waited hungrily. I started toward it, dazed, my arms going wide to embrace the jagged daggers of leaf and blossom and thorn… An end to the racking torture, to the dizzying lights, to the shrieking sound, to—

And then I saw Timtik, who'd never heard my voice amid the symphony of the deadly forest, who was even now moving blank-eyed toward the knife-edged forest plants, to spill the total libation of his blood onto the thirsty soil.

"Timtik!" I cried out reflexively, knowing my voice would go unheard. Timtik's face was glazed with a somnambulist's stare as he tottered toward the notched teeth of the beautiful, voracious blossoms.

When the woods had taken enchanted hold upon me, sword and wallet had fallen unnoticed to my feet. I bent swiftly for them now, in my moment of respite, knowing I'd be too late, that Timtik would be impaled on the thousand teeth before I could slash the thing to flinders and spicules—

Inches from the sword-hilt, my fingers halted, and grabbed instead at one of the remaining two spells which had rolled somehow through the flap of the wallet right to my waiting hand. The spool of thread.

In one desperate movement, I scooped it up, straightened my body and flung it beyond Timtik toward the waiting horror.

There came a whirring, a whirring that grew until it was like wind-driven rain hissing through the air. A cloud of twisting, whirling gray-blue spun upward, outward, downward, soaring, arcing, twining, swelling, growing, knotting, tangling, even as I launched myself in a sprawling tackle that brought Timtik to the earth, inches from certain death.

The spool, empty, fell to the ground and bounced, once.

I heard its fall distinctly, even on soft earth. For, other than that solitary, tiny sound, the stillness of the forest was deafening. Not even a breeze was heard. Silence, absolute and complete. Blinding sparkle was abruptly drab, dull, shadowy.

I got to my feet and lifted Timtik to his. His face was kind of greenish.

"Let's get a move on," I said. "We daren't lose any more time!" I picked up the silver sword, Timtik scurried for the wallet and its sole remaining spell, and we raced nimbly toward the far edge of the forest of hungry glass.

Razor-edge, raucous glass. Each separate leaf and branch frozen into helpless silence by countless windings of blue-gray, taut, slender strands of cotton thread, entangling the glass forest in a skein that could barely have been duplicated in scope by the day-long labor of a hundred billion web-spinning spiders.

CHAPTER TWELVE

WELL, here we are," I murmured despondently, standing on the twitching purple brink. A thirty-yard stretch of moss lay between us and the castle. Even could we have vaulted the gap, there was not so much as a finger hold on that wall; it rose featureless and blank from moss to winged towers, stolid gray granite three hundred feet high.

Timtik flicked a disdainful glance at the looming edifice. "We still have some magic left."

I peeked into the wallet, which opened readily. "Nothing but the tooth," I said. "It must be the right spell, because otherwise, the wallet wouldn't open, right?"

"That seems reasonable," said the faun, doing his impatient hoof-dance on the shore of the mossfield. "If you'd just stop pondering and *act*—"

"Oh…okay," I said, lifting out the bright gold molar. "I kind of wanted to save our *last* spell for emergencies."

"If getting to Lorn before she's incinerated doesn't constitute an emergency, what *does*, for corn's sake!"

Without giving either of us a chance for further argument, I tossed the golden molar out into the moss. At the same instant, the leather wallet vanished with a soft pop. "Why'd you do that?" asked Timtik.

"I didn't," I said. "Maggot must have a Finders-Weepers spell on it."

"I mean that *toss*, Albert! Are you sure it's the right activation?"

"The odds are in favor of it," I hedged, watching anxiously the spot in the moss wherein the tooth had vanished. "I mean— Although I punched the ticket, and squeezed the tube, the beer and the spool were both *throw*-items. So, I guessed this might be the same."

"Well," said the faun, watching the same spot as uneasily as I was, "there's a certain logic to magic; like with the beer."

"What about the beer—?"

"It was the perfect all-purpose destroyer. In the high waves, the Centaurs drowned; in alcohol, the Wumbls pickled through osmosis; and the Cheesers—" Timtik blushed a little. "Alcohol is their primary *waste* product, so they died not unlike being buried under—"

"I get it, I get it," I said. "But the tooth?"

"Well, it's a false tooth, and we need a *bridge*..." he said slowly. Before my groan got too loud, he went hastily on, "And the *shape* is right, Albert. Long roots to reach solidity under the muck, and a flat crown for us to walk on..."

I nodded thoughtfully. "And the beer, the cream, the thread, all grew larger, so the odds are fine—" I scanned the moss, futilely. "So where the hell *is* it!?" I asked, impatiently.

TIMTIK started to shake his head in woeful ignorance, then a little frown puckered his brow. He squatted down on his furry haunches and flicked at a tuft of moss with one sharp claw. The tuft pulled away, and there beneath it, gleaming in dreamy confidence, was the top of our golden bridge to the castle.

"It's been there all the time!" he wailed. "But the spell won't last forever. Can we cross before it vanishes?"

"The quicker, the likelier!" I said, sprinting for the wall, each bare footfall on the soft springy moss feeling as though it were at any moment about to plunge into that weird muck, with its slithering occupants and their caustic drool.

"Hurry," said Timtik, as if I weren't trying to.

"You'd think Maggot'd have made the tooth visible!" I said, nearly to the wall. "Why she left it under the moss—!"

"It's Cort's doing, you dope!" said the faun, catching up to me at the base of the sheer granite scarp. "He has this region loaded with anti-magic. If he can't stop a spell, he can disorganize it a little."

"Timtik—!" I said, wavering. "Will this sword cut through a wall controlled by such a wizard?"

"Like an axe through wax," he said impatiently. "He can't overcome Maggot's spells. All he can do is make us start doubting them. Be confident, and for corn's sake, start *cutting!*"

The silver blade flashed in my hand, described an effortless arc.

And a circle of granite slid ponderously out of the wall, rolled and rumbled across the moss-hidden tooth-top, then plunged sluggishly out of sight beneath the muck-based moss beyond the hidden bridge.

"Come to think of it," I said, as Timtik and I sprang through the gap into the castle of Sark, "Cort went and loused *himself* up! With the tooth moss-covered, there was nothing to alert a sentry up on the walls!"

"I told you not to doubt Maggot," said Timtik. We hurried forward into the dim twilight interior, with Timtik third, myself second, and that all-powerful silver sword in the position of honor.

There was light ahead.

We'd inched along darkened corridors in gloom relieved only by a pale moonlight glow that spilled softly from the diamond on the sword. The light ahead told us we were nearing an inhabited part of the castle. We rushed noiselessly forward, our silence an unspoken consent between us. The light broke around us as we dashed into a great empty chamber.

"Look, Albert!" said Timtik, pointing to four odd-shaped marble things on a rocky shelf. "They're for Lorn!" he said excitedly, as I realized that they were a pair of gauntlets and sabots, with hinges and clasps. "Maggot told me about them. When the Kwistians roast a nymph in the flame-pit, they don't like the smaller body-parts charring while the larger parts cook through, so they bind the hands and feet into these things to keep the juices intact—!"

"Stop!" I groaned. "Does it mean that we're early or late?"

"Let's hope early," said the faun. Then, from high overhead, through a wide orifice in the ceiling, a piteous cry sounded, begging for mercy. Timtik's face went chalky, and I felt sick inside. "That was Lorn," said the faun.

A SHADOW moved across the floor, and we dodged back against the wall. The next instant, two winged men descended almost vertically through the ceiling-hole, and landed lightly on the floor before us, their great pinions folding into place. One had his back to us, but the other, after a startled blink, said, *"Hey!"* pointing at me. "The Earthman! Here!"

As the first one whirled, shaken, the other took a backward step, and his wings began to unfold. Which was stupid of him, because a fifteen-foot wingspread isn't the stealthiest thing in the world to erect unnoticed. I flipped the point of my sword against throat of the nearer man.

"Hold it! If you make a move, your buddy gets it!"

"Ha!" was his only reply as he sprang gracefully into the air.

I shifted the hilt in my hand, drew back the silver blade like a spear, and hurled it.

It caught the ascending Kwistian squarely between the shoulder-blades wherein his wings were rooted, sank in to the hilt, then slithered out and dropped on a suspiciously erratic curve—directly back into my waiting hand, even before the gasping victim's wings folded about him and let him drop to the floor with a resulting thud.

The other Kwistian stood frozen, not moving a feather. "Take us to Lorn, the woodnymph!" I demanded.

The man gulped, then choked out feebly, "At once, sir!"

Timtik frowned. "It sounds too easy."

I glanced upward through the ceiling-hole, then realized that it was superseded by another in the next ceiling, and that a final orifice lay even beyond that, in the floor of the castle's highest room. "Well," I shrugged at the faun, "it's a pretty long jump, Timtik..."

The faun sighed. "Okay, Albert. You're the boss."

"If you'll let me hold each of you by an arm," said our captive, too anxious to please, "I can—"

"Correction," I said. *"We'll* hold *you* by either arm. You might get tired and let go." I clamped the man's right wrist in my left hand, keeping the sword in readiness in my right. Timtik clutched his other wrist with both hands, his face looking as though he dreaded heights more than I did.

"Let's go," I said, then reconsidered. "Wait—! You came here for those marble things... So if you don't return with them, someone else will come and find this corpse—" I looked at Timtik. "We'd better move them."

He ran and got the four marble items, and handed them to the Kwistian, who took them with poor grace.

"*Now* we go!" I said, re-establishing my grip. Then the floor fell away beneath us as the great white pinions labored gustily to raise the additional load.

The next level up was deserted, but the center of the room was a thick column, radiating a lot of heat. Perhaps twenty feet in diameter, it reached from floor to ceiling.

"What's that?" I asked, swaying from the wrist of the rising Kwistian, unwilling to look directly downward.

"It's the base of the flame pit," said the Kwistian. His voice was too smug for a captive, somehow. I suddenly realized that if the room we were approaching held the open mouth of the pit, it might very likely hold the rest of the cannibals, rattling their silverware in anthropophagous impatience.

I FORCED myself to look at the awful distance below my sun burnt toes. My grip, as I dangled, was weakening. This parrot-beaked vehicle of ours was being too cooperative.

"Hold it," I said, touching the point of the sword onto the soft flesh between the base of his beak and his throat. The wings continued to beat the air. "Stop or—!"

"Or what?" mocked the creature. "You won't kill me. Not with a drop like that below you."

I forced myself not to listen to Timtik's panicky moan at those words. "I'm warning you," I said, pressing the needle-pointed blade gently. Pale red blood suddenly started to trickle down the Kwistian's chest, and the great wings faltered.

"*Ukkk!*" he gagged, his thick tongue lolling through the gaping beak. Only a quarter-inch of point was in his neck, but it was enough. Eyes glazed in fear, he fluttered feebly to the floor of the room. I waited till Timtik was standing free, then kept the sword-point in its niche as I said, trying to keep reaction-quaver out of my voice, "Where is Lorn right now? The room above?"

"No—no," he gurgled, afraid to move with that thing imbedded razor-keen in his throat. "She's in the room next to it, awaiting the donning of the marble slippers and gloves."

"How do we get *there?*" I demanded, with tight desperation.

"The only entrance is through the throne room, the room above here. The preparation room has no vertical entrance. He pointed to the ceiling near the rear wall. "It's up there."

As I looked up, the Kwistian suddenly sprang upward with a flip of mighty wings, soaring directly toward the orifice above. He didn't even come close.

The blade, which had left his throat as he rose, just fell lazily through his chest region like a sunbeam through fog. Face gray and dead, he sagged in mid-air, then thumped to the floor beside us.

I shook my head over my latest corpse, then took the bits of marble from his hands and left them beside the lip of the hole through which we'd entered this level. Then I dumped the winged man all the way over it to lie with his companion, below. "We'll cut our way up," I said, heading for the rear wall. "It'll take time, but they won't throw Lorn into the pit till they get those gloves and slippers, and there may be a time-lag till they send a new group to get them."

"You think they won't spot the corpses down below if they find the marble stuff on this level?" asked Timtik.

"I hope they won't," I said, slicing a foothold in the wall.

AT the ceiling, short minutes later, clinging with my left hand while I sliced the granite above with my right, I took care to make the cutout part wider on top than below, like a bathtub plug, so we could push it up quietly. It proved to weigh more than I could budge, but Timtik reminded me about the brunt-bearing propensities of the flat of the blade, and I found, I could lift the granite slab with a light wrist-movement. I held it there while Timtik crawled up over me and through, then balanced it dexterously while I squeezed up after him. I let the segment ease back into place, then stood listening.

A chamber adjoined the sort of closet we seemed to be in, and I could hear murmuring voices and soft feminine sobs.

Lorn, weeping her heart out. We peeped out of the arched doorway together. Lorn was sitting between two tall Kwistian guards. My hand tightened on the hilt of the silver sword. Now, if they would just turn their backs...

"Here they are!"

A third Kwistian had rushed into the room, bearing those marble gadgets we'd left one level below. "I don't know what happened to Teek and Twelrik," he added. "The Extremikilns were on the floor at the next level down—"

"The emperor's getting impatient," snapped one of the two guards. "Get the things on her, quick."

"Right," said the Kwistian, stooping to insert one of Lorn's feet into the proper marble slipper. He received her right big toe in his eye for his trouble. "Hold the nymph!" he cursed, rubbing his injured orb. The others grasped her legs and arms, and he finally got the glossy manual and pedal binders on her.

Not ten feet away, around the corner, we waited, hoping they'd turn their backs. Timtik was shaking with excitement, clutching tightly at my free hand.

"Hurry!" said a fourth Kwistian, joining the group. "Old Cort and the emperor are ready to split their beaks!"

Before we could think out a plan, the men were out of the room with Lorn. Time had been short before. It was all run out, now.

As the chamber cleared of occupants, we dashed to the next archway and looked into the throne room. As we looked in, Cort and the emperor had not yet seen Lorn. I knew who they were the moment I fastened eyes on them. There was no mistaking—even with those razor-edged parrot beaks—the Drendon-transmuted faces of Courtland and Geoffrey Porkle.

Porkle-Kwist was speaking to Courtland-Cort.

"Relax, they'll be here shortly."

"Here they are—!" Cort drooled, as the two guards came swooping with Lorn between them to a spot just before the throne.

"Imperial majesty, the nymph is ready," spoke the first of the two guards. They released her arms. A mistake.

Lorn, her hands bound with cold marble, her feet shod with the same substance, showed him just how ready she was. A vicious swing of her right hand smashed into the half-opened beak of the speaker, sending him sprawling out across the stone floor, yelping with pain.

Immediately, half the Kwistians standing in the throne room leaped toward her with brass tridents ready to strike her down.

"STOP!" said Cort, with a strange motion of his arms. It wasn't a command, I realized, as my limbs congealed like swift drying cement; it was a spell. And all persons present, save Cort and Kwist, froze helplessly, even Timtik, right beside me.

The wizard glowered, then pointed a finger at Lorn and growled, *"You* shall remain... All others: Released!" He said this last with a sharp fingersnap, and my body relaxed, as did everyone else's but Lorn's.

"You fools," said Cort to the shame-faced Kwistians lowering their tridents. "Can't you see that's what she *hoped* you'd do? She doesn't wish to be cooked alive. Take her to the pit, now; I've waited long enough."

"She must be cooked to a turn," said the emperor, suddenly.

Cort flashed a frosty eye at the monarch. "You know I like my nymphs rare!" he said. Something in his tone told me that the sharing of rule with Kwist was a thorn in his side. His face was a dull red with rage. Apparently, though, his power held no sway over Kwist. At least, the emperor had not been paralyzed with the rest of us.

"Pah!" said Kwist. "Ridiculous. Anyone who knows good woodnymph will tell you that well-done is best."

The frost in Cort's eye became a white-hot flame.

"If you hadn't sneaked a look at my Black Art books, majesty," he said, clicking the edge of his knife ominously upon the rim of his plate, "I'd have you so tied up in spells—"

The emperor yawned. "Precisely. *If.* However, a man grows tired of being paralyzed every time his *second*-in-command gets annoyed with him. And that's not the only counter-spell I've mastered, either, remember!"

Kwist gestured airily toward Lorn. The guards had the nymph, paralyzed into enchanted rigidity, at the brink of the pit. They themselves had to avert their faces from the pulsating red glow emanating from within the bowels of the scorched, blackened hole in the floor.

"At least," he said, "we should free her of her spell, that she may enjoy the fire fully."

Kwist smiled nastily, and snapped his fingers sharply. Lorn was resurrected from her magical imprisonment, and her voice rose instantly in a terrible cry of anguish in the blast-furnace updraft that wafted her garment about her in undulating waves of green.

The emperor waved a hand. "Throw the nymph to the fires!"

"Hold it!" I yelled at the top of my lungs. I didn't know if Maggot's powers could stand much more drainage, but I was determined to make a last-ditch stand.

The men holding Lorn turned, startled at the interruption. She staggered from the mouth of the glaring pit, away from the grip of her captors. Kwist spun about and saw me.

"The Earthman!" he cried. "Destroy him!"

AT least half the Kwistians hurled their tridents, with deadly accuracy, at me, an easy target standing stock still in the doorway. And each and every trident was drawn right into the four-foot sword I bore, to glance off harmlessly and clang to the stone floor. An uneasy murmur arose.

Cort stared appraisingly at me. His narrow eyes flickered with malevolence as he pointed a taloned finger at me, and shouted, voice ringing through the great room, "I, Cort, command you to *stop!*" His hands made that strange gesture again, and I stood numbly awaiting that cementing bondage to flow into my body again. But nothing happened. To me, at any rate.

Cort the wizard, however, rammed back into the air as though struck by a pile driver in the solar plexus. He spun along the floor for a dozen feet, then scrambled, pained and shocked, to his feet.

"What happened?" whimpered Kwist, who had sat in dull dazedness on his throne from the moment of my entrance "My spell—" mouthed Cort, blankly. "It backfired!"

"Of course it did," said Maggot, gliding in the great window with her faggot-broom hissing through the air, and great black cloak streaming silkily in her wake.

"The witch!" gasped the emperor.

But Cort gave an exultant howl. "Then the Thrake is dead! She'd never leave it while it was alive!"

Lorn, who in the confusion had struggled out of her marble encumbrances, rushed up to me and flung herself into my arms. "Please, honey," I protested, albeit I held her pressed tightly to me with my free hand. "I may have to kill a few people..."

"No," boomed the wizard. "You are all trapped, doomed!"

"Ha!" said Maggot, cackling shrilly. "What makes you think the Thrake is dead? I could very easily have taught it to feed itself. In fact, how do you know I haven't hooked it up to a high-frequency spell-transmitter that I can control from here, and render you all helpless, ha?!" She certainly sounded convincing.

So convincing that Kwist, who was wildly impressionable, screamed shrilly, "Help...I can't fly anymore!"

Maggot was momentarily distracted. And her power, which had been full on Cort since her arrival at Sark, wavered in intensity. Wavered just as the wizard made a frantic effort to employ his sorcery.

"Maggot the witch—STOP!" he roared, his arms doing that weirdly fluid motion toward her.

And Maggot froze helpless, like a plump, black-garbed statue clutching a broom. At the very instant of her going rigid, my sword vanished from my hand, and I found myself strapped in the heavy lead cuirass once more.

The Kwistians advanced upon us, snarling.

"Albert!" cried Lorn, miserably.

"Odds bodkins!" moaned Timtik.

CHAPTER THIRTEEN

WITHIN forty seconds, I had four Kwistians holding me, Lorn had two, and Timtik looked chagrined to find it took but one man to hold him.

Cort, despite that nasty spill he'd taken, was looking very pleased. In front of all the Kwistians, the emperor had cracked up in a crisis, leaving all the prestige to the winged wizard.

"Cort—" said Kwist, just about recovered from his fright, or at least feigning that appearance.

"Yess…Majesty?" Cort's unmistakable mockery elicited a few snickers from the clustered Kwistians. Kwist turned a pinkish hue, but managed to continue.

"Cort, what does an Earthman taste like?"

Cort's feathery eyebrows rose in shrewd consideration, but not half so high as my pulse rate and hackles. I could see that the idea, while new to the wizard, was not at all displeasing to him. "I really don't know," he mused, staring at me curiously, his yellowish eyes raking over my body from bare feet to tangled hair. "He might be quite delicious…"

"Why," said the monarch to his wizard, "don't we have us the nymph for a main course, and then the man as a soft, succulent dessert?"

"For now, that should be excellent—" said the wizard.

"For now?" echoed Kwist, sensing the glint of sharp speculation in the other's eye.

"Majesty, I was simply thinking… Here in Drendon, we must struggle to stay fed upon a relative handful of these delicious but scarce woodnymphs. But earth people exist by the billions!"

"What a thought!" enthused Kwist, his beak wet with saliva.

"Why," continued the wizard, "with my magic to aid us we can capture dozens every day. If things turn out well, we may just move out of Drendon entirely, and live on Earth, with an infinity of plump, juicy people to feed upon!"

"But—" said the monarch, uneasily, "what of the Edict of Banishment, Cort? I know it's possible for a *few* Drendonites to slip through on occasion, but if we *all* went through, wouldn't there be dreadful repercussions?"

Cort shook his head. "Even Merlin was not that all-fired powerful. As with any spell, the effect wears thin in time. Many centuries have passed since his was woven. A thousand years ago, no Drendonite could return to Earth; a hundred years ago, dozens were sneaking out for short forays every day. And today—It wouldn't surprise me if any of us could return without impunity, to remain so long as we desired."

"Can it have worn so thin, then?" said Kwist, hopefully.

"So thin, and so delicately poised," said Cort, "that the right shock, the right circumstances, could foreseeable collapse the Edict entirely, and return Earth to its primal state, save for the cheering fact that present-day Earth people would have no idea how to cope with the sudden onslaught of fabulous beasts re-returning to ravage the land!"

"Wonderful!" The monarch's joy was manifesting itself in a nervous dance step. "When can we get started?"

"As soon as it is determined whether or not the Earthman is as delicious as he looks!"

I FELT myself turning pink, and avoided Lorn's eyes. I tried desperately to think of something to offset our fates. Then I had it. I thought.

"Aren't you forgetting the Thrake?" I said, and was pleased to see the Kwistians stiffen, monarch and wizard included. "If Maggot can, as she says, turn it on from here, you'll all be in a fine fix, won't you!"

"He's right, Cort!" said the emperor. "We must destroy the Thrake, first, before we plan any further. Its power is the one thing that can ruin us all."

"Am I to assume," mused the wizard, "that you are finally giving me your permission to try the Roton Beam?"

"Never!" gasped Kwist, his face gray with horror. "I tell you, Cort, that so-called long-distance Thrake-destroyer is too incalculable! The heat at the focal point of the beam could ignite the mossfields and destroy all of Sark!"

"But majesty," Cort said, almost whining, "how do we know the Thrake is anywhere near the mossfields?"

"How," countered the monarch, "do we know it isn't wriggling across the moss tufts this minute?"

"All right, all right," Cort said petulantly. "No Roton Beam. We'll have to get at the Thrake indirectly."

"How?" asked Kwist. "Through Maggot?"

"That's our only course," said the wizard. "Without her, the Thrake will die of starvation. And even should it linger a while, Maggot's death can still prevent any long-distance activation of the Thrake's power, such as she claimed to be able to bring about."

"Good!" said Kwist. "You men there, stick your tridents—!"

"Kwist—!" Cort interposed wearily.

"—straight into her heart!" finished the monarch.

As I watched in horror, half a dozen gleaming brass tridents sped toward the rigid form of the plump little witch. And all six, their points blunted, clanged onto the floor, leaving her unscathed. Kwist turned a puzzled face to Cort.

"A counter-spell of hers?"

"No, majesty. *My* spell. The difficulty with the paralysis spell is that the very forces that seal up the person serve also to seal out the world. She cannot, in her present state, be harmed in any way—"

"But that's ghastly!" blurted the emperor. "Spells don't last forever, and when this one wears off—"

"If you'll let me finish?" Kwist shut his beak, and Cort went on, "I was saying that she cannot be harmed at all except for one force, the jaws of the Serpoliths."

The emperor's face went greenish, and not a few of the Kwistians shuddered. "Please Cort," said Kwist, "it's *dinner* time!"

WHEN I stood looking bewildered, Timtik turned his head my way and said, "Those are the mothers of the Kwistians, Albert. Maggot told me all about them. Cort keeps them locked in a black cavern beneath Sark, and only goes in there once a year to bring out their eggs for the hatchery. The eggs hatch into Kwistians, and—"

"Silence, goat-boy!" snarled Cort.

"But how can the Serpoliths—" said the monarch.

Cort shrugged. "I don't know. I never have. Something in them defies most of my magic. Perhaps due to their being the primal ancestors of the Kwistians?"

"Your magic door holds them," Kwist pointed out.

"No," said Cort. "It merely blocks the light, and they detest anything but absolute darkness. To pass through the door is to enter into glaring pain and death for them. And the far end of the cavern is sealed by natural means. So there they stay."

I was at sea about most of their conversation, but had no chance then to figure any of it out. Cort, deciding the dinner hour had been long enough delayed, ordered the guards to take Timtik and Maggot away, Lorn to be reprepared for the flame pit, and myself sent under guard into the room beyond the preparation chamber, to await my return. As dessert.

There wasn't much I could do but let the two tall Kwistians drag me bodily from the throne room. I was taken into the room where Timtik and I had first achieved this level of the castle, and could only sit and try not to listen to Lorn's piteous cries as she was sturdily re-strapped into those marble encumbrances.

The only hope was, of course, Maggot. And Maggot was magicked into evanescent ossification that probably wouldn't wear off until long after the Serpoliths—the sound of that word made my skin crawl—had rendered her pretty nigh useless as an ally. I wished listlessly that I'd paid better attention to Timtik's thunderstorm spell. If I could whomp up a shower every ten minutes or so, I could hold the flame pit at bay for quite a while…

And then it came to me—Timtik could do magic. Not like Maggot could, of course, but he wasn't what you could call powerless, either… If he could be encouraged into trying, he might just be able to louse things up good for the Kwistians. If I could only get to him.

I THOUGHT hard. Something about the Serpoliths was frightening to the Kwistians. With luck, I might maybe turn this loathing to my own advantage. I cleared my throat, said a short prayer, then spoke to the guards. "How's chances of my saying farewell to Maggot and Timtik?"

One of them snickered. "Rotten. You've seen the last of them, Earthman."

I forced myself to look nonchalant, and went on, "I figured as much. You Kwistians only attack unsuspecting people from the air, with those tridents ready to stab in the back. And you fight me, two women, and what amounts to a small boy at odds astronomically in your favor. And now, tough as you look, you're scared silly at the thought of going anywhere near the Serpoliths."

I fell silent and waited. This was the crucial moment. If only they had a spark of pride, a tiny spark of pride—

"Who's scared!" said the first guard. He glanced at the other one. "Come on, Twork! Let's give this guy a quick look at his friends before they're no longer available."

"Gee, Idlisk," said the other. "I dunno—Cort might be mad."

"At what?" said Idlisk. "We take him down, show him his buddies, then bring him back. Where's the harm?"

"Oh—Okay, but let's make it fast. They'll cook up the wood-nymph any minute, and we don't want to be skipped!"

With that, they took me by the arms, sprang into the air and out the tall stone casement in the sunlight, high over the moss. My stomach shrank sickeningly as they plunged down two levels and soared into a huge chamber there. We were two levels below the throne room, near the very corridor wherein Timtik and I had made our entrance. And whether these guys knew it or not, there was a large hole in the stone wall at the end of that corridor, right on the brink of the moss.

I kept that fact in mind as the two guards half-led, half-carried me down that dark corridor. One of them took a wooden flambeau from a wall sconce and ignited its tarry tip, and by this sputtering light we made our way deeper into the corridor, but suddenly turned off at an angle to the path on which I'd first entered Sark.

Shadows from the flaming torch danced wildly on walls barely wide enough apart for a Kwistian to move with his pinions folded, and this narrowness necessitated my being first in the procession. The corridor was damp and had a strangely familiar odor to it, a sick-sweet odor that tugged at my memory as it grew stronger, but I couldn't place it.

Then ahead of me I saw the circular opening leading into a dark muck-floored cavern, and standing a mere ten paces within the cavern were Maggot and Timtik, Maggot still inflexibly rigid, and Timtik sobbing hopelessly into the thick fabric of her voluminous skirt.

TIMTIK!" I called, and he turned his tear-streaked face toward me, looking more small boyish than ever in the flickering orange light of the torch.

"Albert!" he wailed. *"Do* something! The spells are meshing in the doorway, and the light's going fast!"

"What?" I said, baffled by his words. Then I saw that there was, indeed, something strange occurring in the circular plane that was the entrance to the cavern. A grayish cast to the air there seemed to resist any illumination thrown by the torch. "What kind of spell?"

"Two of them," sniffled the faun. "Polarized spells. One turns slowly to right angles to the other, and once it's there, no light can get in here; then the—the S—serpoliths'll come out!"

"That's enough, Earthman!" snapped Idlisk, grabbing my shoulder. "You've seen them. Now come along."

"And," I said, turning to face him, "if I *don't?*"

"You have no choice," he said, reaching for me.

"Make me come," I said, and stepped backward through the polarizing spells into the cavern.

"Hey—!" he said uneasily. "Come *out* of there!"

I noticed he made no move to advance toward me, through the circle of gray that grew gradually darker even as I stood watching him. His torch had developed a fuzzy crimson nimbus, as its light was distorted by the meshing spells.

"Two steps, and I'm yours," I said, tauntingly. Idlisk jerked his head around to Twork.

"We better get Cort!" he said nervously.

"He'll *molt* if you tell him what you did!" said the other. "We shouldn't have brought the Earthman here!"

"Better to get him upset over a slight dereliction of duty than a big one. He'll have *us* flung in the flame-pit if we let the Earthman get away with this!"

"Well…" said Twork. "Okay. You go tell him what's happened, and I'll stay here and make sure he doesn't try and sneak out."

As Idlisk hurried off, leaving the torch with Twork, I turned back to Timtik and Maggot. I knew the reason for Maggot's remaining where she was; then I saw the thick iron gyves on a short chain binding Timtik's hooves to the floor.

"You better scram, Albert," he said wistfully. "Is Lorn—?"

"Not yet," I said. "But look, Timtik, I came down here on purpose—" I glanced back over my shoulder, but Twork was standing well back from the cavern entrance, a dim red-lit figure as the polarized spells neared their locale of total blackout. In an impenetrably black grotto off across the cavern, something slithered ominously. I forced my mind away from that darker darkness, and said, "Timtik, I think you can save us all…"

"You'll be sorry, Earthman," called Twork's voice, as the darkness thickened. "When the Serpoliths come forth, angry with you interlopers, and all that acid dripping from their forked tongues, your death will not come quickly! You'll be begging for the flame pit after one second in the grip of those jaws!" In the tunnel, his voice was a hollow echo. Purplish-gray twilight hid him almost completely.

"Timtik," I said, "you must know some magic that'll get Lorn and all of us safely out of here."

"I know a little—" he said dubiously. "I can— Wait." In the gloom, I saw him frown deeply, then brighten as his memory came across with an answer. "Got it!" he said, then chanted:

"Bonds of metal, hemp or thong,

Loosen as I sing my song,

Set me free, as I belong,

Ere my witching does you wrong!"

THE chains wriggled like galvanized worms, and the gyves sprang open from his hooves and clunked into the muck on the floor. "Come on, Albert," he said. "We'll have to *carry* Maggot out of here, first, and try to save Lorn next."

"We can't," I said. "Twork's just beyond those magic blackout curtains."

"Odds bodkins!" he muttered furiously. "We've got to do something, Albert, and fast!" My nose, which had been twitching with disgust from the moment I'd entered the cavern area, gave a particularly violent wriggle, and called my attention back to the smell. "Pee-yew!" I said, sniffing the air. "This place smells like…" Then I remembered the odor, and identified it. "Like *hell-brew!*" I finished, startled.

Timtik squatted in the dimness to a clot of smelly stuff upon the floor and took a good whiff. "It *is* hell-brew," he gasped, astonished.

The blackness was abruptly complete, an almost palpable blackness, heavy and stygian to the senses. I could hear the slithering Serpoliths bestirring themselves in the grotto.

"You must free Maggot!" I said.

"But how?" he quavered, grabbing my hand in the darkness, as the slithering sounds began converging upon us. "Maggot never taught me the spell for freeing someone from magical paralysis."

"Must you rely on *regulations?*" I demanded. *"Someone* has to coin these spells; why not *you?*"

"We sure have nothing to lose—" he temporized, as the crawly noises with their contrapuntal sizzlings came horribly nearer. "Here goes nothing, Albert—" he said, then intoned swiftly, frantically:

"Now weave I a countermand,

That the wizard's curse be banned!

Move I now my warlock's hand—

Spell, leave Maggot, I *command!*"

I FELT him move, as his arms did some gesture in the blackness which only sorcerers know, then...

"Tikky!" sang out Maggot's voice, through a noise oddly like a distant shattering of glass, as her enchanted bonds were broken asunder.

"I *did* it!" the faun crowed in delight.

"The Serpoliths—!" I yelled, as a terrible scratching of scaly bodies crackled on the slimy stone of the cavern.

"Oh, of course!" said Maggot. "Lights, lights!"

There was a sputter, and two gleaming fluorescent tubes shone bright as elongated moons just beneath the cavern's domed ceiling. I barely got a glimpse of the Serpoliths, as—rasping out discordant screams of ocular agony—they sped back into the black recesses of the grotto.

"Swell!" I said. "Now, quick, let's save Lorn!"

"Wait a second, Albert!" said the faun. "Maggot, look at the stuff on the floor of this place. It's hell-brew, or I'm not the warlock I thought I was. Tell me, Maggot, is there some kind of connection between the Thrake and the Serpoliths and the Kwistians? And where *is* the Thrake?"

"Dead," said Maggot. "Fell into the cauldron fire. But as to the connection— I guess it doesn't matter if I tell you now, now that the poor little thing's gone..."

"Lorn," I urged, "they'll be tossing Lorn in the—!"

"You see," Maggot said to Timtik, ignoring me, "I was by the edge of the moss one day, gathering herbs, when a thing I took for a beautiful white stone came bobbing up from the muck. I thought I'd found a Serpolith egg, and—entertaining thoughts of raising me a *friendly* Kwistian for reconnaissance and such—I took it home with me, and kept it warm by the fireside, and one day it hatched. But it hatched into the Thrake. I was quite disappointed until I discovered its wing-stopping power over Kwistians, but—"

"Then I'm right!" interrupted the faun. "Maggot, you wonderful old darling witch! You were right, but you didn't know it. That was a Serpolith egg you had, but it didn't turn into a Kwistian because you hatched it out of the *darkness* it craved, kept it in Drendon where it only gets dark once in a lifetime!"

Maggot caught the fever of his deductions. "And the racial memory of the hatred all Serpoliths have for the Kwistians brought out this strange power it had over their flying ability?"

"Right!" said Timtik. "So the Thrake's death doesn't matter!"

"It doesn't?" I asked, fascinated despite myself.

"No," he laughed giddily. "Maggot, you told me that Cort controls the yearly crop of new winged men by coming down here where the baby Serpoliths are, and taking them into the castle to change, in the daylight, into—not adult Serpoliths, but—Kwistians! But *you* took an *un*hatched egg into the light. Can't you see it, feeling the sunlight through its shell, knowing it must alter its development before the shell broke away? So it became the smooth-bodied, tentacled Thrake, but still needed the food its own kind ate, the recipe which you discovered by trial-and-error, and which you named hell-brew. And, in its puny form, it couldn't threaten Kwistians as the fully-grown Serpoliths do, with fang and acid and venom. So it developed this wing-paralyzing power, and—"

"Tikky!" Maggot's jaw dropped. "What you're trying to say is that, if we expose the eggs in this cavern to heat and to light—"

"We'll have more Thrakes than the Kwistians have feathers!" he chortled, jumping up and down.

MAGGOT whispered a magic word, and she, Timtik and I were suddenly equipped with flashlights, with which we hurried into the dark grotto, bright yellow beams flaring ahead of us. Agonized hissing met our ears.

"We've got to get rid of the Serpoliths, first," said Timtik.

"Easy as pie," said Maggot, with a mystic gesture. A black tube of darkness appeared on the ground, extending from the grotto toward the rear wall of the cavern, where for the first time I noted a rusted metal door set into the stone. As the tube appeared along the ground, the rusted bolt burst, and the heavy metal door creaked open, exposing—oozy black muck, the underside of the morass beneath the mossfields, where the acid-tongued Serpoliths lived. I knew, then, what had happened to my legs in that brief dip into the mossfield.

"Flee!" commanded Maggot, and every single Serpolith trapped at the end of the grotto by our flashlight beams slipped frantically into the tube of darkness and out into their muddy ancestral home. As the last scaly tail slithered into the glutinous black ooze, the door slammed itself and the tube of darkness vanished.

We played our lights on the rear wall of the grotto, and without counting, I realized that at least a thousand Serpolith eggs lay there, waiting to hatch.

"Odds bodkins," said Timtik, wide-eyed with delight, "if we hatch *these* out, the Kwistians not only won't be able to fly—
They won't be able to *move!*"

"Don't just stand there with your face hanging out, Albert," said Maggot. "Have you forgotten that Lorn is about to be roasted alive?"

"Of course not!" I said. "But what can I—?"

"Delay things!" she commanded. "You can do it!"

"How?" I choked.

"Do a tap dance, or card tricks! Just hold them off for another ten minutes, perhaps." Then, forgetting me completely, she returned her attention to the faun and the stacks of eggs. "Come on, Tikky! Let's get a fire started!"

I turned and grimly hurried back to the disc of blackness masking the cavern mouth. I took a breath, said another prayer, and then stepped through.

"There he is!" said Twork, to Idlisk and Cort, who were just approaching him down the tunnel. I worried for a fractional moment that Cort would spoil everything when he saw the Maggot-evoked fluorescents in the cavern, then realized that the only light in the tunnel was torchlight. Cort's magic door worked both ways, thank heaven.

"Chickened out, huh?" smirked the wizard. "Couldn't stick it out with your friends when the going got tough!"

"No," I said, making my voice panicky, which wasn't hard. "Those fangs, that acid! I couldn't take it!"

"Now who's a coward," chuckled Twork, grabbing my arm and leading me away from the cavern mouth.

"Is Lorn—?" I said to the wizard.

"For the next thirty seconds, she lives," he said, as the two guards lifted me in sudden soaring flight behind him. We reached throne room level just as Lorn was brought out of the preparation chamber.

IN the center of the floor, the flame pit was almost hidden by a leaping column of yellow-orange fires; the stokers had done a horribly good job.

"Now," said Kwist, from the throne, "toss that nymph in there, and let's get dinner going!"

Now or never.

I threw back my head and laughed. The occupants of the room, Lorn especially, looked at me in consternation.

"Hysteria?" asked the emperor of Cort.

The wizard eyed me coldly. "Something amuses you?"

"In an ironic sort of way," I said. "Here you all are, about to glut yourselves on this nymph, and spoil your appetites and taste judgment!"

"Spoil them for what?" said Cort. "Surely not for *you?!*"

"Who else?" I said, trying not to think too deeply on the topic. "Unless you were planning on cooking Kwist next?"

"Cort—!" said the emperor, uneasily.

"He's only goading you, majesty," said the wizard. "Or trying to change the subject. Which is: Just how good *is* an Earthman for dinner...?"

"Let's cook him and see," said Kwist, matter-of-factly.

"No," said Cort, "we should *taste* him first."

"T-taste?" I murmured.

"To immerse you totally into the flame might spoil your flavor, burn you to a crisp," said Cort, smiling gently. "We must experiment, find what sort of cooking suits you best. We will do it in parts. Fry a foot, broil a leg, bake a hand—"

"You mean cut me up and experiment?"

"Oh, *not* cut you *up*," soothed the wizard, cruelly. "We're not barbarians. We'll leave you fully alive, of course."

"No," Lorn cried. "No, have mercy on him!"

"Will someone *cook* that nymph?" roared the emperor.

"Please, *please!*" squealed Lorn, as the muscular guards bore her backward toward the hungry fires of the pit.

I'd lost. I averted my eyes. And saw the square-cut diamond in the center of the lead breastplate, coruscating blindingly, waiting to be pressed, as I should have had the sense to press it the moment Maggot's powers were restored. But Twork and Idlisk had my arms held tight.

There was only one chance. Their irritability-level.

"Careful, birdface!" I snapped at Twork, twisting in his grasp. "You almost bumped my diamond stud!"

The parrot-beaked guard snarled, "I'll bump it if I feel like it!" His hand whipped up, and the heel of it smacked hard against the twinkling diamond. Then his beak opened in a silent scream, as the silver sword flashed into magical existence in my hand, the tip of the blade appearing as snugly in Twork's chest.

HE'S loose!" blubbered Kwist, as I wrenched away from a terrified Idlisk. Then, as Twork crumpled to the floor, Idlisk leaped for me again, claws flexed to tear through my flesh. I swatted him behind the ear with the mountain-stopping flat of the blade. He went spinning across the floor with a shattered skull, to vanish suddenly in the gaping maw of the open flame-pit, with a noxious odor of burning feathers.

The men holding Lorn pulled back from the gray clouds that marked their companion's line of departure, and she yanked free and ran toward me. Cort raised his arms impressively over his head and shouted *"Stop!"* at me in his loudest wizardly roar.

Some swift reflex brought up the flat of the sword between myself and the wizard even as he spoke, and the spell that rushed upon me was deflected into a group of quaking Kwistians, all of whom stiffened horribly and went down like ninepins at the feet of their associates.

Then Lorn was clasped to me in one arm, her marble-clad hands nearly braining me as she flung them wildly about my neck, and I held her tight, ready to stay there fighting for her life until I dropped in my tracks of exhaustion.

"Can power fend power forever?" sneered Cort, still spoiling for revenge. His fist came up at the length of his arm, and a pale blue stone in his ring suddenly arrowed a blinding white needle of force at me. The sword-blade caught it, but could not deflect it, and the hilt jerked in my hand, then held steady. Cort's mocking laughter crashed about the room as I stood there with legs braced, fighting the awful surge of raw power that threatened to destroy me if the sword gave out.

Beneath my fingers on the hilt, I could feel the copper and the ivory bands switching from first place to last, as those balance-of-power storage tanks or whatever strove to cope with this merciless overload.

"The edge!" Lorn yelled into my ear. "Use the *edge!*" she demanded again, as two flanking bodies of Kwistians started rushing in upon me while I was powerless to do aught but fight Cort's ring-power, using the blade as a shield instead of weapon.

I didn't get it, but I'd have a trident in either kidney if I waited to ask stupid questions, so I twisted the hilt, and caught the sizzling white beam with the razor-edged silver blade. White power cracked asunder in midair, as all the brunt that had poured into the flat of the blade released instantaneously from the edge. Cort's grin faded into gray-faced horror as the raw force spattered outward like so much shattered glass, and—as the hurtling shards of white light blasted the incoming Kwistians into hunks of bloody flesh and charred bone—his ring contained nothing but a scorched hole where the blue gem had rested.

"Quickly," he yelled to Kwist, as I advanced upon him. "The laboratory! We'll stop them yet!"

Pinions whacking the air, they soared smoothly upward through the final orifice of the castle levels, into the tower room housing Cort's laboratory. The other Kwistians were already soaring out windows into the relatively safe-from-me area above the mossfields, or downward into other rooms of the castle. It was a wonderful rout.

"Wait here, honey," I said to Lorn, as I strode grimly toward the nearest wall, and began smilingly hacking out a series of hand holds in the stone like I'd been doing it all my life...

CHAPTER FOURTEEN

As I reached the ceiling, cut out a circle of stone, and stealthily raised it with the flat of the force-absorbent blade, I heard the wizard and the emperor in agitated discussion.

"Cort, what'll we do?" the emperor was whining.

"The casement's right here, Kwist," growled the wizard. "If he comes here, we'll simply fly somewhere else!"

Below me, as I awkwardly tried to ease through the gap without dropping the hellishly heavy slab on myself, one of the winged men looked downward through the entrance orifice and his eyebrow feathers stood straight up on end.

"The witch!" he choked, and sprang into the air, headed—I assumed—for another level of Sark, to warn his companions. Only, he didn't rise any farther than that initial spring had taken him. The great white pinions remained stubbornly shut, and with a gurgle of fear, the man's fingers clawed futilely at the air before his ill-advised leap dropped him neatly through the opening in the floor.

But I could have guessed that outcome. If Maggot was truly down below, on her way up, it meant that the eggs in the Serpolith grotto were already hatching like popcorn popping, each into a wing-numbing Thrake.

I finally got both legs through the gap after me, and dropped the slab back into place. My entrance had been behind a long lab table, where neither man could see me; nor was the crash of the stone noticed amid the growing shouts of frightened Kwistians below.

"We can't fly somewhere else," Kwist was replying in panic, "if the Thrake becomes activated, Cort—"

"How can it?" grated the wizard. "Maggot was the one who might have activated it, and Maggot is dead! By now, she's a mess of bone and acid-eaten flesh!"

"*I resent that!*" came a familiar voice, from the room below the lab.

Emperor and wizard rushed to the brink of the orifice and peered down. "She's alive!" gasped Cort.

Kwist clutched Cort's arm. "Do something!" he whimpered.

"Let go of me so I *can!*" yelled Cort, pulling free. He reached down a long crystal spear from a rack on the wall, a spear whose faceted surfaces glinted with a hundred rainbow sparkles. Just as he stepped back to the brink of the floor-entrance, I stood up silently behind the lab table, silver sword ready in my hand. Kwist gave a shriek of fright and ran to the casement.

"Fly, Cort, *fly!* It's our only—My wings! They won't open! It's the Thrake! Maggot's done it!"

I saw Cort's own white pinions tremble a bit, and the perspiration spring out on his brow as nothing more happened. "She wasn't kidding!" he mumbled, low and scared. "She *did* activate it from here!"

"Cort—!" screamed the terrified, sobbing emperor. "Don't put it off any longer. Use the Roton Beam."

"You mean it?" rasped Cort, still keeping a wary eye on me, his crystal spear poised for defense.

"*Yes!*" the emperor screamed desperately. "The hell with the risk. I'd rather lose Sark and the mossfields than stand here with paralyzed wings while this Englishman hacks me to pieces!"

I STARTED around the lab table, my sword ready, to stop the wizard. The trouble was, I had no idea where he was about to move, which made interception difficult.

Then, just to one side of him on the floor, I saw an object I recognized. Its metal-and-glass top was supported from below by a tripod. It was the spitting image of one of those gadgets

Courtland had used to start sending people and houses to Drendon in the first place. Some vestigial memory of his Earth-self had stuck with Cort-Courtland, enough to let him construct another of those dimension-warping machines. Of course it would destroy the Thrake; it would destroy anything in Drendon by the simple expedient of warping it out the dimensional doorway to Earth-normal.

"Hold it!" I said, striving to put myself between Cort and the gadget. "That's more dangerous than you know—!" I don't know why I blurted that. Some subconscious reasoning must have told me that events were coming a full circle, if this thing were used, this thing that had started all our troubles.

"Try and stop me!" said the wizard, slamming home a switch. That shimmering haze I'd seen once before, long ages ago on Earth, began to form on one side of the tripod. Then I saw the danger. It had no second tripod-gadget to regulate its focal range. Amid the eye-blurring shimmer there appeared a bright blue helix of light, a helix that twirled like a motor-driven corkscrew and went spiraling swiftly out the open casement, seeking out the Thrake.

Except—*The* Thrake was no more. But a minor army of Thrakes lay wriggling their puny tentacles down in the Serpolith cavern in the base of the building itself. Kwist saw at once that something was wrong.

"The beam, Cort! Look at the beam!" he cried, much too late. Even as the wizard turned and stared, stunned, the accelerating corkscrew beam was bending in flight like a hawk that has overshot its prey, and snaking right down at the base of the castle. As wizard and emperor sprang fearfully back from the open casement, the beam—now an audible blue bolt of destruction—lurched into the hole I'd cut in the base of the castle.

I braced myself, giving that zooming helix about one second to find its way down the corridor, off down the tunnel to the polarized spell-door, and then strike with all its fury at the wriggling blue heap against the grotto wall.

It took two floor-shaking temblors of concussion before the whole granite base of the castle burst into flame, and the mossfields of Sark ignited.

"Fire!" yelled the emperor, as myriad waves of lacy blue flames shot skyward from every surface outside the casements. Cort had already dashed like a madman to the tripod and half-torn the switch from its contacts the instant of the helix's down-dip, but— The shimmering halted, the hungry fires did not.

A MOMENT later I heard a shout, as Kwist whipped open his fifteen-foot pinions. "My wings work! The beam did it!" He stepped toward the casement and stopped, aghast. Wings or not, there would be no flying out into that sky-high ocean of leaping blue flames. "Cort—" he squeaked. "We can't—!"

Cort, already foreseeing the difficulty, had leaped on beating wings to the ceiling. And there, his crystal spear whisked out a hole as if the granite were wet cardboard.

"Look out below!" I had the presence of mind to shout as the slab dropped unerringly through the open floor. A second later, Maggot, with Timtik riding tandem on her broom, bobbed up through the gap and deposited her passenger beside me.

"Thanks for the warning, Albert," she said, flashing her fangs in comradeship. "Excuse me," she added politely, as she broomed through the hole again. "Got to get Lorn. My broom only carries one extra rider."

Then she was swooping down out of sight, even as Kwist went soaring smoothly up through the ceiling-hole through which Cort had already made a hasty exit.

"Timtik—!" I said, as a horrible notion came to me. "If the broom carries only one extra—Who goes with her? You, me, or Lorn? And worse, who gets *left?*"

Smoke and licking heat were staggering me by now. I could barely see straight as Maggot and Lorn came swiftly up into the room. The castle walls were cracking in the blaze, and here and there a smoking shard was splintering from the rocky walls, which were themselves turning hot pink.

"All aboard, Tikky!" sang out the witch, as Lorn hopped from her perch and rushed to fling her arms about my neck.

Down below, toppling walls increased in thunder, and the lab floor was starting to grow horribly hot against my bare feet. "Maggot," I said, as Timtik hopped onto the broomstick behind her, flinging his arms far as they'd go about her plump waist. "What're you going to do, make three trips?"

"Don't be silly," she said, turning her wrinkled face to me. "The castle will sink into flaming muck in less than thirty seconds. Why'd I even come back a *second* time?"

"But Lorn and I—! What about *us?*"

"Aren't you coming with us?" she said, blinking.

"With you! *How?*" I yelped, dancing from one burning foot to the other, a clumsy polka in which I was accompanied by a likewise barefoot Lorn.

"The silver sword, silly!" she alliterated hissingly. "Hold the crosspiece like handlebars and point the blade where you want to go. The flat edge also absorbs the force of gravity!"

WITH a ripple of voluminous black skirt, she and the faun rocketed up through the ceiling into the clouds of smoke boiling there, and were gone.

"Honey," you'll have to hold me," I yipped, still dancing. "I need both hands for the sword."

Once again those slim beautiful arms encircled my neck, and the woodnymph pressed up close against me.

Shifting the hilt slightly, I took hold of the left crosspiece with my left hand, then the right one with my right, and then—after a quick prayer that the thing would work—I pointed the tip of the silver blade at the center of the hole in the ceiling and poked it slightly in that direction.

My next sensation was not unlike that of a man whose cufflinks have gotten hooked to an ascending express rocket. A jolt that sent yelps of pain through my deltoids managed to lift me and my woodnymph before my arms tore from their sockets, and then we were arrowing through smoke—then icy air that burned along my face and wrists like sandpaper, so sickeningly swift was our movement.

A glance downward showed me a tiny flicker of blue flame that was the entire mossfield of Sark, and I gave a frantic twist to the crosspiece that dropped us like a plummet to a—relatively—safer height.

Lorn still clung gamely to my neck, though my horizontal flight above the rising heat waves billowing from the nigh-endless blue flames left her dangling like the vertical part of a capital T with me and the sword forming the crossbar. Ahead of us, I barely had time to recognize Maggot and Timtik swooping along before I was beside them, then past them.

"How do you *slow* this damned thing!" I shrieked as we blurred by them.

"You don't!" came Maggot's voice from far at our rear. "You either go fast or not at all…" came the fading amendment to her statement.

In the stinging curtains of haze and heat before me, I saw two sets of flip-flopping wings, and suddenly I was almost right on top of Cort and Kwist, the sole survivors of the carnage at the castle, their pinions whacking mightily upon the air as they hurried to get beyond the flaming fields.

"Look out, Albert!" said Lorn, even as I saw Cort twist in his flight, and bring up that crystal spear in an attempt to impale me by my own motion. I wrenched the crosspiece, and Lorn and I skewed off sideways and upward past that glittering shaft, then looped wildly end over end before I could undo the torque I'd put upon the blade. I looked up. Damn. We were re-approaching the rear of the wizard again.

"I'm not *chasing* you—!" I screamed futilely, as Cort swung about to a "standing" stance in mid-air, his wingtips a feathery white blur of motion, and lunged with the spear again.

THIS time I tried twisting the blade the other way, and almost lost hold of it as an even tighter loop swung us down so near the blue fires that my toenails turned brown. I yipped and wrenched and we rose again, beneath our foes.

"Cort—!" yelled the emperor, but Cort was already folding his wings neatly and dropping out of my ascending vector, to snap them open like twin parachutes as I roared past, and once again jabbed at me with that crystal spear.

The tip of the spear caught the trailing end of Lorn's "diaphanous draperies," and there came a loud shredding sound all at once.

"I thought that thing was indestructible," I said.

"It is, given the proper care," said the woodnymph, burrowing her face into the side of my neck, her arms strained keeping hold of me. "But I've been through an awful lot today, Albert, and—Oh, look!"

I saw, through the dizzy spinning sphere of sky and flame which had temporarily become my loopy environment, that the trailing tail of her garment had fluttered onto Cort's head, and that he and the emperor were struggling to get it off him, the two flapping gamely to stay aloft, high aloft.

"Albert—" said Lorn, her voice as green as her gown. "Can't you stop this—looping?"

"I'm trying, I'm trying!" But if I pull out at the wrong time—" I gasped, breathless with vertigo, "we might end up in either the fire or the stratosphere! I'm trying to…pull us out in a…horizontal direction."

"Well, do it! Quickly!" she wailed.

I shut my eyes and gave a wild yank on the bar, and then groaned in despair as the flexible tip of the blade started to vibrate. Our flight instantly changed from a closed loop to the more involved pattern of an aerial roller coaster.

And again our flight path, still roughly circular, despite its added pogo stick itinerary, came back toward Cort and Kwist. They were just getting the last bits of trailing veil free from the wizard. I saw with horror that we were due to smash right into them if I didn't do something, fast.

SO, moving faster than was safe I tried another yank on the bar—and my perspiring hand slipped, skidded from the grip, and struck the diamond stud.

There is nothing I can think of, offhand, that is less fun than finding oneself suddenly in mid-air above a flaming mossfield, a terrified and nauseated woman clinging to your neck, and nothing to help you remain aloft except a solid lead cuirass strapped to your chest. Magic or not, lead don't fly. Lorn and I flipped end over end and started down—

Approximately ten feet we dropped, and landed with a soft tugging plop in the center of her veil-remnant, which was at that moment being held almost net-wise by emperor and wizard.

With an ounce of thought, Cort would've just let go his end, and let us drop into the blue fires below. But I guess he'd been spear-practicing so long that he didn't grasp the simpler method of getting us dead. So he lunged at us with spear in one hand, but (I guess to keep his target handy) kept hold of the veil with the other.

This release of the right hand grip on the veil, however, turned the "net" from a supporting square to a sagging triangle, off which Lorn and I slid backwards, shrieking in two-part terror.

The crystal spear whizzed over the veil-top where we'd just lain, and almost skewered Kwist in mid-air, and just as my groping fingers caught hold frantically of the veil-edge, Kwist—dodging the spear—let go his end. And there we were, me and Lorn, dangling down at the lower end of a trailing bit of gauzy green drapery beneath the heels of the flying wizard, whose pinions tripled their stroke to take up the extra load.

And still *again* he didn't think of just dropping us! With his left hand gripping its claws into the veil, he poked at us with the spear in his right, just as I got my non-clinging hand onto the diamond stud and shoved, hard.

The silver sword leaped into existence once more. We were off, flying madly, wildly—at a never-varying ten-foot radius from Cort.

Seems the veil was partially snagged on the sword handle, letting us fly solely in a circle about the wizard, like a stone at the end of a string.

Cort—counterforced into an involuntary mid-air pirouette—drew back that spear for *another* thrust at us as we whirled in a helpless circle about him, a sitting target insofar as his relative motion was concerned.

"*Do* something, Albert!" begged Lorn, the furthest out in our living centrifuge.

"*Such as!?*" I shrieked as we whipped around the turn for what was probably our nineteenth lap in five seconds.

THEN I saw the spearpoint coming at me and tried to duck. Which, oddly enough, was the perfect move to have made. My attempted move lifted my arms up, with the sword in them… The sword, by virtue of the snag, lifted the veil… And the spear, by virtue of its magical cutting power, sheared away the fragment of cloth snarling us, and let us fly into the blue on a violent tangent, which, stomach-turning or not, meant momentary safety.

I braked our slanting skyward motion more carefully this time, and had the sword under the grim control of more-or-less sane thinking as we zoomed back in the direction we'd originally been headed, this time trying to stay high over the winged duo.

By now, though, the delay in spear poking and merry-go-rounding-in-the-sky had let Maggot and Timtik close the gap toward the Kwistians.

Cort was just steadying to a halt from his spin, amid a down-flutter of downy feathers that had been dislodged during his travail, when Maggot and Timtik sailed smoothly past, and a small white object was tossed from Maggot's hand to the wizard.

"You forgot something, dearie," she crooned sweetly, her ugly old face flashing its best witchy smile.

Cort, reacting like anyone to whom an unexpected missile is lobbed, caught the thing and stared at it, along with a baffled Kwist.

"That," said the emperor, "looks like a Serpolith egg—?"

"It *is…?*" said Cort. "I don't underst—"

At that moment, the blistering heat that had been rising everywhere took its toll of the unhatched beast's willpower, and the shell began to crackle and crisp away under the brunt of its imprisoned thrusts.

"But Cort—" said Kwist, as a tiny blue tentacle appeared in the side of the shell, "that's no Serpolith…"

"No," the wizard agreed, "it looks more like a—" His long eyebrows shot up. "A *Thrake!*" he squealed, just as the small blue creature made its short crowing sound, the sound of joy Thrakes always make when their wing-dampering power caught a victim. Or two victims. And the last I saw of Cort and Kwist, they were suddenly wrapped neatly in their folded pinions, and dropping down, the egg and its half-hatched Thrake with them—into the hot, flaming field that was the final ruined chattel of the winged men of Sark.

CHAPTER FIFTEEN

THE mossfield fires still raged when the four of us, flushed with windburn and reeking of smoke, sailed down from the skies to the hut of the witch. I had just a little trouble landing, until I figured that a sudden uptilt of the sword would allow us to drop to the ground before our new up-swerve began. It worked nicely, with Lorn and I taking an easy fall into high, soft grass, and the sword, released, stopping its aerial shenanigans and plopping hilt-first into my waiting hand.

"Whooie!" I signed, leaning my head on the sword and shutting my eyes. "That's all the flying I want to do for the rest of my *life!*"

A pair of warm lips touched down upon mine, then Lorn snuggled her forehead beside my neck, and curled up on the cool grass beside me. Well, not too cool; a lot of heat from the flaming fields was radiating into the forest itself.

Maggot's hut, which she'd left on "automatic," had altered its amorphous form to suit its caloric environs, and was now a Grecian-type statue, with a spray of water spouting like an umbrella from the stone maiden's head, and running in an icy cascade over the exquisite form, finally splashing gaily into a circular cement trough that kept the water from running away over the grass.

"Hmmm," said Maggot, "that's the first time I've ever seen it in *that* shape—Of course, we never had such a peachy fire before...But I don't intend to get drenched on my way indoors!" With a witchy wave of her arms at the pseudo-statue, she chanted:

"From this graceful vision rest us;
Be a hut, of neat asbestos."

In a twinkling, a cheery little rough-thatched hut swelled out of the stone statue's components, looking—with each haphazard shingle a different color—like a cubical patchwork quilt. "Much better," said Maggot.

"One thing—" I said from the comfortably lazy sprawl beside Lorn on the thick grass, "even if that hut won't burn, we can still get warm inside, with that fire out there."

"What fire?" said Maggot, distractedly.

"The one which is busily spreading from moss into shrubbery and pretty soon will turn the whole enchanted forest into a sort of bosky hell," I replied.

"You know," she nodded, "you're right." She turned to Timtik and said casually, "Tikky, douse that blaze for old Maggot, like a dear boy."

"Me?" The faun was astounded. *"Me* put out *that?"*

Maggot looked surprised. "Have you forgotten everything I ever taught you, Tikky? What of your thunderstorm spell?"

"Gosh—" he faltered. "On such a big scale—" He looked at Maggot, then shrugged, flexed his fingers, and turned to Lorn. "Give me a hand?" he said.

The witch's eyebrows rose a half-inch. "What's this? Help? That's a solo spell, Tikky."

Timtik looked abashed. "I know, Maggot, but—I can't assume the primary position. When I cross my fetlocks, my hooves give way."

"Oh, is *that* all!?" chuckled the witch. She shuffled into her hut, and a moment later returned with a soiled silken cloak in one hand. Probably once black velvet, it was faded now, and rank with mildew. "Under you go!" she said, whipping the cloak over the faun, completely obscuring him from view.

"Abracadabra-presto-chango!"

SHE whisked it away, and Timtik stood there on a pair of normal boy's legs, his horns and goat-parts vanished.

"Odds bodkins!" he yelped. "Maggot—! You changed me to a—!" he blurted in a rush.

"Save the eulogy!" interrupted the witch. "This is no time for compliments. It's getting a mite warmish." She fanned herself busily with one hand. "I'd whomp up a rain myself if I thought the old sacroiliac could take it."

Timtik, assuming the primary position with ease, waved his arms, his hips did the around-the-island motion, a howling chant rang triumphantly from his throat—

A fork of lightning stabbed across the sky, thunder cracked and rolled, and the blue-flaming fields and the smoldering fringe of trees were suddenly smothered in a wet torrent of icy waters that turned them into steaming mulch. Rain fell everywhere from the swift-moving black clouds, everywhere in Drendon save an area about fifteen feet square in which the four of us were.

The storm raged one minute, then the skies went clear blue and sunny once more. Timtik, who had been clapping his hands in glee, suddenly sobered. "Maggot—I know I don't *need* the new feet, and all, now the spell's done, but—Could I keep 'em awhile longer? I never had any before, and—"

"Oh, shush!" said the witch. "I was just jumping the gun, Tikky. The only reason I never made you normal before was the Edict of Banishment. But now, with the Kwistians done for, Merlin's spell is cancelled out—them being the reason for it—and you and I can go back with Albert and Lorn, and join in all the wedding festivities, and—"

"Hey!" I hollered, sitting bolt upright. "I like Lorn a lot, but I never asked—I mean, we've never discussed—"

A glittering witch-eye banked with fires of red lightning suddenly locked upon mine. "You *intend* proposing, don't you, Albert?" Maggot's fingers flexed impatiently.

"Uh—" I said. "I would—love to marry Lorn."

"Good," said Maggot, all charm and bustle again. "Now't *that's* settled, we'd best hurry off to the proper sector for the Great Reversal. I can feel Merlin's spell weakening by the minute! Let us away, so we'll be in the right Drendon-spot to pop back Earthside. Wouldn't want to wind up with Genghis Khan's time. Ugh!"

"You don't mean Drendon's coming to Earth-normal?"

Maggot shrugged. "Depends. Remember, Albert, so-called 'normal' on Earth *isn't;* Drendon-normal is the way Earth *should* have been if Merlin hadn't messed things up."

"Then that allegorical orange peel—"

"—about to fit right back on the orange, yes," said Maggot.

"But that means centaurs all over Greece, and dragons all over England," I gasped.

"Ah yes!" the witch crooned dreamily, knobby knuckles clasped to her hoary breast. "And werewolves in the Carpathians, vampires in the Balkins, ocean serpents in the fjords, mermaids in the Pacific, sirens and sorceresses in the Mediterranean, kobolds in every cave."

"BUT WHAT'LL it do to present civilization?" I said weakly.

"It'll *preserve* it!" snapped Maggot. "How can one country concentrate on building ICBMs to blast another with, when all the citizenry is busy with things like keeping gnomes from swiping the silverware, or kelpies from dropping bricks on their heads?"

"You know—" I said thoughtfully, "you've *got* something!"

Maggot snapped her fingers. "Almost forgot about Lorn. Can't have her going back to Earth looking like that. Stand aside, Albert."

Up came the cloak, out came the words, and as the gray-spotted black garment whisked away, Lorn stood in a royal blue dress with a lemon-colored belt, long black lashes lying against a pale rose cheek, lovely and very blonde hair a golden aurora about her head, and her figure a pulse-maddening conformation set neatly atop legs smoothly encased in silk stockings and feet in silly little French-heeled shoes.

"My goodness," said Lorn-Susan, blinking. "This is comfy. And not half so drafty as my diaphanous draperies."

Maggot lead the way into the woods. Lorn-Susan and Timtik and I followed, hurrying. Maggot had the key to my part of Earth-normal ready in her hand, and as we got to the proper place—that former hotsy-blasted clearing—she paused before inserting the twig-like thing into the ground.

"I think," she said thoughtfully, "that 'Lorn' and 'Timtik' are unlikely Earth-names. So, for that matter, is 'Maggot'. We'd best call ourselves the—um—'Baker' family, if only because I like to cook. I'll be Maggie, you'll be Timothy, you'll be Susan…"

I looked at her, frowning deeply. Her matter-of-fact choosing of those very names almost made me think she'd been aware of her dual existence all along, but before I could ask her about it, Timtik-Timothy tugged my hand.

"You know," he whispered, grinning impishly, "you're kind of lucky, Albert. How many guys can call their mother-in-law an old witch and get away with it?"

While I was trying to think of an answer, Maggot turned the key.

* * *

I WAS standing in my study staring at a can of beer that had popped into existence in my hand and I knew, then, that I was back at the time before Annabel's arrival, back at that moment I'd entered my home to get a beer and a sandwich. I rushed into the kitchen, and a swishing feel along my legs made me glance downward. My trousers were whole again, and neatly pressed, and I was once again in shoes and socks after that long barefoot itinerary.

"Damn," I said, setting the beer on the sink and looking out the rear window toward Susan's house. Except that no mysterious man was adjusting a tripod-thing in the back yard, the scene was exactly as it had been, so many ages ago...

I dropped the beer onto the sink, and was out the back door and halfway over that fence before the can could bounce twice. A lurched dash through their yard brought me to the front of the house, and I sprang to the porch and thumbed the bell, hard. In the living room, a weepy-eyed Susan jumped up from the couch, dabbed at the corners of her eyes with a kerchief, then came to let me in.

"Albert!" she said, her face coming alive with joy at the sight of me on the doorstep. "Have you thought it over—Made up your mind?"

"Well..." I said, uncertainly.

She glanced behind me, and tugged at my coat.

"Hurry," she said. "The unicorn looks mean."

I went rigid up my back and across my scalp, but I did manage to turn my head and see the splendid white beast with its shaggy mane and long white spiral spike on its forehead standing out under the lamppost at the corner, its eyes like two red coals of anger. Then Susan shut the door and led me into the parlor, where the cookies and lemonade awaited us, as they always had.

"You shouldn't come out without your cloak of darkness," she said. "You know how edgy the unicorn gets in the fall; he might have skewered you." She said it with no more concern than she'd have mentioned my dashing a bit carelessly through traffic.

"Susan—" I said stupidly.

Then Maggie Baker and her son Timothy came out of the kitchen, she wiping plump hands on her pink apron, he munching a sandwich.

"Hi, Albert," he said in his froggy little voice.

"I'm so glad you came back, Albert," said Maggie, with a warm smile at me. An odd smile. "So many young men think true love is dull. Do you still think that cookies and lemonade and sitting sedately on the sofa are too lacking in adventure?"

"I think just sitting down quietly safe inside a house is one of the loveliest occupations invented by mankind."

"You always were a good boy, Albert," she said, with a satisfied sigh. She patted the top of my head, then she and Timothy wandered off upstairs.

"You know," I said, after a little thought, "some women will stop at *nothing* to get their daughters married!"

"Why, Albert!" came a sedate gasp from Susan. "Whatever in the world do you mean?"

I turned my head to tell her, just in time to catch the slightest of twinkles in her eyes.

All at once, I decided the hell with protocol and pleasantries and polite behavior, and I vaulted from the number one cushion right onto the end of the number two cushion, and grabbed the girl very fiercely in my arms.

"You mustn't!" said Susan, her eyes wide and alarmed.

"So scream for help!" I growled, and kissed her.

THE END

If you've enjoyed this book, you will not want to miss these terrific titles...

ARMCHAIR SCI-FI, FANTASY, & HORROR DOUBLE NOVELS, $12.95 each